Guardians of Stone

Guardians of Stone

ANITA CLENNEY

Charlottesville, Virginia

Montlake
Romance

305717504

R

Text copyright © 2012 Anita Clenney
All rights reserved.
Printed in the United States of America.
No part of this book may be reproduced, or stored in a retrieval
system, or transmitted in any form or by any means, electronic,
mechanical, photocopying, recording, or otherwise, without express written permission of the publisher.

Published by Montlake Romance
P.O. Box 400818
Las Vegas, NV 89140

ISBN-13: 9781612186542
ISBN-10: 1612186548

This book is dedicated to my agent, Christine Witthohn of Book Cents Literary Agency. I couldn't have done this without you.

PROLOGUE

"WHY CAN'T I GO WITH YOU?" KENDALL ASKED.

Her father hesitated and then tucked the covers up to her chin, even though it was warm inside. "Not this time, pumpkin. It's too dangerous." He ruffled her hair, but his face was tense. "Besides, your aunt Edna wants to see you."

"What about Adam? Won't it be too dangerous for him?"

"He's coming with you."

"OK." Adam was her best friend. She trusted him more than anyone. If he was coming, it would be all right.

Her father studied her for a minute, his forehead wrinkled. Seemed like it was wrinkled all the time now. Adam's father's was too. She and Adam didn't know why, but they were both worried. Adam said he had a plan to figure out what was going on.

"Go to sleep, pumpkin. Tomorrow you'll see your aunt." Her father dropped a kiss on her forehead. She really thought eleven was too old for good-night kisses, but tonight she didn't mind. For some reason she felt jittery. Her father stopped at the door and looked back at Kendall. "Are you sure you don't remember anything before you bumped your head and passed out?"

An image of a castle flashed through her mind followed by a blinding light. She didn't know if it was real or a dream. Or one of her visions. But it made her head hurt. She didn't tell her father. He didn't like her visions. "I don't remember anything."

1

"Good," he whispered in the voice he used when he didn't realize he'd spoken out loud. He watched her for a minute longer and then nodded. "I love you, pumpkin."

"I love you too, Daddy. Don't worry about me. I'll be fine with Aunt Edna."

And Adam would look after her. He always did.

CHAPTER ONE

H ER FIRST DATE IN SIX WEEKS BLOWN TO HELL. KENDALL Morgan pressed the cell phone to her ear. "When do you need me?" She cast an apologetic glance at her good-looking new neighbor who'd finally gotten around to asking her out.

"Now." Nathan's voice was firm, with an edge that hinted at secrets. "Please," he added. Probably an afterthought.

She couldn't ask her boss to wait. No one asked Nathan Larraby to wait. She made her excuses to her date and settled for a chaste kiss and tantalizing whiff of hot male. Promising a rain check, she grabbed her bag and jacket and left his apartment. She hurried down the street to her Volkswagen, not bothering to take the extra few minutes to go to her own apartment a few doors away so she could change. When Nathan said now he meant now.

Her date's curtains were open, so she couldn't help but see as he pulled his shirt over his head. Nice chest. Darn. Well, it probably wouldn't have worked out anyway. It never did. Her sixth sense made intimacy a risk. Body fluids were often strong conductors. Kissing could be hell sometimes. Sex…a nightmare. There were things that helped, but it was always a crapshoot. Not conducive to "happily ever after."

A car eased away from the curb, distracting her. It didn't belong to any of her neighbors. She knew most of the people on this street. With the exception of her and the new guy, everyone else was old. She'd seen the vehicle a couple of times before. It was big and dark, like the ones Nathan's bodyguards used. He was protective of everything around him, but surely he wouldn't spy on his employees.

It took fifteen minutes to reach Nathan's estate in the rolling Virginia hills. She pulled up to the gated entrance. The guard, a man with more muscles in his neck than Kendall had in her whole body, nodded once and let her in. The entire estate was surrounded by an iron fence that would have done justice to a maximum security prison and protected by an extensive surveillance system. After the mile-long drive in from the gate, she parked in front of the mansion and started up the steps.

Nathan met her at the door wearing a suit that probably cost as much as her apartment. His light brown hair was cropped close and, as usual, his handsome face tense. In the months she'd worked for him, he never laughed, rarely smiled. He was all mystery and no clues. If she wasn't so busy working on his relics, she'd turn her *talents* to decoding him. He raked her over once with dark, smoky eyes. "Hope I didn't interrupt anything important."

"Just a date." Since she'd started working for him, she hadn't had one that he hadn't interrupted. Maybe he *was* spying on her.

"My apologies." A muscle twitched in his jaw. He hadn't shaved and the faint shadow made him look sexy. He escorted her inside, through the elaborate atrium that led to his library, which was adorned with first editions, priceless historical documents, and rare art. If Aunt Edna got a glimpse of this place, she'd be hearing wedding bells. Maybe that would stop the barrage of personal ads Kendall had been getting since her aunt discovered e-mail.

Two men on Nathan's technical security team were just leaving the room. Fergus stood behind them, his face worried.

"...trace the data security breach," one of the men said.

Nathan pushed back his sleeve and looked at his watch. Not a Rolex, as Kendall would have expected, but silver on a worn leather band. "Meet me back here in two hours with an update."

The two men left and Nathan motioned Kendall inside. He took her jacket and handed it to Fergus, who nodded his head as if she were royalty. Every inch the proper butler. "Miss Kendall, I hope you're well."

"Yes, Fergus. Thank you."

"Lovely dress. Were you at dinner?" He glanced briefly at Nathan, and Kendall thought she saw the barest hint of a frown. He probably realized Nathan had interrupted her meal. Sometimes she wondered if Fergus had his own sixth sense. He seemed to know everything. A good trait for a butler, she supposed.

"Yes, I had dinner." And had been looking forward to dessert.

"I'm sorry if you had to cut your evening short—" Nathan's apology was interrupted when the front door slammed. Fergus hurried out as footsteps rang across the floor.

"Larraby, this had better be good. I left a nice warm bed and a hot..." The man entering the room stopped short when he saw Kendall. "Meal," he substituted. She knew that wasn't the word he would have used had she not been there.

Her senses started tingling as she sized the intruder up. Dangerous. A rebel. Steel-gray eyes met hers—intelligent, calculating, cool. A mask for the anger and insolence lurking inside. She blinked, distancing her mind. She didn't pry without good reason. After all, she wouldn't appreciate someone digging around in her thoughts. The stranger's gaze dropped to her slinky red dress, lingering longer than it should. Kendall squirmed under his appraisal, which was every bit as intrusive as her evaluation had been.

Rumpled dark hair and clothes—black T-shirt and faded jeans—backed up his claim that he'd been in bed.

"Kendall, I'd like you to meet Jake Stone. Jake, this is Kendall Morgan. She's my relic expert."

Kendall nodded a greeting. Was that lipstick on his neck?

"We don't have much time," Nathan said, picking up a leather satchel from the marble credenza behind him. He seemed more intense than usual. Perhaps because of the latest security breach. "The jet leaves in one hour."

"Jet?" Kendall inquired.

"You're going to Italy." Nathan nodded toward the solemn butler, who set down two duffel bags. "Fergus has your clothes and equipment packed."

Kendall still hadn't gotten over the awkwardness of having Fergus pack her clothing for these spontaneous trips, including bras and panties. She would prefer to do it herself, but he always beat her to the punch, choosing her things from the wardrobe that Nathan insisted she keep here. Between Fergus and the backpack she kept loaded and ready in her car—she knew better than to answer Nathan's summons without it—she was usually well prepared.

"And you'll need this." Nathan handed Jake the satchel.

Jake frowned. "She's not going with me. I work alone."

"You're sending him with me?" Kendall said at the same time.

"Hold on." Jake threw up a defiant hand. "I don't have time to babysit a skirt."

A skirt? Arrogant jerk.

"I need both of you for this job," Nathan said, returning Jake's glare. "Follow orders, or you can go back."

A look crossed between the two men. Kendall didn't need her sixth sense to feel the testosterone seething underneath. Both men were over six feet, muscular, probably an even match strength-wise, but Jake's collar-length hair, worn jeans, and boots made him look like a badass, while Nathan looked like more like Batman hiding behind Bruce Wayne.

Jake glanced at Kendall, his eyes flat. "Let's get it over with, then. Why are we going to Italy?"

"I'm looking for a box," Nathan said.

Kendall tried to see inside his head, but as usual, it was like hitting a wall. "What kind of box?"

Nathan hesitated before answering, and she knew it would only be a half-truth. "An old one."

"That's all? An old box?" Jake leaned a hip against the sofa. "You gotta have more than that."

"It contains something powerful," Nathan said.

"A relic?" Kendall asked. This was where her expertise came in.

"I can't say yet."

Jake's eyes narrowed. "You and your damned secrets."

Who was this guy? No one talked to Nathan like that.

Nathan motioned to the sofa. "Both of you, sit."

Jake set the satchel on the table and dropped onto the sofa, knees spread wide. He folded his arms across his chest and lifted a mocking eyebrow. Kendall held his gaze and sat, not far away from him, as she knew he expected, but in the middle of the sofa. She regretted her decision immediately when the cushion dipped, putting them shoulder to shoulder. His scent slithered up her nose. She scooted back a few inches and tugged at her dress, ignoring his leer. Bastard.

"The box is ancient," Nathan said. "It was guarded for centuries by a secret order."

"A secret order?" Kendall's pulse kicked up a notch. "What kind of order? Like Templars?"

"I don't know what they were. Monks? Knights? No one seems to know much about them." Nathan pulled a cross from his pocket. It was silver, a couple of inches long, and hung from a chain. Kendall's senses started buzzing. "I think this is connected to them," he said, handing it to her.

She took the cross and the buzzing grew louder. The metal felt cold. There was an opening in the center, and the edges were rounded. Or perhaps just worn with age. It was ancient. She could tell from the saturation of emotions attached to the piece. Sadness, betrayal, fear. There was something else she recognized, but the sensations flying at her like shrapnel came too fast to make sense. Sometimes it took awhile to get a clear picture. Sometimes it never came at all. She turned it over and saw a worn mark. A circle perhaps. A memory flashed through her mind, as if there were something she should know. "Where did you get this?"

"I've had it for a while." He didn't offer more but surprised her by kneeling in front of her. His eyes met hers, dark with secrets. He took the cross from her hand and placed it around her neck, his fingers as warm against her skin as the cross was cold. "Keep it," he said, his voice low.

Goose bumps covered her arms. She wasn't sure whether her reaction was caused by the cross or his fingertips. She looked over and caught Jake's insolent stare.

"So where in Italy do we start looking for this mysterious box?" he asked.

Nathan rose and walked to the credenza. He unlocked a drawer and took out two thick envelopes. "I'm still working on the precise location, assuming the place still exists. We'll start at Saint Peter's Square in Vatican City. I've found someone who claims he knows something about the group. You're meeting him there."

"Vatican City?" A thrill ran through Kendall, followed by immediate dread. She'd visited once as a girl. The trip hadn't gone well. The vast amount of history and relics had given her sensory overload. She hadn't been back since. Hopefully, it would be a better experience as an adult. It might be smart to drink a couple of glasses of wine first to dull her senses.

"I don't know how much this guy knows," Nathan said, "or if it's accurate, but we have to start somewhere."

Jake muttered something about needles in haystacks, and then said, "I guess we're going to Italy, Ms. Morgan. Try not to slow me down." He looked at her legs again and lifted a mocking brow. He was trying to intimidate her.

"Do you always stare at women's legs, Mr. Stone?" she whispered.

"Only when they're worth looking at."

Nathan walked back to the sofa and placed the envelopes on the table in front of them. He took the opposite seat in an ornate chair that once belonged to a king. Kendall had found it for him a month ago. In addition to his relics, at Nathan's request, she had taken charge of his antiques.

"You're pretty certain this box is in Italy?" she asked, picking up her envelope.

"All the clues lead there, and I believe if we locate the secret order, we'll find the box." Nathan watched as she opened her envelope. Inside were maps, euros, dollars, a black AMEX card, and two passports under fake names. Jake slit his envelope and Kendall saw that it appeared to hold the same. Next, he opened the satchel, and Kendall glimpsed the handle of a gun. His eyebrows rose in surprise.

Strange. Nathan didn't like guns.

"Anything else we should know about this trip?" Jake asked, examining the contents of the satchel, which he didn't appear inclined to share.

"We might not be the only ones looking for the box," Nathan said. "Someone has been buying up valuable relics."

"Someone besides you?" Jake asked.

Nathan ignored the gouge. "I believe he's involved in the black market...among other things."

It was the "other things" that caught Kendall's attention. Jake's too, judging by his narrowed eyes.

"Is he dangerous?" Jake asked.

"Anyone can become dangerous if given the right motivation," Nathan said. "We don't know for sure if this man even exists, but some of the rarest relics in the world have disappeared. The owners usually disappear too. Everyone with a collection worth having fears him. He's like the Grim Reaper of relics. That's how they refer to him, the Reaper."

"Sounds like a comic book villain," Jake said.

"I've heard about the relics that have disappeared," Kendall said. Anyone involved with artifacts and antiquities was familiar with the thefts.

Nathan studied Kendall and Jake, his expression serious. "If you do find this box, don't try to open it. It can't be opened unless it's on holy ground."

Jake gave a derisive snort. "Anything can be opened with a crowbar and some dynamite."

"Don't try to open it. That's an order." Nathan's voice was sharp.

A wave of hostility rolled off Jake. He didn't appear to care for orders, which was unfortunate since Nathan was good at giving them.

"What the hell's in this box?" Jake asked. "A demon?"

Nathan rubbed a knuckle across his chin, something he did when he was troubled. It was one of the few things about him that she could read, and for some reason it disturbed her. "I can't say, but we have to find it before anyone else does."

The fact that he didn't discount Jake's demon theory had her and Jake sharing the closest thing yet to a commiserating glance.

"So we're looking for an old box that may or may not be somewhere in Italy. We have no idea what's inside it, but we might have to fight someone called the Reaper to get it. And it can't be opened except on holy ground. Nice."

"Just find the damned box as quickly as possible. I'm running out of time."

"Why the urgency?" Kendall asked. She was used to Nathan's spontaneous trips, but this trip was unusually rushed.

"Timing is crucial," Nathan said. "I think someone else is close to finding it."

"Maybe it's a demon with a time bomb," Jake muttered, his weight shifting as he stretched long, muscular legs.

Kendall scooted over to keep from sliding toward him. "When you say holy ground, do you mean a church?"

"Your guess is as good as mine. I'm just going by rumors." Nathan rubbed his eyes. He looked tired. Again.

He always seemed tired lately. Last week, when she went to his office to show him a new amulet that had come in, she found him asleep at his desk, in the middle of the day. She knew something was troubling him. It must have been this.

Nathan slid a drawing across the table. "This is what I believe we're looking for." The sketched box appeared to be made of wood, with a circle engraved in each corner.

As Kendall watched, the lines of each circle began to move, coiling like snakes. The room faded. She heard Nathan and Jake talking, but their voices sounded far away. She saw a castle covered in vines as if forgotten by time. It was guarded by a line of giant warriors. A shadow crept up the castle walls and over the towers until the place was drenched in darkness. The darkness was blood. Bones rained from the sky, covering the ground. Whole skeletons, arms, legs, skulls. She dug her nails into her palms and tried to breathe.

"Kendall, what's wrong? Did you see something?" Nathan leaned toward her, concerned, while Jake watched with narrowed eyes.

Kendall swallowed. "Blood and bones."

Bones, Jake thought. It figured. He could handle blood, but he despised bones. Give him a fresh corpse any day. But how the hell could she see blood and bones from a picture of a box? She must be the psychic he'd heard worked for Nathan. She looked ready to faint. Her hands gripped the drawing so hard that Nathan eased the paper away. He looked as shaken as she did. She was probably just a good actress. It wouldn't be the first time someone had tried to con their way into Nathan's money.

"Excuse me." She jumped up and hurried from the room. Nathan stood, and both men watched her go.

She might be a fraud, but she had killer legs. And breasts. In fact, the whole package was hot. Blonde hair, the color of wheat, just below her shoulders. Long enough to be sexy, not so long that it got in the way. Green eyes, slanted like a cat's, and a mouth made for kissing...and other things. He looked up and saw Nathan watching him. It didn't take a psychic to know his boss had the hots for his relic expert. And that he was hiding something dark. Jake knew danger when he saw it.

"So I'm babysitting a nut job?"

"Watch it, or I'll send you back where I found you."

Where he'd found him or where he'd *put* him? "Then who'll find your treasures?"

A flush appeared above Nathan's collar. "Kendall can sense things you and I can't begin to understand."

"Or she could be after your money." It must be the money. She didn't have that starry-eyed look most women got around Nathan.

"Keep your bloody opinions to yourself. And that goes for your hands and everything else. Just do your job and keep her safe."

So that was how it was. "Guess I'm playing bodyguard?"

"You're more than a bodyguard. You have talents. So does she. I need both of you."

If her abilities were real, she could weed out the scum before they got near Nathan's money or his bed. Eliminating her competition?

"What's with this?" Jake asked, taking the Glock out of the satchel. He jammed the clip in the gun and put a round in the chamber. "Thought you didn't like weapons." That was one of the reasons Nathan's security guards were so well trained in martial arts and hand-to-hand combat. Jake tucked the gun in the back of his jeans, covering it with his T-shirt.

"The circumstances call for extra measures."

"You mean we might end up dead."

Nathan stared in the direction Kendall had gone. "I don't anticipate trouble, but stay alert. I expect you to keep her safe."

Not a bodyguard, huh?

Nathan watched Kendall step back into the room.

"Sorry." She returned to her seat, this time farther away from Jake.

Nathan moved closer and sat on the edge of the heavy table. Jake could tell he wanted to touch her, but didn't. "Are you all right?"

She nodded, but she still looked pale.

"What else did you see?" Nathan asked, his eyes scouring her face. Boss man was uptight for someone who didn't expect trouble.

Kendall licked her lips and took a deep breath. "Darkness."

Jake gave a harsh laugh. "That's about as clichéd as a psychic can get."

"I'm not a psychic," she said, glaring at him. "I find things."

"What are you, a bloodhound?" Jake asked. He knew he was being an ass. Must be sexual frustration. Nathan's call had come at a bad time. Jake had been so busy worrying about his freedom he hadn't had time for women. Until tonight that is, and Nathan had ruined that.

"She's better than a bloodhound," Nathan said. The blank look he kept on his face slipped for a second, revealing something close to reverence. "She can sense the history of things. Sometimes even the location."

"Better not let the government find out." Jake didn't want to be impressed, but if she was for real, that was one hell of a gift.

Exactly the kind of gift the man who'd ruined his life would revere.

CHAPTER TWO

THEY LANDED IN ROME WITHOUT A HITCH. NATHAN DIDN'T believe in hitches. His money and contacts saw to that. They breezed through security to the rental car Nathan had waiting for them outside the VIP lounge. A silver Maserati.

"Want me to drive?" Kendall asked.

Jake grunted no. He'd requested no driver for a reason. One of the perks of working for a rich boss was the cars. He really wanted to try out the Lamborghini, but Nathan never let anyone drive his favorite car.

Jake threw his duffel bag in the back and considered offering to load Kendall's, but she was too quick.

"Are you always this charming?" she asked, slamming the trunk.

"You should see me in bed," he said, eyeing her jeans and soft sweater, which were as sexy as that red dress she'd had on before. What the hell was wrong with him? He'd gone longer than this without sex.

"No thanks." She reached for the passenger door. "You might not want me here, but we have a job to do. Let's do it and go home."

Jake opened his door and slid inside. "Got a man waiting for you?" With a body like hers, she must have men lined up. She had their boss's silk boxers in a twist.

"No. What's the address for the hotel?"

Jake turned the key and the engine purred to life. "You can't *sense* it?"

She glared at him and dropped a big bag at her feet, the kind that went over your shoulder or your back. She'd kept it with her the entire time, guarding it like the crown jewels. "Assuming we can find the place, how do we get in?"

"You have *your* talents, I have mine." He'd gotten inside places where he didn't belong more times than he could count. This should be no different. Get in. Get the box. Get out.

"And if we get caught? If this order still exists, they probably take their privacy seriously."

"We'll pretend we're a couple of tourists, husband and wife on a honeymoon. We got lost hiking."

"This will be my first time undercover," she said. "How about you?"

The memories came from nowhere, the cries of frightened girls, the sound of gunfire, the beatings, and constant fear of death. "No." He was glad she didn't ask any more questions. They drove in silence, ignoring the throngs of tourists admiring the views. The peak season for tourism had passed, but there were still crowds. The hotel was only a short distance away. It was elegant. No surprise there. Trust Nathan to put them up in fancy rooms, and then send them on an assignment with no direction and little intel. Better than the first assignment for Nathan. He was lucky he'd had a tent in the woods and a change of underwear.

They left the car with the valet and started inside, carrying their own bags. Jake refused to let anyone else touch them. Again, Kendall had grabbed hers before he could offer to help. She stopped once and turned around, frowning. Jake followed her gaze but didn't see anyone other than the valet pulling away in the Maserati. While Jake checked them in at the front desk, Kendall called Nathan to let him know they had arrived. He probably already knew. Jake suspected Nathan was tracking their every move.

The clerk confirmed the reservations under their aliases, and when Kendall joined Jake, the man's gaze immediately dropped to her breasts before returning to her face. "If you need anything, anything at all, please call, regardless of time, day or night."

Did she have this effect on every male? "I thought he was going to kiss your hand," Jake said as they walked toward the elevator. Everything about the place screamed money, from the marble floors to the elaborate paintings and décor. It was nice, but he'd rather have a cabin beside a mountain lake.

"He was extremely accommodating," Kendall said. "Nathan has great taste in hotels. Have you stayed here before?"

He shook his head as they stepped inside the elevator. A man entered behind them and out of habit, Jake put himself in front of Kendall. When the man leaned forward to push the button for his floor, he looked at them and did a double take. Another admirer of Kendall's breasts, Jake guessed. He didn't blame him. Kendall was the hottest thing he'd seen in months. But still, she was with him. Didn't matter that he was just a bodyguard. They could be married for all this jackal knew. Jake turned to give him what his team had called his hell-frozen-over stare, but the man was already looking at the floor, tugging his ball cap lower.

That didn't stop Kendall from watching him. She kept sneaking glances until he got off the elevator on the floor below theirs. The guy was young and tall and had a few muscles. So what? Or maybe she had a thing for beards. Jake didn't trust beards. Too often they were used for hiding.

"If you hurry, you might catch him," he muttered as the doors closed.

"What?"

"You were all but drooling. You looking for a little action on the side?"

"Is that all you think about?" Kendall gave him a disgusted look and stepped away.

"Sometimes I think about food and hockey." And how to keep silly psychics alive.

It was only after they got off the elevator that Jake wondered if his irritation over the guy had been something more. He seemed familiar. Could he be one of Nathan's men checking up on them? If he'd paid more attention, maybe he'd know. He needed to stay focused. Nothing would foul up an assignment faster than lust. But he was still thinking about how good Kendall smelled when they stopped outside their door.

"There's only one room," Kendall said, looking alarmed.

"It's a suite." He opened the door and they went inside. The living area was almost as fancy as the lobby. A waste of money a woman would appreciate.

"This is bigger than my apartment."

Jake dumped his pack and duffel bag on the floor. "There are two bedrooms, each with a bath. And there's a kitchen and sitting room. Choose whichever bedroom you like, or we can share."

Kendall glared at him and opened one of the doors. Jake glimpsed a plush king-size bed. "This one," she said, and shut the door in his face.

He waited a second and tapped.

She cracked the door and peered out, her eyes as green as pond slime. "What now?"

"I need to check your room."

"For what?"

"Bedbugs." He pushed the door open and moved past her, giving the room a thorough check. But there were no bad guys under the beds or hiding in the shower. No bugs. Of any kind. "All clear."

Kendall was standing by the door, arms folded over her chest, watching. "Did you think it wouldn't be?"

"You never know."

"Thank you. Now please leave. I'm going to shower and take a nap. I didn't sleep much last night."

"Yell if you need help scrubbing your back."

She made a rude sound and slammed the door.

"Sweet dreams, Legs."

Jake didn't nap. He was used to operating on short bursts of sleep. He checked the rest of the suite, and then continued studying his maps. What did that box contain that was so important? Nathan didn't send him after things that weren't important, and he'd never authorized Jake to carry a gun. That didn't stop him from carrying one, but this time something wasn't sitting right in his gut. And his gut was usually dead on.

But not always.

A couple of hours later, he put the maps away and tapped on Kendall's door. He needed food. She probably did too. After another minute of knocking and no answer, he cursed and turned the knob. He'd explained to her that she had to stay close.

When he stepped inside her room, his heart slammed against his ribs. Her duffel bag and backpack were upside down and all her things spread across the bed and floor. Papers, makeup, flashlight, a bottle of water…all kinds of junk. There was no wallet. He didn't know if it was a robbery or a kidnapping, but either way, he was screwed.

They hadn't been in Rome two hours and he'd already lost her. It must have happened while he was in the bathroom.

After checking the hotel bar, gift shop, and concierge with no sign of her, he stopped at the front desk and told them his girlfriend was missing. They took him back to the security office, where a guard checked the cameras to see if she had left the building over the past two hours. There was no sign of her leaving. Jake's thoughts were frantic, but he forced himself to stay calm. There was no telling what kind of person they were dealing with. Someone could have smuggled her out of the hotel in a suitcase.

They must have been pros to work so quietly and so quickly. He hadn't even heard her cry out.

The phone rang and the security guard picked it up while Jake considered his next move. The local police would be no match. He would have to call Nathan. He had more resources. They'd have to check the airports, hospitals…

The security guard hung up the phone. "One of the guests reported a suspicious woman on the floor below yours. Didn't you say your girlfriend has blonde hair?"

"Yeah." Jake followed the guard to the ninth floor. The elevator doors opened and Jake slipped out first. Partway down the hall they spotted her hiding behind a marble sculpture, staring at a door.

"That her?" the security guard asked. Kendall hadn't seen them.

Jake nodded. He wanted to wring her neck.

"What's she doing?" the guard asked.

He didn't know, but he was sure as hell going to find out. "We have friends staying on this floor. Probably can't remember which room they're in."

The security guard frowned. "She could've called the front desk and asked."

"Yeah, well, she's got looks, but brains…What can I say? You can't have it all."

Surprisingly, the guard accepted the explanation and left. Slack security, Jake thought. He'd have to warn Nathan about his choice of hotels. He crept down the hall toward Kendall. She was so focused on the door she didn't hear him sneak up behind her. He grabbed her arm. "What the hell are you doing?" he growled in her ear.

She jumped, but he held on to her. He hadn't realized how worried he'd been until he felt her squirming in his arms. And that made him even more pissed than he already was. He let go of her, and she whirled, eyes flashing, face hot. God, she was gorgeous.

"Care to tell me why you're hiding behind a sculpture instead of in your room where you're supposed to be?"

"I'm uh…" She glanced at the door.

"You were looking for the guy in the elevator." Jake shook his head in disgust. "You're looking to *accidentally* bump into him so you can get laid, and here I was worried that you'd been chopped up in little pieces and smuggled out of the hotel in a suitcase."

Kendall scowled. "If I was that desperate to get laid, I wouldn't chase down a stranger. Heck, you're sniffin' at me every ten seconds."

That completely derailed him. All his "sniffin'" was just talk. But damn. Would she? If he got her in bed, maybe he could get her out of his system. She was screwing up his focus.

"I'm not looking to get laid. Something about the guy bothers me. I wanted to see if I could figure out why."

"You mean your psychic mumbo jumbo?"

"It's not mumbo jumbo," she said. "Why did you think I might be chopped up in pieces and smuggled out of the hotel?"

"Your room looks like it's been searched."

"I was looking for my phone."

"To call him? Or take his picture?"

She started to speak, but the door she'd been watching began to open. Jake grabbed her and pulled her around the corner into a small sitting area. "I need to teach you a thing or two about surveillance, Legs," he whispered.

"I'm not an idiot. I tried this already but I couldn't see the door."

"There." He pointed at a mirror behind them that reflected the door yet kept them hidden. "Always know your surroundings and use them to your advantage."

"Shhh, it's him."

The guy from the elevator stepped out of the room. He still wore the ball cap and was pulling out his keys. His phone rang and he looked at the number before answering. "You're here?"

He continued walking as he listened. "I know you're worried, but I can't call it off now. I'm too close. But things have gotten more complicated. I think I just saw a ghost." His voice faded as he moved past them and down the hall.

After the man got in the elevator, Jake kept staring after him. He couldn't shake the feeling that he was missing something. He realized he was still holding Kendall, and she hadn't tried to move. Should he read anything into it? He let a hand slide down her stomach, testing the waters.

"If you want to keep that hand, you'd better move it."

When he did, she pulled away and stalked down the hall toward the elevator. He was so mesmerized watching her go that by the time he got to the elevator, the doors were closing. She stared at him through the shrinking crack, not even attempting to stop it. He punched the button for the next elevator, and when he got to the room, he heard her stomping around inside her bedroom.

She was going to be trouble. He could feel it in his bones.

He didn't even bother to ask her about food, given the mood she was in, so he ordered room service and, after he'd eaten, took a shower and tried not to think about her at all. He thought about the guy downstairs. He wasn't sure what it was that bugged him. The phone call maybe. Was the "ghost" he referred to Kendall? He had seemed surprised in the elevator. Maybe it was more than her breasts. Just thinking about them had Jake imagining her slicked up next to him in the shower. He gave a snort of disgust, shut off the water, and climbed out, cursing Nathan for not calling a couple of hours *after* Jake's date so this lust would've been out of his system. He needed to concentrate on the assignment, not sex. He wrapped a towel around his waist and plodded into the bedroom. He yanked the curtains closed, blocking out the city lights, and loosened his towel when a scream erupted from Kendall's room.

The words on the stone began to glow, growing brighter and brighter until a stream of light burst from within, filling the room. She huddled close to the floor as the glow surrounded her. Then her father was there, staring at her, the look on his face one she'd seen too much lately. Fear. She stretched out her hands, desperate to feel him, to wipe away the fear, to know he was alive. A shadow slipped up behind him, and she felt the evil swirling inside the dark mass. Her father hadn't seen it yet. She had to warn him.

She opened her eyes and saw a figure leaning over the bed. His head was covered and he wore a robe like a monk's. She opened her mouth and screamed.

Kendall's door flew open and she shot up in bed. Jake burst into the room wearing only a towel, his gun raised. He scanned the area, and then lowered the weapon.

"What happened?"

She looked quickly around the room at the luxurious furnishings, her bag on the table, the lamp by the bed, Jake half-naked by the door. No monk. She put a hand over her heart. "Nothing. Did you break my door?"

"No. You screamed."

"I'm sorry. I had a dream." She glanced at the towel clinging to his hips.

"You have nightmares?" Something in his tone made her think he was no stranger to them either.

"It was nothing." Her heart was still pounding so hard she was surprised he couldn't hear it.

"A ploy, then."

"A ploy?"

His towel slipped an inch. "To get me in here. If you wanted sex, you could've just asked."

He got out before the pillow hit the door.

Kendall looked around the room, still expecting to see the dark figure reaching for her. He must have been part of her dream. Or vision. She lay back on the bed, dreading sleep, afraid the dream would come again, even though she couldn't remember what she'd dreamt of other than the monk. Too much talk about monks and secret orders, she supposed. She rolled onto her side and curled into a ball, staring at the door. She was tempted to go after Jake and let him distract her. Not with sex but a good fight.

She woke in the morning feeling like she had run a marathon. Judging by the tangle of sheets, she had. She rose and walked outside to get something from the kitchen, which had been fully stocked with her favorite foods. The hotel's service was amazing. Nathan must be paying a fortune for this place. A piece of paper had been shoved under the suite door. A note from the maids? She picked up the paper and read: "Your search will end in death."

Surely Jake wasn't this desperate to get rid of her. Had someone followed them? She concentrated on the note, trying to get a sense of who had written it. A dark-haired man, that's all she got. Jake had dark hair. But this seemed beneath Jake. She went to his door and knocked. He didn't answer. He was probably at breakfast. She turned the knob and saw the door wasn't locked. Slipping inside, she started searching the room for a sample of his handwriting. She didn't want to confront him without proof. Their working relationship was already strained. He must have a signed invoice or a notebook or something. She didn't find an invoice, but she did notice his duffel bag on the bed.

She experienced a twinge of guilt as she unzipped it, but snooping wasn't like digging into someone's head. Anyone could snoop, and if she was going to trust him with her life, she needed to know more about Jake Stone. She knew a few things. He was intelligent, strong, and didn't take well to orders, which made her wonder why he was letting Nathan tell him what to do. He was angry, at whom she didn't know. Other than Nathan. The tension between them was as thick as sludge. Whatever Nathan was holding over his head didn't sit well with Jake.

His duffel was neat and efficiently packed. The work of Fergus? Three pairs of black combat pants, a couple of pairs of jeans. One pair of khakis. A leather jacket. A second pair of boots. Black, military. There were several T-shirts, all dark colors, along with socks and underwear. There weren't any pajamas, but that didn't surprise her. He didn't seem like a pajama kind of guy.

She spotted his backpack on a chair. She might have more luck finding something handwritten there. Inside were the usual items a badass bodyguard might carry: a rolled-up jacket, thermal blanket, rope, gloves, compass, knife, matches, lighter, bottled water, and first-aid kit. The little wooden doll she found at the bottom of the pack didn't seem to belong. She picked it up, studying the workmanship. It had been hand carved, with amazing detail etched in the face.

She couldn't breathe. Dirt covered her body, filling her mouth and nose. She freed her hands but the more she clawed, the more dirt fell. Panic, blackness. Then nothing.

Kendall dropped the doll inside the pack, pulse racing. She tried to rationalize the vision. It was connected to the doll. Why did Jake have it and who did he know that had been buried alive? She saw a piece of paper in one of the side pockets and started to reach for it when she heard a sound coming from the bathroom. She zipped the backpack and jumped up to leave.

"I told you, all you gotta do is ask," Jake said from the bathroom door. Of course he was naked.

Kendall quickly turned her back. "Geez, do you ever wear clothes?" Her first instinct was to turn back around and throw something at him, but that would mean looking at all that nakedness. "I knocked but you didn't answer."

"I didn't hear you. My head was underwater."

"Underwater?" She edged toward the door.

"I was soaking my sore muscles. The tub's the size of a small pool. There's plenty of room for two if you're game."

"No thanks." She wasn't about to ask what he had been doing to make his muscles sore. "I'll come back when you're dressed."

"No need. I'm not shy."

She heard a sound that she hoped was a towel being wrapped around his body. When she turned, he was tucking the edges around his waist. She'd seen more of him in the last few hours than she'd seen of all the men she'd dated in the past two years.

"Did you write this?" She thrust the note at him, trying to keep her eyes on his face. She hadn't seen a chest that sexy since...maybe never.

"What's this?" Frowning, he took the note.

His hands were sexy too. Nice fingers, well shaped. Everything he had was sexy, she thought, immediately banishing the bare image. She folded her arms. "Are you trying to scare me off?"

"You think I wrote this?"

"You didn't want me here. Remember your 'I work alone' speech?"

"Are you crazy? I didn't write this. Where did you find it?"

Being called crazy went a long way toward neutralizing lust. "It was on the suite floor this morning."

He cursed. "Well, Legs. Either someone's warning us to back off or they want us dead."

"Unless you wrote it," Jake added, studying the note. It was written on hotel paper. So much for staying undercover.

"Why would I write it?" she asked.

He shrugged. "You didn't want to work with me any more than I wanted to work with you." Something they'd have to fix. Trust was crucial in the field. Their lives could depend on it. And if he botched this assignment, he was as good as dead. He put the note down and opened his duffel bag, pulling out boxers and socks.

She eyed the underwear. "But I haven't been acting like an ass. You've been trying to intimidate me since we met."

He sat on the side of his bed, dropped the boxers next to the note and rubbed the remnants of last night's headache nudging the base of his skull. He wondered if she'd hit him if he asked for a massage. Soaking in hot water hadn't helped his aching muscles. "Sorry. I don't like this job. Nathan knows more than he's saying."

She cast another suspicious look at his boxers lying on the bed but seemed to decide that he wouldn't put them on with her still in the room. He was tempted to do it just to get her reaction, but that wouldn't help matters now.

"I don't like all this secrecy either," she said. "But it's no reason to act like a lecherous scumbag."

"I haven't been that bad."

"Yes you have."

"I'll try not to act like a lecherous scumbag if you'll stop sneaking off to spy on strange men."

"I wasn't—"

Jake held up a hand. "Whatever the reason, just don't." He waved the note at her. "I can't keep you safe—or alive—if you don't stick close. Now, how about we let bygones be bygones and get breakfast. I'm ready to eat this bed." Preferably with her in it, nasty glare and all. "Then we're going to find this damned box and go home. I think your guy in the elevator must have written the note."

"I got some weird impressions from him," she said.

So had he, but his attempt to sneak into the guy's room through the balcony had been interrupted when the couple next door caught him picking Elevator Guy's lock. Jake had had to escape without taking time to put on his climbing gear. Leaping from balcony to balcony, nine floors in the air with a heavy pack strapped on his back, was murder on the arms and legs. "Can't you do your psychic...uh, bloodhound stuff on the note and find out who wrote it?"

She rolled her eyes. "I tried before. It wasn't clear. I can try again."

She took the note and ran her hands over it, her fingers stroking the paper. It was kind of sensuous. Then he saw the look on her face change, and it reminded him of when he was a kid, watching the blind lady across the street read to him in Braille. Kendall's eyes flew open.

"What?" he asked leaning forward.

"Death."

"Damn." She'd had him there for a second. "Can't you come up with something more original?"

"You've been suspicious of me from the start. I don't know what you think I'm after."

"For starters, Nathan's billions."

"You don't have to believe me," she said, "but the guy in the elevator is connected to the note."

"How come you didn't *see* this before?" Jake asked.

"I don't know why it works the way it does." Her face softened and her lips thinned to the point that he wondered if she was going to cry. "He's going to die."

"Die? What do you mean?" Everyone died eventually.

"Someone's going to stab him."

"You saw this?"

She nodded and rubbed her arms.

"When?" Jake asked. "Tomorrow? Next year?"

"Soon."

Jake stared at her, not sure what to say. "Is that why you were hiding outside his room? Waiting to warn him?"

"No. I didn't know until just now."

"Did you see who stabs him?"

She shook her head.

"Does this happen a lot? Seeing someone's death?"

"Not often. I'm not a palm reader. I get more impressions from objects than people, but lately my senses have been going haywire."

"If you know someone's going to die, do you tell them?" Talk about the bearer of bad news.

"No." She looked so haunted he wanted to pat her hand or something, but he didn't want her to think he was hitting on her. He didn't blame her. She was right. He had been an ass since they met.

Nathan chose that moment to call. Jake told him about the note. Nathan seemed alarmed but not surprised, which made Jake wonder again how much Nathan knew and wasn't telling them. After listening to Nathan's instructions Jake hung up. "We're meeting our contact at eleven. Get ready to leave."

"I'm not packed."

"Then get packed. Take everything; we're not coming back. I'll have to figure out why this guy wrote the note and why he wants us dead."

"It may be just a warning," she said, her face still looking like a lost little girl's. If he didn't get her out of this funk, she wouldn't be any good at finding anything. He reached for his towel. "I'd suggest you leave now unless you want to watch me dress."

Sure enough, she shot him a dirty look and slammed the door on her way out.

Mission accomplished.

CHAPTER THREE

AFTER THEY DRESSED AND PACKED, THEY LEFT. THEY STOPPED at the front desk and asked the clerk if he could tell them who was in Elevator Guy's room. Jake expected to be told that the information was confidential, but the man punched a button and gave them a name—Thomas Little, from Chicago. Thomas had already checked out of the hotel. It was probably an alias, but Jake called and left the info on Nathan's cell phone. His people could find out who Thomas really was.

"This hotel's security sucks," Jake told Kendall after they'd walked away.

"I'm surprised they gave you his name," she said, glancing over her shoulder.

"What's wrong?" Jake asked, but his neck was prickling too.

"I think we're being watched."

He scanned the area but didn't see Thomas or anything out of the ordinary. There was a couple trying to console a crying kid, a tour group, and a woman sitting in a chair, her back to them, only her legs visible. Nice legs. No one seemed to be paying attention to Kendall and Jake, but no one genuinely spying on them would. They hurried outside, and when the valet pulled up, Jake handed him some euros and they left.

"You're good at spending Nathan's money," Kendall said.

"He has so much he won't miss it." He drove around the streets in circles, taking quick turns in case they were being followed.

Kendall's phone rang. She looked at the display and then shoved the phone in her bag.

"Aren't you going to answer it?" Jake asked.

"No."

Was she avoiding a man? "Boyfriend troubles?"

"Sort of."

She had a boyfriend. He wasn't surprised. But he was disappointed, even though it shouldn't have mattered. "Is he pissed that you went to Italy without him?"

"I don't have a boyfriend, just an aunt who won't rest until I'm married."

Ah, so no boyfriend. "Any prospects?" Perhaps their filthy rich, handsome boss?

"No."

"Why not?"

"You think I need a boyfriend?"

"No. I just figured...forget it." Maybe the psychic thing turned men off. "I see you found your phone."

"It was under the bed."

"How'd it get there? Were you hiding from ghosts? You know if you get scared my bed's always open."

"Do you do this with all women?"

"Jealous, darlin'?"

"Hardly." Kendall's fingers played with the strap of her bag. "You don't have any alcohol, do you?"

"You planning on getting drunk? We haven't even had breakfast." Was he that irritating or was the vision troubling her? He didn't blame her for being bothered over what she saw. Who wanted to foretell someone's death? Still, she would have to let it go and move on or they could be next.

"I had a bad experience at Vatican City when I was younger."

"What happened?"

"Too much history, too many relics. It was overwhelming."

"Does Nathan know?" Jake asked. He doubted Nathan would send Kendall somewhere that would upset her. He was too protective of her for that.

"No. I haven't told anyone."

"I can go alone," Jake offered. "You can stay in the car." Though he preferred to keep her in sight.

"No. I'm curious to see if it's different now that I'm grown. But I'm nervous too. I can't afford to mess up my senses now. There's too much at stake."

"If you start feeling bad, we'll leave."

"I fainted the last time," she said, sounding embarrassed.

"If you faint, I'll throw you over my shoulder and carry you out." If it wasn't for that threatening note, he'd stay in the car and let her meet Nathan's contact. Jake hated crowds.

And it was crowded. Families and tourists swarmed the place like flies. After finding a place to park, he and Kendall started walking. "We're early, but if someone's looking for us, what better place to hide than in a crowd?"

"Have you been here before?" she asked, looking toward the dome of Saint Peter's Basilica.

Jake shook his head. "We have two hours to kill. Let's grab something to eat then look around." They stopped at a little restaurant nearby. Neither of them ate much, and after a few minutes they paid the bill and left.

She looked uneasy, but as they approached the obelisk and the colonnade, she seemed to relax. Jake wasn't much for organized religion yet had to admit the place was impressive. And intimidating. He could imagine how it could affect a child with Kendall's gift. If she had a gift at all. The jury was still out on that.

While waiting to meet their contact, they saw as many sights as they could without a tour guide. She didn't appear overwhelmed this time. Her face glowed as she moved from place to place. It was easy to see why Nathan had hired her, besides the fact that she was gorgeous and could supposedly find things no one else could. Jake could feel history reflected in her face.

He checked his watch. "It's almost time."

She didn't hear him. She was staring at a statue of Saint Peter, her eyes intent on his face. What did she see that everyone else didn't? Jake touched her arm to get her attention and a tingle ran through his hand. A voice whispered in his ear; a male speaking Hebrew. One of his team members—ex-team members—had spoken some Hebrew. Jake dropped her arm and took a step back. The voice disappeared. He blew out a breath. He was just getting caught up in her fervor. Or he'd overheard someone speaking Hebrew as they walked past.

He pulled her from the trance, and they made their way back to the obelisk, where they were supposed to meet Nathan's contact. A lone man stood a few feet away, watching the crowd.

"I think that's him," Jake said.

As if on cue, the man rose and walked toward them. He was midthirties, with light brown hair and a few pounds overweight. He could easily pass as a local or a tourist.

"You are Kendall and Jake?" he asked.

Jake was relieved that the man addressed them in English. "Yes. Edward?"

"Edward Romano. There's a little trattoria here if you're hungry. Nothing fancy, but very good food."

"We already ate," Jake said. "We don't have much time." He wanted to get the info and get out of here. He was jittery from staying in one place too long. They found the least busy spot and listened as Edward told his story. One of his ancestors had helped build the castle where the secret order lived. According to family stories, the group was shrouded in mystery, a brotherhood of some sort, but no one was sure if they were monks or knights or Satanists. The few who had tried to investigate had disappeared. The locals believed the place was cursed.

Kendall looked intrigued. "So it's a real castle?"

Edward nodded. "Or it used to be. I don't know how much of it remains. It could have been destroyed."

"You haven't been there?"

"No."

"What kind of stories did you hear about the order?" Kendall asked.

Edward looked over his shoulder at the bustling crowd. "Power and evil. The Protettori were feared."

Kendall frowned. "That means protectors, I think."

Edward nodded. "I don't know if that is what they were really called or a name given to them by the villagers. The stories are still whispered today."

"Did your ancestor leave any records that might help us find the box?" Jake asked.

"If he did, they're lost now. He died a year after the castle was built. The stories go that everyone who had contact with the Protettori ended up dead. Everything I know was passed down by word of mouth."

"Your English is excellent," Kendall said.

"I studied at Cambridge. I wanted to see the world. To explore."

"But you're back here now." Kendall watched Edward, her gaze steady.

"Italy is home. There's something about the place, a pull. I hope you find what you're looking for. I don't know what the Protettori were about, but they were protecting something. I'm nosy enough to want to know what."

Her gaze met Jake's and he knew she was thinking the same thing he was. The box.

"You've never tried to find out yourself?" Kendall asked.

He looked alarmed. "No, the place is cursed." His expression settled into an embarrassed grin. "I may be well educated, but I'm still as superstitious as my *nonna*. I'll point you in the right direction. If you find anything interesting, I would appreciate it if you would share the information." He gave them a rough map that would get them to the area. "It's well off the road. You will have to hike in. And be careful. The stories say the path leading there is enough to kill a man."

"Hope you brought hiking boots," Jake said as they left.

"You didn't like him," Kendall said softly after a moment. "Are you naturally wary of strangers or was it something about him in particular?"

"You digging around in my head?" He could already see the drawbacks of traveling with a psychic or whatever she was. He didn't want anyone knowing his thoughts or his past.

"I could just tell that you didn't like him."

"Just wary, I guess." He couldn't tell her it was because Edward's eyes were the same dark brown as the dirt in a lonely, forgotten grave. "You should be wary too, considering that note."

Kendall didn't hear him. She was staring over her shoulder at the colonnade.

"We can't keep playing tourists," Jake said. "We have to find that box."

She stood rooted to the spot, staring at Saint Peter's Cathedral. "Fake." She said the word so quietly Jake almost didn't hear.

"What's fake?"

Kendall shook her head. "What?"

"You said something was fake."

"I did?"

"You don't remember?"

"No."

"Does that happen a lot?"

She pressed a palm against her forehead and looked back at Saint Peter's Square. "I think that's the first time."

"Don't tell me it's not really Saint Peter buried there."

She didn't answer. Now she was scanning the crowd, searching the faces. "Someone's watching us."

Jake hoped she was just a paranoid psychic, but he was getting that same prickle in his neck that he'd had at the hotel. He scanned the masses looking for Thomas or anyone out of place. There was no longer any question that someone else was after the box. The only thing that worried him was how far he'd go to get it.

"Come on. Let's go." He grabbed her arm and pulled her through the crowd. A few feet later, Kendall gasped.

"What now?" he growled.

"Someone touched me."

"We're in a crowd. Someone probably bumped you." He'd been elbowed several times since they arrived.

"This was different." She looked shaken.

He pulled her away from the spot, and when he glanced back, a man looked right at them before disappearing behind one of the columns. Thomas? Too far away to tell. If Kendall hadn't been with him, he would've gone after the man, but he couldn't do that with her in tow. "Come on. If someone's there, we'll lead them on a wild goose chase."

They moved quickly, darting through groups of people, joining one party, and then slipping into another, gradually moving closer to where he'd left the Maserati. When he was sure no one was following, they hurried to the car. He put on a hat, had Kendall duck low in the seat as they left, and then drove for miles before stopping at a rental company to switch cars.

Following Edward's directions, they headed north in the most nondescript BMW Jake could find. The drive took them through towns and scenery that the average tourist would have killed to see, but Jake and Kendall had other things on their minds besides ruins and history: the box, Thomas Little, and his warning note. If it was his. Jake looked at Kendall, who was holding her bag on her lap. Could she have written the note and pretended Thomas had done it? Jake couldn't think of a good reason for her to lie. Either way, the situation made him uneasy. If she had sensed the author of the note simply through touch then her sixth sense was real, and he wasn't comfortable with someone who might take a peek into his past.

Kendall perked up as they approached a quaint town with cobblestone streets and tiny shops. "This town is charming."

"Glad you approve. This is home for the next several hours. There's an inn up ahead."

"Did Fergus make reservations?"

"No. I called while you were packing. But Fergus gave me a list of places to stay." The ever-resourceful Fergus. "How long has he been with Nathan?" Jake sometimes wondered if Nathan could take a piss without the man.

"For as long as I've known him."

"How long's that?"

"I started working for him a few months ago."

About the same time Jake did. Watching Nathan and Kendall together, he had assumed they'd known each other longer.

"You sleeping with him?"

Now why the hell did he say that?

Her green eyes widened and then narrowed, the glare sharp as a cactus. "No, not that it's any of your business."

"Don't get your panties in a bunch. I was just making sure you were alert," he lied, and then checked to see that she wasn't touching anything that belonged to him, just in case her gift was legit. Her hand was resting on the seat. The car was rented in his name—his alias. Did that count? "How did you meet him?"

"I was working at the Smithsonian. Nathan had lent us a collection. When he came to pick the pieces up, one of them was missing."

"Let me guess. You did your bloodhound thing and found it?"

"Yes." She didn't roll her eyes or glare at him. Maybe she was starting to relax. "It had gotten mixed in with another collection. He was impressed and offered me a job."

Jake barked out a laugh. "I'm sure it had nothing to do with the fact that you look like a swimsuit model." Better than a swimsuit model. They usually didn't have enough to fill a bikini.

"It wasn't like that. We just connected. I guess we have a lot in common. I wasn't looking to change jobs, but his offer was too good to refuse. I needed the extra money for my aunt Edna. She was about to lose her antique shop."

So there was a heart of gold hidden inside that sexy exterior. "Did Nathan know about your abilities then?"

"I don't know how he could have. It's not something I advertise."

Smart. It wouldn't be wise to draw attention to a gift like that. There were lots of unscrupulous people who would do anything to get their hands on someone with her ability. It was probably a good thing Nathan had hired her. He had the means to protect her. Just like he protected himself. He was harder to get to than Fort Knox. Digging up his history wasn't any easier. He was the damned poster child for reclusive billionaires. "How much do you know about Nathan's past?"

"Not much. He likes his privacy. I can't say that I blame him."

If he had all those billions to worry about, maybe he'd be the same. Come to think of it, he was the same, just without the money. "You don't seem starstruck around him like most women. They fall over themselves to get near him."

She gave a delicate shrug. "He's my boss. That's all."

That wasn't all. She might believe it, but he didn't. "You haven't read him?"

"Of course not. I don't pry."

Then what was she doing going through his pack? She hadn't taken anything, but he didn't like that she'd looked. Well, fair was fair. He'd checked hers out too. "Maybe you should. Someone's after him. His network has been attacked twice in the past few weeks." Whatever Nathan was hiding, Jake wasn't the only one who was interested.

"I wish I could help him, but I can't control how my gift works."

"Do you know where he grew up? He sounds British. Not as stuffy as Fergus, but the accent is there."

"I know. He sounds like Jason Statham."

Jake frowned. "The actor? Is that a good thing?"

She smiled. "It's definitely not bad."

Jake grunted under his breath. So she liked British accents. Hell, he wasn't British, but he had more hair.

"I think Nathan spent part of his childhood in England and Scotland with Fergus. Nathan has never mentioned his father or mother. I think something unpleasant happened in his past."

Jake knew about unpleasant pasts. He'd tried forgetting his, but it had a way of coming back.

"This is nice," Kendall said when he pulled up to the inn.

Nice wasn't important. Safety was. The inn sat off the main street, backed up to a hill. It had a clear view of the town, which was small, but drew enough tourists that they could blend in. The long lane that led to the inn would allow him to see anyone approaching, and the trellis on the side would make for a quick exit if needed. The downside was that it could also be used to get in. "This town draws a lot of tourists. That's what we're doing, Kara Monroe, being tourists."

"Are these aliases really necessary?"

"Thomas or someone found out we were at the hotel. We don't want him to find us here."

"I don't think we have to worry about it with the way you drove," Kendall said.

"Just trying to keep you safe." Jake slapped a fist against his heart. "I vow to protect you with my life."

He expected Kendall to smirk or roll her eyes, but she just looked at him, those green eyes steady on his, and a thrill of something ran through him.

While she gathered her backpack, he opened the door and went around to the trunk, continuing to survey the outside for security problems. There were a few vehicles parked out front. He would have to check out the other guests. Tourists probably. When he made the reservation, the innkeeper said a small tour group was staying there.

Jake threw his pack over his shoulder and gathered their duffel bags. This time Kendall didn't beat him to the task, though she did take her bag from him before they approached the door. The doorbell jingled as they stepped inside. The lobby was friendly, yellow walls with pictures of smiling men and women. He could never figure out exactly what the people in Italian paintings were doing. Frolicking, he guessed, whatever that was. He wasn't sure, but he had a pretty good idea what it would lead to.

The man behind the desk appeared to be even friendlier than the walls. "You must be Jason Sutter and Kara Monroe. Welcome to Italy. I am Roberto."

Roberto was in his early thirties, immaculately dressed, and looked like he'd just gotten a manicure. And Jake suspected he was wearing eyeliner. After his welcome, the innkeeper's attention remained focused on Jake.

Kendall pressed her lips together and Jake knew she was hiding a grin.

"What brings you to our little inn?" Roberto asked, looking Jake over head to toe.

Jake threw an arm around Kendall's shoulders and yanked her close. "We're honeymooning."

Kendall gave a strangled gasp and Jake tightened his hold, pulling her closer. Damn, she smelled good.

"Honeymooning? You're married. But your names…"

"She kept her maiden name," Jake said.

"Then I must change your room. I assumed you were just… friends."

"Room?" Kendall asked, her eyes doing that cactus thing again. She shot Jake a glare when Roberto turned his back. She could patent the damn things.

"Our honeymooners always get the special room," he said, sitting down in front of his computer. "I will switch with another guest."

Kendall had managed to pull away from Jake, which was fine with him. Her perfume was gnawing through his skin like a damned piranha.

"Won't the other guest mind?" she asked.

"She hasn't arrived yet," Roberto said. "I only gave her the room because someone canceled and it was our last." With a wink, he added, "It will be our little secret." He turned to his computer and started muttering to himself.

"Heaven's sakes, Gilbert, I know I put them in here." The voice was loud, with a twang that could only come from the American South. A woman entered the room. She was well into middle age, her strawberry blonde hair teased so high it looked like a wad of cotton candy stuck on her head. Her dress was a big floral thing that made her look like a hockey player in drag. She was digging in a tiny little purse while a skinny man trailed behind her. "Oh," she said catching sight of Kendall and Jake. "More guests. Are you here for the tour?"

"This is Jason and Kara from America," Roberto said. "They're honeymooning."

"Honeymooners," the woman crooned. "Remember when we were honeymooners, Gilbert?"

Her husband nodded, but his expression didn't indicate whether it was a good memory.

"Oh, we're Gilbert and Loretta Jenkins," the woman said. "From Georgia. We're *tourists*." She said the word with the same satisfaction one would expect from a person announcing that she was a movie star. "This is our first trip to Italy. Granddaddy passed away and left me some money, so I said to Gilbert, 'Gilbert, let's go to Italy.' And Gilbert says, 'I reckon we could.' So we've been touring Italy for two weeks now. Oh, there they are." She pulled out a bottle of Tums. "I've developed acid reflux. I guess it's all this Italian food."

"There," Roberto exclaimed. "I have fixed the problem. I think you will enjoy this room much more. It is very romantic." He grinned, and Jake wondered if Roberto was imagining what would happen behind closed doors. He would be disappointed at the lack of action. Jake would definitely be.

"Let me give you a quick tour of the downstairs," Roberto said.

Of course, loud Loretta tagged along, giving her opinion on everything. The inn was more Jake's speed than the fancy hotel. It had wide plank floors and clean walls, except for those frolicking paintings. He studied the people they passed—all old as far as he could see—while Kendall and Loretta commented on the furnishings and décor. Some of the guests were still lounging over lunch, the heaviest meal served.

"Have you eaten?" Roberto asked.

"We grabbed something on the way," Jake said.

Roberto nodded. "I'm sure you're anxious to get settled. Most of the shops are still closed. They will reopen later in the afternoon. Dinner is at eight. Some of our guests eat in town, but for those who stay in we have a variety of food choices. There should be several of the tour group dining in before the tour this evening. I warn you, it gets a little noisy." He tapped his ears. "Some of the older guests are hard of hearing."

"Me and Gilbert are gonna grab a quick snack in a few minutes," Loretta called. "Why don't you join us?"

"We'll probably be *occupied*," Jake said, pulling Kendall close.

Roberto led them to a room on the second floor. It was a corner room, with one window facing the front and the other near the trellis on the side of the inn. As soon as the door closed, Kendall turned to Jake.

"Why did you tell them we were honeymooning?" she hissed. "Of all the stupid things to say."

"I got distracted by your perfume."

"I'm not wearing perfume."

Then she had the sexiest smelling skin known to man.

She surveyed the room, eyes lingering on the bed.

"You can sleep on the sofa if you'd prefer," he said. "Looks small but you could curl up."

Her eyes narrowed, accusing. "Roberto said he just gave the last room to someone else, so why didn't you book two rooms instead of one in the first place?"

"He didn't have it when I called. Don't worry, I won't attack you. I like my sex friendly."

"This is insane," she said, looking at the large bed.

He left her stewing and went to check the room. He was inspecting the lock on the window when a blue car rolled up the drive and pulled to a stop. He was vaguely aware of Kendall moving toward the bathroom as the car door opened and a leg appeared. Female. There was something about that leg…Before the rest of the woman could exit the car, Kendall cried out, and Jake ran to the bathroom.

Kendall stood in the middle of the floor, smiling. "Look at the tub."

"You're admiring a bathtub? I thought you'd been attacked."

"Sorry." She squatted beside the tub, gazing at it like a mother looking at her newborn. "Isn't it gorgeous?"

It was a tub. It was white. What was the big deal?

She reached out and ran her hand along the edge. "It's old, like one I had before…" She flinched and jerked her hand back. She stood and wiped her hands on her jeans. "How's the rest of the room?" she asked, her voice shaky.

"Secure." Jake frowned at the tub, expecting a tarantula. "What just happened?"

"What do you mean?" she asked.

"You looked like something bit you."

"No. I'm fine."

She wasn't fine, but it was his job to protect her, not sort out her quirks. "You ready to go downstairs?"

"You told Loretta we weren't coming."

"I changed my mind."

"Why?"

"I want to check out the other guests. I like knowing who I'm sleeping under the same roof with." That leg troubled him. He wanted to see its owner. Someone had followed them to the hotel, maybe even to Saint Peter's Square. In spite of precautions, it was possible that they'd been followed here.

"I need a few minutes," Kendall said.

"Don't leave the room without me." While she did whatever women did in the bathroom, Jake checked out the inn. After eavesdropping on guests and learning more about bowel movements and ghosts than he wanted to know, he slipped outside and walked the perimeter. When he came back, he ran into Roberto in the hallway.

"The room? It is fine?"

Jake nodded. "Yes, it's fine. Thank you. We decided to grab a quick snack and then look around the area. Maybe go for a hike or visit some castles. Kara loves castles. There's my lovely bride now," he said through clenched teeth as Kendall appeared on the stairs. Couldn't she follow any damned instructions? She had changed into khakis and a shirt that hugged her breasts. Perfect breasts. Firm. Just the right size. But he didn't need to be focusing on her breasts no matter how perfect they were.

"There are several castles in the area," Roberto said. "A few within walking distance or a short ride."

Jake pulled his eyes from Kendall's perfect breasts. "Anything haunted? She likes ghosts."

Roberto tapped a manicured finger against his cheek. "We have the haunted tour in town. It runs for the next three nights.

There are reports of ghosts. Like the graveyard down the street, but—"

"We were hoping to find something…darker," Jake said. "Have you heard of the Protettori?"

Roberto froze. "Where did you hear about them?" he whispered.

"From a friend who's interested in old legends."

Roberto took a quick breath, his eyes wide. "You don't want to go there, even if you could find it. The place is cursed."

CHAPTER FOUR

K ENDALL RAISED HER EYEBROWS AND LOOKED AT JAKE.
"Cursed? You've been there, Roberto?"

"No. But I've heard stories since I was a boy. Whispers about *them*. There was a family in a nearby village who claimed an ancestor had helped build the castle."

"What stories?" Jake asked.

"That there were ghosts and strange lights, and if anyone went there, they disappeared, never to be seen again."

"Do you know where the place is?" Kendall asked.

Roberto looked wary. "Beyond the hills."

"Which hills?" Kendall asked.

"Those." He pointed out the window at the rolling hills dipping harshly across the landscape, covered in thick trees that gave way to mountains. "I don't know exactly where. I was forbidden to go near as a child. Please stick to the tourist sites. Let me get you a brochure." He hurried to the lobby and returned a moment later, opening a brochure. He pointed to a church. "This church and graveyard is on the haunted tour. It has catacombs and everything."

"I love catacombs," Kendall said.

Of course she would.

Jake started to usher Kendall toward the dining room, where he could hear some lingering diners talking and laughing. He stopped and turned back to Roberto. "I saw a car arrive after we got here."

"Yes. The guest who was supposed to get your room. Another American. Lots of Americans. Lucky I speak good English."

When they neared the dining room, Loretta spotted them immediately. "Hello honeymooners," she called, and every head in the place turned.

"Come join us," she said, patting a chair next to her.

Jake would've bolted right then and there, but Kendall gave him her warning glare and put her hand on his arm. Before Jake knew it he was seated next to Gilbert Jenkins, who was as quiet as his wife was loud.

"Oh look, there's Brandi," Loretta said. "She's the last to join the tour group."

A redhead entered the dining room. She was midtwenties and pretty, with curves toned to muscle and hair fiery enough to make a man wonder if she ran hot in the bedroom. She glanced at their table and looked like she wanted to turn around and leave. Jake wondered if she was trying to avoid Loretta or them. Curious. She must have been the one who arrived in the blue car. She was wearing a green skirt that gave him a good look at her legs. Nice. And familiar. The nice part didn't bother him. The familiar did.

"Brandi, this is Jason and Kara," Loretta said. "Brandi's a nurse." Brandi took a seat at a nearby table.

"Where are you from, Brandi?" Kendall asked.

"Wisconsin. This is my first trip to Italy. What brings you here?"

"We're honeymooning," Jake said, rolling the words around in his mouth like rocks.

Brandi's gaze dropped to Kendall's hand. Kendall quickly hid it in her lap as Brandi shifted her attention to Jake's bare ring finger. They'd have to find some wedding rings or come up with a reason for not wearing them.

"This is a nice place for a honeymoon," Brandi said. "I think it's the most charming inn I've ever visited."

"Everything I've seen is charming," Loretta said. "I love Italy." She took a bite of pizza and sighed. "So are you two sightseeing today? I heard you asking Roberto about a cursed castle. Do they do tours? I'd love to see a cursed castle."

Jake wished he could suffocate the woman. "Someone mentioned it on the way here. Tell me about this tour group," he said to distract her.

Loretta's eyes lit up. She wiped her mouth, smearing what lipstick had survived the pizza grease. "There's a bunch of us from Georgia. We've had a few others join the group. Like Brandi here. The more the merrier, I say. We've seen the most wonderful ruins and castles. There was a haunted church in Rome. It had catacombs and everything. It was so exciting. Wasn't it exciting, Gilbert?"

Gilbert shrugged. "Just a bunch of lanterns and bones."

"When were you in Rome?" Jake asked, giving Loretta and Gilbert closer scrutiny. They were the last people anyone would suspect as attackers. A perfect disguise?

"We left there yesterday," Loretta said. "What a great city. Brandi, have you been to Rome?"

The redhead was focused on her phone, apparently reading a text message. She looked up. "Not yet."

Loretta took a long drink of water. "You should see the Colosseum. It was like I could hear the cries of the gladiators. And Vatican City, now that's a lovely place." She tapped on the brochure Roberto had given Jake and Kendall. "You should join us tonight. It might not be as nice as Rome or Vatican City, but we might see some ghosts. Are you coming, Brandi?"

"I can't. I have some things to take care of tonight," Brandi said, putting away her phone.

Loretta adjusted her hair, which was tilting to one side. "Too bad. Jason, Kara?"

"Sorry, we have plans," Jake replied.

"Maybe tomorrow night, then. It starts at eight thirty." Loretta drained her bottle of water and wiped her double chin. "Get me another bottle of water, Gilbert. I shouldn't have ordered pepperoni pizza. They make it with real peppers, you know."

"I'll get you a bottle," Brandi said. "I was going to get one myself." She returned with four bottles of water and set one in front of each of them. "You'll need to stay hydrated if you're planning to do much walking."

"Is anyone up for shopping later?" Loretta asked, finishing the last bite of pizza crust. "I saw a little store in town that sells clothes. I need some new pants. Mine shrunk."

If she kept eating they'd have to remodel the inn to get her out the door.

Brandi's phone rang. She pulled it from her purse, looked at the display and frowned. "Excuse me, please." She hurried from the dining room.

Jake watched her go. Something wasn't hitting him right about the nurse. There was a carefulness about her speech and stance, even her facial expressions, that usually indicated a person was hiding something. He'd used the tactic many times himself when he wanted to keep his identity hidden. Nathan…He'd damned near perfected it.

Jake considered following Brandi but Loretta chose that moment to choke. Kendall pounded her on the back and Jake handed her his bottle of water.

After Loretta caught her breath, she pushed back her chair and stood. "I think I'd better lie down. I'm not feeling so well. My acid reflux is acting up. Come on, Gilbert."

Gilbert rose like a piece of petrified wood and followed.

"If you change your mind, we'll see you at dinner," Loretta called.

"Like hell," Jake muttered after they'd moved out of earshot.

Kendall picked up her bottle of water and stood. "I'm going upstairs to check in with Nathan."

She seemed to check in with Nathan a lot. Jake looked down the hall where Brandi had disappeared. "I need to do something. Then we can try to find the road to this castle."

He followed Brandi's scent to the library, a large room filled with bookshelves and an assortment of cozy chairs scattered here and there. Long windows looked out over the grounds of the inn. Brandi stood at the window, talking on her phone. The afternoon sun streaming through the glass lit her hair, making it look like a flame. She hadn't realized she had company yet. Jake stayed outside the doorway, listening.

"It's too risky. You said yourself that you think someone is watching you. Just let it go, please. We don't even know for certain..." Brandi tensed. "You're sure?" She dropped onto a chair, her body stiff. "My God, after all this time." She listened for a minute, tugging nervously at her hair. "Even if you're right, don't do this. It can't change what happened, and what if he finds out?" She turned, catching sight of Jake, and jumped up, her eyes wide. "I have to go."

"Sorry I startled you. I just stopped to get a book...for my wife." The term didn't sound as awkward as before.

"Oh, what does she like to read?" Brandi asked, laying her phone down. "Maybe I can help you find a book."

"Mysteries and thrillers," he guessed, wondering what that call was about. Was she having an affair and worried about a spouse finding out? Or was it something darker?

"Let's see. How about Dan Brown? I saw one earlier. My brother loves..." She stopped and pulled out a book. "Here it is." She handed it to him, her face blank except for the nerve jumping under her eye. Jake took the novel, and when he turned, he saw Kendall watching from the doorway. Damned if he didn't find himself moving away from Brandi like a guilty husband.

"Brandi helped me find a book for you to read," he said, handing it to Kendall.

"A book? Thank you." She didn't look thankful.

"I think we'd better get moving, love," he said, taking Kendall's arm. They said good-bye to Brandi and left the library. He looked back and saw Brandi staring out the window, her forehead wrinkled in a frown.

"What were you doing with her?" Kendall asked when they were in the hallway.

"Careful, darlin', you sound like a jealous wife."

Her eyes flashed. "I'm not jealous."

"I was eavesdropping."

"Did you learn anything?"

"She has a brother who likes Dan Brown."

"I found out something better."

"I didn't realize it was a contest." He put a hand behind her back as they started up the stairs.

"Brandi lied about being in Rome."

"How do you know?"

"Roberto just brought up some extra towels and he said she'd mentioned something about the airport in Rome being crowded. Why would she lie? After that note, I'm starting to suspect everyone."

That was the best way to stay alive. "Maybe she just meant she hadn't seen any sights in Rome." Jake unlocked their bedroom door.

"You're defending her?" Kendall said, stepping inside.

"I'm not defending her. I'm just being logical." He picked up Kendall's backpack and handed it to her, and then grabbed his own.

Kendall slung hers over her shoulder. "Sounds to me like you're thinking with something besides your brain."

"Stop jumping to catty conclusions. I actually think she's up to something too. I just overheard a strange conversation, but that doesn't mean she's guilty. She could be having an affair. We'll keep an eye on her." And it might not be a bad idea to find another place to stay. "Let's see if we can get a location on this castle, and then we'll figure out what Brandi's hiding."

The town looked like a postcard. There weren't many people out. Just a few tourists wandering idly about. Most of the shops were still closed for lunch. Jake stopped at a store and they picked up supplies, including bottles of water and snacks they could throw in their packs.

"Isn't that Brandi?" Kendall asked.

Jake looked up and saw the redhead turn onto a side street. "That's her." A man was walking behind her. Jake saw him for only a second, but he got that prickly feeling in his neck again.

"That man's either with her or following her," Kendall said.

"Wait in the car. I'll see where they're headed." He made sure Kendall was locked inside and then jogged toward the street Brandi and the man had taken. They had vanished. There wasn't enough time to check it out. He and Kendall were already losing daylight. He hurried back to the car.

"Lost them," he said. "She's probably cheating on a husband. This is far cry from Wisconsin. Good place to have hot sex without anyone finding out."

"You think about sex a lot."

"Next best thing to doing it." Something he hadn't done for a while. "Let me know if you want to give it a try."

"Don't hold your breath. I don't mix dating with work."

He didn't either, usually. But what he had in mind wasn't dating.

Kendall looked back at the street where Brandi and the man had disappeared. "She's up to something."

"Is this your sixth sense talking?"

"More like female intuition. She's hiding something."

"Most people are."

Small towns and villages changed to rural farmland as they drove toward the hills. The gentle roll of the land became more rugged, the trees showing the golden colors of fall. Suddenly he wished they were here for something more fun than searching for an ancient box. Italy was a paradise for lovers. He'd never been one for sightseeing, but with Kendall it might be fun. She had a way of digging into history, making the past come alive. The best part would be the nights in bed, lots of them, he would hope, and—hell, what was he thinking? Daydreaming like a damned teenager. She'd just said she didn't mix dating and work. He sure as hell didn't need any distractions. He needed to focus on his own search for answers to his past.

He checked their surroundings. According to what Edward and Roberto had said, they were getting close to the area where the Protettori had lived. Jake glanced over and saw Kendall staring straight ahead, not blinking. She looked like she was in a trance.

"Is that jet lag or a vision?" Jake asked.

"Turn here," she said, looking at an isolated stretch of land.

He slowed the car. "You mean that goat path?" He hadn't expected a paved road and a welcome sign, but hell.

He eased the car off the road and parked behind some trees. This road wouldn't get much traffic, but no need to advertise their presence. The area was hilly, covered with rocks and trees. Beautiful in a treacherous kind of way. A good place for a secret society. He opened the trunk of the vehicle and pulled out his pack.

"We can't stay long," he said, checking the position of the sun. He put on his pack and tucked the gun in the back of his jeans for quick access. He preferred a holster if he was covering rough ground, but guns were easier to hide than a holster. "I'll go first. Don't want Jill breaking her crown."

She slung her bag over her shoulder. "If I remember correctly, it was Jack who fell," she said, moving ahead of him.

He started to remind her about the note, but if she wanted to play GI Jane, best let her get it out of her system now before things got more dangerous. They followed a thick grove of trees to a set of rough steps cut into the hillside. Watching her climb, he had to admit she was as sure-footed as a goat.

"Where'd you grow up?"

She looked back at him, her face glowing, not even out of breath. Impressive.

"I was born outside Washington, DC, but we traveled all over the world. Wherever there were relics to be found."

"You've been doing this since you were a kid?"

She nodded and scrambled over a pile of rocks that would've turned an ankle of a less agile woman. "My father spent his life searching for relics. My earliest memories are of pyramids and tombs."

"He was an archaeologist?"

She nodded. "It was his passion."

"Was?"

"He's dead." She hurried on, forcing him to follow.

"Did he have your...gift?"

She gave him an irritated look that said she thought he was being sarcastic. When she saw he wasn't, she nodded.

Must be genetic. Would she pass it on to her kids? Jake's mind immediately went to the possibilities a gift like that would bring. If it were real, that is. He still wasn't convinced that it was. It wouldn't just be the US government looking for her. What about other governments? Criminals? Terrorists? Someone with that kind of power would be invaluable.

The terrain became more rugged as they walked. He spotted entrances to several caves along the way. He was about to tell her they needed to turn back when he felt a prickle move up his spine. He noticed Kendall had slowed as well.

He did a quick check and at first didn't see anything. Then he spotted a man standing two hundred yards away, hidden in the trees. It was hard to tell his size. He was stooped, his body and face obscured by loose cotton clothes, and he held a walking stick in his hand.

"Don't hit me," Jake warned, a second before he pulled Kendall into his arms. She grunted with surprise and dropped the open bottle of water she held. Jake's lips touched the soft spot beside hers. From a distance it would pass for a kiss. "We're being watched."

She stiffened. "Where?"

"He's under the trees. Relax. Put your arms around me."

She put her hands on his waist. "What's he doing?" she asked, her breath warm on his face.

His mind and body were on guard, but he was still aware of how good she felt pressed against him. He lifted his head a couple of inches and checked again. "He's still there," he whispered against her cheek. "When I step back, slowly start walking." He stepped away from her but kept his eye on the man.

"He looks like a goat herder," Kendall said, picking up the bottle she'd spilled and putting it in her bag.

The man didn't approach but started waving his arms and yelling.

"I don't think that's a greeting, but we'll pretend it is." Jake waved a hand and they kept walking.

"I think he's warning us to go back," Kendall said.

"Not a bad idea. We can come back tomorrow when we have more daylight."

The man yelled a minute longer. Then he turned and disappeared into the trees.

"What was he saying?" Kendall asked.

"He said *pericolo*. That means danger, and I think he yelled something about a curse." Jake didn't believe in curses any more than he believed in psychics, although he wasn't sure where Kendall fit into that philosophy. He believed in strength, wits, and common sense. And a good supply of weapons. But he knew evil existed. He'd seen its work. A memory tried to intrude, but he stopped it before it got to the grave.

Kendall watched the spot where the man had vanished. "That was weird." She sounded intrigued, not alarmed. If she had searched for relics all her life, she wouldn't be intimidated by a goat herder warning about curses and danger. That didn't bode well for him, since his job was to keep her safe. He looked at the sun sinking in the sky. "We need to go back. Edward said the trail may be dangerous. It's already been a hard hike. We don't want to get caught here after dark."

"Just a little farther. I can feel it."

They continued, following Kendall's mysterious internal compass as the sun sank lower in the sky. It was time to leave. He could come back later, without her. Before he could turn her around, they came to a narrow ravine.

"Someone doesn't want company," she said.

"You just now figuring that out?"

She walked to the edge and looked at the opposite side of the canyon. "We'll have to find another way across. Did you bring climbing equipment?"

"No." He had some rope, but he had no intention of letting her climb down. If she broke her neck, he would be the one to pay. "If we go back now and get equipment and supplies, we can come back tomorrow when we have more daylight. We're not prepared for an overnight trip. We're almost out of water."

"Look," Kendall said, pointing. "There's a bridge."

He'd already spotted it but hoped she hadn't. "We don't know what condition it's in. It might not be safe."

She moved cautiously along the edge of the ravine. He followed, grumbling with each step. If he had known she'd grown up climbing pyramids and excavating tombs, he never would've agreed to protect her. Not that he'd really had a choice in accepting the assignment. As usual, Nathan held all the cards.

Jake grabbed her arm and pulled her back as she approached the bridge. It was about fifty feet across and the same distance in height. Below, sharp rocks waited to rip skin and crush bones. "The bridge could be booby-trapped. If it breaks, you're dead."

"I'm not going to cross without testing it. I'm not stupid. I grew up around this kind of stuff. Egyptians were creative when it came to protecting their dead." She knelt and examined the bridge, pulling on the sides. Then she tested the first plank with her foot. "It seems steady enough. But only one of us should cross at a time."

"Are you that desperate to find the box?"

She did that staring off into space thing, as if she could see a message in the trees. "Yes. We have to find it before he does."

"Who?"

"I don't know."

"Did you see someone?"

"No."

"Do you ever get anything definite?" He raked his hand through his hair in frustration.

"Mostly bits and pieces, like a big puzzle." She dug in her bag and pulled out a coil of rope.

Damn. She'd brought her own.

She looped it expertly around her waist and tossed him the end. "Secure this."

He caught the rope and held it in his hand. "We don't have enough time—"

"I'm going with or without you."

Damned female. "Wait, I'll go first." He tied the rope around a sturdy tree, but before he could approach the bridge, she started across. If he could've reached her, he would have strangled her, but she was already several planks in and he couldn't risk adding his weight to hers. "Watch out for loose or rotten boards." If she fell, the rope would only do so much good.

Jake's heart thudded in rhythm with the swaying bridge as Kendall moved across. She was nimble, he gave her that. Her body was perfectly balanced as she tested each board. Still, his hands didn't unclench until she reached the other side.

She dropped her backpack and untied the rope around her waist. "Your turn," she called. She tied her end of the rope to a tree and waited for him to join her.

He was glad she was safe, but part of him wished she'd found at least one rotten board to scare some sense into her. The rotten board was waiting for him, halfway across the bridge. He'd knotted the rope around his waist but was so busy fuming at Kendall that he didn't notice the crack in the plank until it gave way and his foot smashed through. Kendall started back toward him to help.

"Stay there," he said, barking out the command as he pulled his foot free. He made it the rest of the way without incident, but his pride was bruised. Hell, he'd crossed spans wider than that going hand over hand on a rope. And here he had to go and fall in front of her while he was crossing a damned bridge.

"Are you OK?" she asked, making matters worse.

He scooped up her backpack and hooked it over one shoulder.

"What are you doing?"

He bent and threw her over the other shoulder like a sack of dog food. "I'm taking you back."

"Put me down," she yelled, pounding her fists against his back.

"It's my job to protect you. I'm not letting you get us both killed."

She bit him on the shoulder. He cursed and dumped her on her feet. Not just because the bite hurt like hell, but also because his burst of temper had cooled enough for him to realize he couldn't put their combined weight on the bridge.

She swatted her hair out of her face, looking like a volcano might spurt out her ears.

"This is why I didn't want you coming on this assignment with me," he said through clenched teeth. "Do you have any idea what Nathan will do to me if you get hurt?"

Her eyes glinted like jade daggers. "I'm not an idiot. Did you even bother to look under the bridge?"

No, he didn't. He'd been too busy trying to keep her off it.

"It has steel supports and that rope is weatherproof." Her fists dug into her hips. "And the planks are in good condition."

He threw her backpack on the ground. "Not all of them." His ankle still hurt from the one he'd stepped through.

"Go back if you want, but that box is close. I can feel it." She snatched her backpack and took off.

He had no choice but to follow. He had to keep her alive, but by God, this was the last time he'd play bodyguard. He moved alongside her when the path widened. "You know we need to go back. You're just too damned stubborn to admit it."

She glanced at the setting sun and a worry line creased her forehead. "I know, but just a little farther. We're so close."

"Ten more minutes, that's it. I'm not risking our necks because of your *feelings*."

She kicked a weed out of her way and kept walking, but her shoulders didn't have that feisty set anymore. "You sound like my dad. He was always warning me not to get distracted by my feelings."

Now she was comparing him to her father. Things kept getting better.

"The path is getting easier now," she said, changing the subject.

That was usually when the sky fell, but he gritted his teeth and they kept moving. They walked for another few minutes. The trees grew thicker and the water he'd drunk pressed for an exit.

"Wait here. I gotta take a leak before we head back. You might want to do the same." They'd both drunk a lot of water.

She looked longingly at a fat clump of bushes.

"Mother Nature's bathrooms. You go first. I'll turn my back."

"I'm not going with you right here."

"I don't want you out of my sight."

"I'm a big girl. I can go to the bathroom by myself."

Yeah, but they didn't know what else was in these woods with them. "Don't go far."

She went one way while he walked a few yards through the bushes in the opposite direction. He scanned what he could of the surroundings while he took care of business. The thick trees and sinking sun made it increasingly hard to see anything. He could barely see his own piss. It would take them over two hours to get back to the car. If they left now, they would have just enough time to get there before dark. A rumbling noise sounded close by, as if the earth were moving. Imagining hidden traps and pits with spikes, he rushed back.

"Kendall?"

She didn't answer, so he started through the bushes after her. If he caught her with her pants down, next time she'd be quicker. She wasn't there. Her tracks were clear where she'd stopped and squatted. There was a circle of saturated ground and tracks leading back to where they had separated. The tracks continued in the direction they'd been walking. A few branches had been snapped off. She'd come this way. Her tracks continued for several yards, stopping at a cliff covered in ivy. It had to be at least twelve feet high. Too high to jump. There were no tree limbs strong enough to climb. Where had she gone? He pulled the thick ivy aside and saw it was actually a stone wall.

Then Jake noticed a second set of footprints a few feet away. A man's. The goat herder maybe. But there was no indentation from his walking stick. Jake pulled out his gun and cautiously bent to study the tracks. Big feet, average height. These prints weren't as fresh as Kendall's. She wasn't followed, but where was she? Both sets of tracks stopped near the same spot.

Jake heard the rumbling sound again. He jumped to his feet and raised the gun. The curtain of vines moved and Kendall's face appeared. "I found a door," she said. Her grin changed to surprise when she saw the gun pointed at her chest.

He lowered the gun. "You damned idiotic…" he sputtered, looking for words. "Are you insane? I had no idea where you were." He shoved the gun into his jeans and glared at her.

"Calm down. I saw the footsteps leading to the wall and thought they were yours."

"They're not mine."

"Oh."

She looked slightly alarmed, which was good. A little fear might help him keep her safe. He studied the opening in the wall, more intrigued than he wanted to admit. "How did you find the door?" One of her *senses*?

"I saw this." She pushed back the vines on a section of the wall. There was a mark etched in the stone. A circle. "I knew it must be there for a reason. The stone seemed loose. When I pushed it the door opened."

"You should have waited for me. What if it didn't open again? You're forgetting this place is supposed to be cursed."

"You believe in curses?"

"I believe in traps."

"The bridge was safe. If the door didn't open from this side, I would have climbed the vines."

And she probably could have, but that didn't change the fact that she wasn't following orders.

"Maybe the footsteps belong to the goat herder," she said. "He could be the one who's been taking care of this place. You should see this side of the wall."

"Keep your voice down. Anyone who's gone to these lengths to keep people away won't be happy to find us here."

She moved aside so he could climb through the opening. Even though the trail behind them had a rugged beauty, this side of the wall was like entering heaven after escaping hell. The area was well tended. Plants and shrubbery grew along a small path. The trees formed a lacy canopy, allowing the setting sun through in soft streams. One large tree sat in the center, its leaves already golden with the chill of fall.

"It doesn't look cursed," Kendall said. "It looks magical."

A little too magical. It was probably a trap. "It wasn't magical getting here. I want to look around too, but we need to head back or we'll be stuck on the trail after dark."

"My God."

He turned and saw Kendall staring at something in the distance. He moved closer and saw a tall statue a few hundred yards away.

"I've seen this before," Kendall said, her voice hushed with awe.

The damned thing about it was he'd seen the statue too. Sketched on a piece of paper he'd found in a palace in Iraq. Then he noticed there were more statues, lined up as far as he could see. He looked at the first one again, puzzled. Kendall gasped, pulling him from his shock. The sound was so loud he was afraid she'd been shot.

"There it is," she said.

He saw what looked like a mountain of rock covered by vines. Then he noticed windows and doors peeking through the vegetation. It was a castle built against a hillside, like something out of a fairy tale. It was three stories tall, with towers rising at each end. Beyond it, he could see a garden with fountains and a maze.

Kendall moved toward the castle in a daze. "It's like the one in my vision. Without the blood and bones."

"You saw this place?"

She nodded. "When I touched the drawing of the box. We have to be careful. There's danger here."

That was obvious by the obstacle course they'd encountered getting here. "We need to leave. Now."

"*Alt!*" a voice growled behind them.

CHAPTER FIVE

KENDALL SPUN, HER HEART RACING. THIS WAS NO GOAT herder. He was tall, and he wore a long, dark garment, something between a robe and a ninja outfit. His hair was dark and hung past his shoulders. Tattoos covered one side of his face, making it as hostile as the dagger sheathed at his side. Narrowed, amber-colored eyes drilled into hers. "Who are you?"

Jake moved in front of Kendall, his body brushing hers, close enough that she could feel the tension vibrating through his muscles. "My wife and I are honeymooning. We were hiking and got lost."

"How did you get past the wall?" the man asked.

"We uh...climbed," Kendall said. "The vines..."

"You must leave," he said. "I'll escort you out."

Kendall looked at the dagger. "What is this place?"

"It is private." The man continued to stare with those strange eyes. Jake stared back, his tourist face never wavering.

"Couldn't we take a peek around outside first?" she asked. "Those statues are amazing."

"She's always loved old places, haven't you, love?" Jake planted a kiss on her hair.

"No one is allowed here," the man said, but his focus was on Kendall.

"Could we see the garden before we go?" Jake kept his tone friendly. "I'm studying plants native to Italy."

The man looked up at the sky, which was darkening quickly. He frowned and moved his hand closer to his dagger. "Just the garden. Then you must leave."

Jake took a step, keeping her close to him.

"Not her," the man said. "Women are not allowed."

No women? Ordinarily, that would have had Kendall fuming, but an ancient mentality fit perfectly with an ancient secret order.

They were in the right place.

She saw the struggle in Jake's eyes. He didn't want to leave her alone, but he wanted to get closer to the castle. "Do you mind?" The look on his face gave her no comfort—the fake smile paired with the set of his shoulders that made him look relaxed but masked tension.

"I guess I have no choice." She was still irked, even though it meant they'd found the secret order.

Jake shifted his pack, and one hand darted quickly behind him. He turned to her and his façade slipped. "Stay here," he whispered. "Don't move from this spot. I'll see if I can find a way inside the castle." He grabbed her in a newlywed hug, dropped a hard, quick kiss on her lips and fondled her butt. He was back in character again as he followed the stranger.

She watched them walk to the garden, feeling the gun Jake had shoved down the back of her pants digging into her skin. He pretended to study the trees, but she knew he was searching for a way inside. Every minute or so, he glanced back toward her, presumably making sure she hadn't moved. She started to sit on a big rock near one of the walks so she could rest her feet, but she was afraid she'd shoot herself in the butt. She stood, studying the place, trying to equate reality with her vision. It was the same castle, without the horror. It reminded her of something from a fairy tale. She could almost picture Merlin inside, practicing his spells.

The place might not be cursed, but there were secrets hidden here. She could hear them whispering. She wasn't sure if they were trying to get her attention or warn her away, but the feeling persisted that she had been here. That often happened with her visions. Sometimes she wondered if she was traveling to another dimension in her sleep. She checked on Jake again. As if he sensed her watching, he turned and met her gaze. He continued to move around the garden, while keeping her in sight.

She was burning with curiosity about the place. Were there others in the order besides this guy? He didn't look like a monk or a knight, more like a warrior or a guard. It wouldn't be easy getting past him, but they had to get inside. She was certain the box was here.

She flexed her sore feet as the shadows lengthened around her. She might as well call Nathan and give him an update. She pulled out her phone. No signal. She walked a few feet and tried again. Nothing. She heard a sound, and when she looked up, she saw a robed figure move behind one of the statues.

"Hello?" she called softly. "*Salve?*" It was probably her imagination or her senses playing tricks. She looked toward the garden. Jake's back was turned as he examined the maze. She hurried toward the nearest statue. It was at least nine feet tall. Some kind of warrior. She looked behind him, but there was no robed figure. The only things she saw were the other statues lining the castle grounds as far as she could see. The robed figure must have been her imagination, or perhaps her sixth sense. Sometimes it was hard to tell the difference.

She studied the statue again. He wore a garment similar to the ninja monk's. He had a sword clasped in his hand and his face was coldly handsome. She touched the stone, letting the texture settle against her hand. The images rushing through her head startled her. Places and faces that felt more like human memories than the impressions she usually got from an object. The stabbing pain in her stomach startled her even more. She grabbed hold of the sword to keep from falling and put her other hand on her stomach, expecting to feel blood.

She wasn't bleeding. She heard a low voice and realized it was Jake and the ninja monk returning. Shaking off the effects of her vision, or whatever it was, she started back to the spot where they had left her, but the ninja monk was already looking around, his face pulled into a fierce frown.

"Where is your wife?" he asked, his hand settling over his dagger.

Jake looked over the man's shoulder and saw her. His face went taut. Call it bad timing or karma, but a crash sounded behind her. She whirled, expecting an attack and saw the statue's sword lying on the stone walk.

A soft roar had her spinning back around to see the ninja monk racing toward her, a look of horror and fury in his eyes. Jake reached for his gun as he ran after the monk, but he came up empty handed. His face was every bit as fierce as the ninja monk's. Kendall knew why he'd left her the gun. He didn't need it.

Kendall tried to get the gun out of her waistband, but it was stuck on her belt loop. The ninja monk advanced on her, his face set like stone. "Who sent you?" he demanded.

Jake slipped between her and the monk, his hands turned up in submission. "I apologize for my wife. She loves exploring." His fierce look was gone, yet his jaw looked tight enough to shatter his teeth.

Kendall bent to pick up the sword but couldn't lift it. "I'm sorry. I was just looking at the statue and the sword fell."

The monk wasn't looking at the sword. He was staring at Kendall's cross, which had slipped free of her shirt. He looked pale now, his tattoos harsh against his skin. He slowly stretched out his hand and touched Kendall's cross. "Where did you get this?" he whispered, turning it over.

"A friend gave it to me." She put her hand on the chain, afraid he might try to take it.

"We'll go now," Jake said. "We're sorry to have troubled you."

"It has begun," the ninja monk said, still mesmerized by the cross. He shook his head. "No. You must stay."

Jake's whole body stilled, but there was tension running through him, like an arrow just before it was released.

The ninja monk let go of Kendall's cross and folded his hands in front of him. "I've been waiting for you."

Kendall exchanged a blank glance with Jake. Had Nathan already found the castle and told this man they were coming? Why hadn't he called to let them know? Kendall didn't know if they were supposed to use aliases or if the monk knew what they were looking for.

"Forgive my manners. I am Raphael."

"Who told you we were coming?" Jake asked, the tension easing slightly from his body.

"My...employer." Raphael raised his head and smiled. It wasn't an easy smile, more like he'd found it buried in the ground and brushed it off for the occasion. "Would you like something to eat or perhaps a drink? We don't have much to offer. We don't often have guests." He glanced at the cross again, as Jake continued to watch him with narrowed eyes.

"Thank you," Jake said. "But we should get back to our car before it gets dark."

"You must stay," Raphael said. "At least until morning. The trail is dangerous after dark. I would hate for you to suffer an accident." He glanced at the statues. "Please. You will be my guests."

Jake gave Kendall a quick glance. His newlywed persona slipped for one second and she knew he was considering whether to shoot Raphael or take him up on his offer. He smiled, still in character. "We could use the rest. We haven't had much sleep. Honeymooners, you know." He gave Kendall a grin that her body would have believed if it hadn't been so distracted with relief that she was still alive.

"I thought no women were allowed," she said.

Raphael's amber gaze dropped to her chest, where she could feel the cross pressing against her shirt. "I will make an exception."

"Who owns this place?" Jake asked.

"It belongs to a...foundation. I watch over it for them. They're very private."

Like a secret order.

"These statues are magnificent," Kendall said, keeping her voice level.

"Yes."

"What are they?"

"Sentinels."

Sentinels? As she had thought, although she wasn't sure what purpose they would serve other than intimidation. "I'm sorry about the sword. I don't know why it fell off."

"No matter," Raphael said. "Come. I will show you inside. Then you must rest." He looked at Kendall's cross again and smiled, another stiff movement of his mouth that left the rest of his face untouched. A chill rolled over her skin, and she didn't move away when Jake's warm hand touched her back. Raphael turned away for them to follow, and Kendall slipped the cross inside her shirt. She felt Jake ease the gun from her waistband and tuck it in his.

Raphael led them to the castle and through a set of heavy wooden doors that were crossed with metal strips. The only light inside came from lanterns, candelabras, and low-burning sconces on the walls. Was there no electricity? Raphael grabbed two lanterns and handed them to Kendall and Jake. The lanterns helped, but the entryway was still shadowed. It was large, the ceiling two stories tall with columns lining the walls. A fountain gurgled in the middle of the floor, seated in a small pool. Corridors ran right and left, and circular steps lined each side of the entryway, leading to the second floor. Kendall took in as much as she could, but the low light made it difficult to see.

There were the usual things one would expect in a castle: armor, swords, daggers, and other weapons, as well as heavy furniture and thick drapes covering long windows. She felt bits of memories calling to her, but the message wasn't clear.

"How long has this foundation owned the place?" she asked.

"A long time." Raphael didn't look back but kept walking. His shoulders were powerful, his movements easy. He reminded her of Jake.

They passed a room with an open door, and Kendall felt her senses warm. She stopped and tried to look inside. "What is this room?"

Raphael turned, his face even dourer than it had been before. "The library."

She held her lantern higher and saw bookshelves covering the walls. Two long tables sat in the middle of the room. She shifted her light and saw a tapestry woven in rich colors hanging on the near wall. "May I go inside?"

"It's not for public use." He closed the door, pulled out another awkward smile and walked on. She had to get inside that room. Something in there was connected to the box. Perhaps it was hidden there.

Raphael showed them several other rooms, including a kitchen that looked rather bare. Many rooms he passed without opening. Those were the rooms she really wanted to see. Those, and the library. Jake didn't seem to have questions. He just watched everything, his eyes alert.

Their guide kept moving, and Kendall hurried to catch up. Raphael led them to the second floor. Paintings and tapestries covered the walls, but he didn't stop long enough for her to examine them. He continued on to the third floor, not even stopping until he reached another set of stairs.

"There's a fourth floor?" Kendall asked.

"No. This is the tower. It is the only room available."

The only room available out of three floors? Kendall glanced back at all the doors they'd passed and then looked at Jake. He nodded, and she followed Raphael, with Jake bringing up the rear.

Raphael stopped and opened a door. "I am sure you will want to rest after the long walk." He motioned for them to step inside. The room was small, like something she imagined would be in a monastery, but there weren't any crosses on the wall. There was a small bed covered in a worn brown blanket. Two equally worn rugs covered the floor, one by the bed and another in front of an empty fireplace. There was a small window above the bed and an old desk against one wall. After the impressive entryway, this room was a disappointment. Obviously, they weren't prepared for guests.

"The night will be warm," Raphael said. "No need for a fire."

Kendall already felt chilled and night hadn't even fallen.

"The bathroom is there." He pointed to a door just inside the bedroom. "I apologize that it's not better equipped."

The door was cracked, so Kendall pushed it open and peeked inside. Her jaw dropped. It was a garderobe. There was no toilet or shower, only a porcelain basin tucked into a corner.

"I will bring water and soap for you to wash up, and something to eat," Raphael said, and then he left.

"This is crazy," Kendall said after the door closed. "First he tells us we have to leave—no women allowed—then he insists we stay, says he's been expecting us and gives us a tour. It feels more like we're prisoners than guests. Should we sneak out? He makes me uncomfortable."

"I think you have the same effect on him."

"There's something about his eyes. I've never seen that color before." She looked at Jake but he appeared unperturbed. "You seem awfully calm about this."

"We're where we wanted to be. Inside. Half an hour ago, that seemed impossible without breaking in, which is what we would have had to do if Raphael hadn't seen that cross. Unless you've decided the box isn't here."

"It's here. I can feel it."

"Then we stay. He's right about the trail. It's too dangerous to travel at night."

"Sorry. I know you wanted to go back earlier."

"What's done is done. And we're in. Let's make the most of it." Jake moved around the room, examining everything without touching.

Kendall followed, touching everything she examined. "This is like something out of *Grimms' Fairy Tales*. We're in a tower without even a bathroom." Or toilet paper. "Just a garderobe." Thank goodness she'd brought tissues and disposable wipes.

"What exactly is a garderobe?"

"A castle's version of an outhouse. Except this one dumps straight down the castle wall."

"Well, Rapunzel, it's a good thing we used the facilities outdoors."

She didn't know why she was making such a fuss. She'd made bathrooms out of desert and jungle floors all over the world. But she hadn't had a hot man a few feet away, sharing the same space. "Maybe this isn't as sinister as it feels. We know Nathan was still trying to find this secret group when we left. He probably beat us to it and told Raphael we were coming."

"If that's the case, it would have been nice if Nathan had told us," Jake said.

"If he didn't discover the location until after we hit the trail, he couldn't have reached us. Cell phones don't work here."

"You're quick to defend him."

Kendall shrugged. "He's a good man."

"Is he? I thought you hadn't read him?"

"I have five other senses and for the record, I can't read anything on Nathan. He's like a locked room."

"That's comforting. What about me? You read anything on me?"

"You're angry, a rebel, and you like sex."

He stared at her a minute, his expression unreadable, and she wondered if he was trying to block her. It was possible. She was almost certain Nathan had.

"I don't think Nathan alerted Raphael we were coming. It seems more likely that Thomas or whoever is following us warned him. We have to remember we're probably in enemy territory here. We're here basically to steal a box that they believe belongs to them."

"Then why is he being so accommodating?" Kendall asked.

"That's obvious. He wants your necklace."

"I wonder why he's so intrigued by it."

"Nathan said it was connected to the group. He must recognize it. And he probably wants it back." Jake walked to the door and turned the old key that was in the lock.

"You think he might slip in and kill us in our sleep?"

"I'm not taking any chances." He moved to the bed and pulled back the covers.

"What are you doing?"

"Looking for spiders and snakes."

He was probably being sarcastic, but she knew spiders and snakes were no joke. A black mamba had almost bitten her when she was a girl. Kendall continued to check the room, trying to find something that might tell her about the place and trying not to look at the door to the garderobe, which she already needed. The long hike had made her thirsty. She'd drunk a lot of water.

"Are you going to sleep now?" she asked Jake, who was lying down.

"I'm testing the bed. I'll take this side."

She'd rather he take both sides. Sleeping in the same bed with Jake would be danger of an entirely different kind. She touched the iron headboard and a dark stain began oozing from the center of the bed. Blood. Then she heard a baby's cry. She went hot and cold at the same time, feeling as if she was being pulled out of her skin. She thought she heard an echoing scream. A woman. She jumped in alarm, blinked and saw Jake still lying there with his feet crossed, arms over his chest. No blood, but he was staring at her as if she'd sprouted a tail. She hated it when the visions came without warning.

She grabbed her bag and went into the garderobe. At least it had a door. There were only two windows—open, no glass— high in the wall. In olden days, these would have helped with the smell. It looked like it hadn't been used in ages. She hoped it hadn't, but it didn't make sense that Raphael had given them this room when she'd seen others that looked more up to date. They must have occasional guests, no matter how private this foundation was.

After making sure there was no one below, she made use of the garderobe. She'd admired a few of these from afar. Sitting on one dulled the appreciation. She brushed her teeth with the emergency toothbrush she always carried, using the last of the water from the bottle Jake had given her. As she put the items back, she noticed another bottle in the bottom of her backpack, the one from the inn. Good. They would need it.

When she got back to the bedroom, Jake was opening the door to admit Raphael. He glanced at the key in the lock as he entered the room. Kendall wondered if he realized Jake had locked him out. Raphael carried a tray with cheese, bread, and wine, and he had a basket slung over his shoulder. He set the tray down and dropped the basket near the door. It held a roll of toilet paper, a bar of soap, two towels, and two bottles of water. "For you. Food and supplies. I apologize that we aren't better prepared. We do have good wine. And the water is bottled from a local spring." The water had the same label as the bottles they had bought in town and the ones provided at the inn.

Raphael opened the bottle of wine and poured two glasses, setting them on the tray. This was the best opportunity she'd had to study him. His hair was braided on each side, keeping it out of his face. He was striking, his face fierce and beautiful at the same time. Those tattoos and amber-colored eyes that watched her every move gave him a feral look.

"Has a woman been in this room?"

Raphael's eyes widened then narrowed to slits, making them look sinister. "No women."

He was wrong or lying. There had been a woman. She'd given birth in that bed. "Those are interesting tattoos," she said, looking at the little dots and lines patterned across his cheek.

He took a couple of steps back. "This should be all you need. Sleep well. I will see you tomorrow." He hurried to the door.

She turned to find Jake studying her over a glass of wine. "You definitely make him nervous. Why were you grilling him about his tattoos?"

"I wanted to see his reaction. His tattoos have something to do with this place."

"'Course they do. Secret orders usually have some kind of identifying mark."

"He said the place belongs to a foundation, not a secret order."

Jake cocked an eyebrow. "He's not gonna admit it's a secret order. That's the secret part."

"He's unusual, to say the least. And did you notice he knew we spoke English before we opened our mouths?"

"Probably heard you talking from the other side of the bridge."

"You seem particularly crabby."

"Chasing reckless women through the woods has that effect on me."

"I'm not reckless. I know what I'm doing."

"Then why did Nathan send me?"

"Because two heads are better than one." But he was right, Nathan expected Jake to protect her. This job was far more dangerous than any other she had done for Nathan. She didn't just know this because he'd sent a big badass bodyguard with a gun to accompany her. She could sense it. "I want to look inside the library."

Jake raised both brows this time. "I assure you, Raphael does *not* want you in his library."

"I think there's something inside that's connected to the box."

"This one of your feelings?"

She nodded. "I don't know if it's the box itself or a clue, but I need to see. If we don't find this box, something bad is going to happen."

"If Raphael catches you in his library, something bad is going to happen. All the more reason to wait until he thinks we're asleep." Jake set down the glass of wine, which he hadn't drunk, and picked up the basket Raphael left. "Since we'll be sleeping together, I'm going to attempt washing off. I'd hate to get you sweaty."

"Sleeping together?"

"Unless you want the floor. Lock the door, will you? And I wouldn't touch the food or wine."

"You think it's poisoned?"

"I wouldn't put it past him."

As soon as the garderobe door shut, she grabbed a flashlight. She understood that he was just doing his job, but she was just doing hers. Some risks had to be taken, and Raphael hadn't forbidden them to leave the room.

Creeping to the door, she made sure Raphael wasn't lurking outside, and then hurried down the stairs to the second floor. The castle was deadly quiet except for those whispers tugging at her ears. If only she understood what they were saying. She didn't encounter Raphael. He must have been busy standing watch. As difficult as it was to find the place, she couldn't imagine Raphael ran into too many trespassers like her and Jake. *Trespassers.* The word made her head swim, but she didn't have time to sort through it now.

Most of the pieces of artwork in the hallway were copies of famous paintings, many of them of Christ, his birth, his baptism, the Garden of Gethsemane, the Crucifixion, and the Last Supper. They were amazingly authentic looking. It was frustrating trying to examine them so quickly and with only a flashlight, but she had to get back before Jake discovered her missing. And she still needed to see the library. She slipped down to the first floor. The door to the library was closed but not locked. Looking over her shoulder, she turned the handle and slipped inside, closing the door behind her. Her skin began to tingle as she approached the tapestry. The scene was vivid. Blood and water ran from the spear wound in Christ's side, and the Roman soldier was looking up at him as Mary knelt at her son's feet. Kendall let her fingers brush the tapestry. A sharp pain struck her side and she doubled over, unable to breathe.

"What do you think you're doing?"

She jumped and her flashlight catapulted into the air. She knew immediately that it was Jake by the masculine scent that said, "I'm in charge and I'm pissed." He caught the flashlight with one hand and stepped closer, his body taut with anger.

"Are you insane?" he hissed. "I told you to wait until tonight."

"I couldn't," she said, holding one hand against her side.

"What if Raphael had found you?"

"I would have made up some excuse," she gritted between her teeth. "And he didn't tell us we weren't allowed to leave the room."

"He didn't have to. Have you seen the way he looks at you? He would have that cross off your neck the minute your head left your body." He jabbed his finger at her for effect.

Kendall gulped and put a hand to her throat. "Get your finger out of my face."

He did but replaced it with his nose. "This is your last warning. You don't go anywhere alone, do you understand? You don't even take a crap without telling me. I'll be damned if I'll explain to Nathan that you're dead. If I have to, I'll tie you to the damn bed. You can do your divining from there." He looked down at her hand, and his frown softened. "Why are you holding your side? Are you hurt?"

"I picked up something from the tapestry."

Jake turned his light on the tapestry and then looked down at her side again, his brows lifted in surprise. The embrace caught her off guard.

"I appreciate the hug," she wheezed, "but really, the pain is almost gone."

"Be quiet," he breathed in her ear. "We have company." She felt him reach around and pull out his gun. Footsteps sounded in the hall, slowing outside the library door. A second later, the door opened.

She leaned her forehead against Jake's shoulder and concentrated on the mesmerizing thump of his heartbeat, trying to steady her own. Dum dum. Dum dum. Dum dum. Strong, warm, vivid colors...then dark, gray, and cold. She lifted her head, disturbed at what she'd sensed. The figure left, closing the door behind him.

"I don't think that was Raphael," she whispered.

"Whoever he was, he's gone. Hurry. If we get caught, he'll try to throw us out. I'd hate to have to kill someone just so we can find a box."

"I hope you're being sarcastic."

He didn't answer. He left their hiding place and checked the hallway. "It's clear, stay close." Jake led the way, stopping near a small door on the third floor. "Do you hear that?"

"Hear what?"

"Sounded like someone singing." He frowned and put his ear to the door.

"I don't see Raphael as a singer." Kendall joined him, listening at the door. "I hear it. You sure it's singing? Maybe it's crying. Someone could be in trouble. We should investigate."

"No."

She grabbed his shirt as he started to walk away. "Someone could be hurt. Raphael could be keeping prisoners here."

She felt something dark settle over him, an emotion so thick she didn't need lights or any paranormal abilities to feel it grip him. And just as strongly, she felt it leave. He had pushed it away. Fear, memory, whatever it was.

"We'll check it out later, after Raphael's asleep," Jake said.

"What if Raphael doesn't sleep?"

"Everyone sleeps."

"Vampires don't."

"If he's a vampire we'll definitely kill him. Come on. I'm not letting you foul up this assignment." He took her arm and pulled her down the hall. Walking quietly—he more so than she, since he moved like a ghost—they hurried to their room. He opened the door and they went inside. He locked the door, and then stuck the key in his pocket. "That's so you don't leave again."

"You think that will stop me?"

He gave her a rather nasty grin, pulled the key from his pocket and stuck it down the front of his underwear. "Go ahead."

"Bastard."

"Sticks and stones…" He pulled an empty water bottle from his pack. "You got any water left? I need to brush my teeth."

"I found another one from the inn." She handed him the bottle and watched him walk to the garderobe door. "Would you really kill Raphael?"

He stopped, hand on the doorknob. "Not if I don't have to. If you follow instructions, we'll get out without having to hurt anyone. You use your mojo and find the damn box. Let me handle the dangerous stuff."

"I know you're trying to help in your own brutish way, but this tough-guy stuff is getting old. I'm not a china doll and I have a brain in addition to the breasts you keep staring at."

His mouth twitched. "What did you feel when you touched the tapestry?"

"I felt as if I'd been stabbed in the side."

"Uh…that was Christ's crucifixion."

"Yeah."

"You *felt* it?" His expression was a combination of disbelief, fascination, and alarm.

"Just the stabbing, although I'm sure it was just a hint of what it really felt like." She shuddered thinking what it would have been like to experience the other. Crucifixion was a cruel death.

"And this happens to you a lot?"

"No. Usually it's simpler, like touching a figurine and knowing that it was made in the twentieth century, not the tenth. That's why Nathan hired me." She gave a frustrated sigh and turned away. A second later, she heard Jake close the door.

A small desk and chair had been placed against one wall. She pulled out the chair and sat. A jolt shot through her body, flattening her against the back of the chair. She felt her arms moving, even though she could see they were still pinned in her lap.

Trembling hands held a piece of paper. She couldn't read the words, but she could feel the anguish written there. A tear dropped onto the page, and then the hands folded the letter and reached under the desk…

The vision vanished abruptly. Her hands were free, her body released. She jumped from the chair and turned to find Jake, but he was still in the garderobe. What was happening to her? She'd never had so many intense visions this close together. It must be this place.

She lowered her body into the chair again, slowly letting her full weight settle. She waited. No vision, nothing. The desk appeared ordinary. Two drawers, four legs. She opened each drawer and found it empty. She tried to recall the writing she'd seen on the paper. Italian maybe—she wasn't sure. She remembered the hands reaching underneath the drawer, so she ran her fingers along the bottom. At first she didn't find anything. Then she felt the crinkle of paper. She got out of the chair and squatted. A scrap of paper was stuck to the bottom of the drawer. She moved the chair and scooted the desk out from the wall, tipping it back to expose the underside.

"You dismantling the furniture now?"

She whirled and saw Jake enter the room, shirtless.

Holy mackerel. His bare chest was as sexy as she remembered. Broad shoulders tapering to sculpted abs that made her itch to touch them. The faintest dusting of hair shadowed the center of his chest and another trailed from his navel, disappearing under his jeans. And she remembered what that looked like too. She jerked her gaze away. "There's a piece of paper stuck here."

Without making a noise, he appeared at her side. "What is it?"

"Part of a letter, I think."

He squatted and took a look. "Do I want to know how you knew it was there?"

"No. I'm trying not to tear it."

"I'll push the bottom of the drawer away from the paper; you try to work it free."

The space was small for two people. Her cheek was pressed against his shoulder as she reached underneath the table.

"Good thing I washed off, since your nose is almost in my armpit."

"Yes, thank goodness," she agreed, joking, but in truth, his scent was playing havoc with her senses. He smelled clean, but masculine, and that sexy line of muscle running along his side made her want to touch skin instead of paper.

She freed the paper except for one edge. "Can you push up on the drawer a little more at the back?" She turned and caught him sniffing her hair.

"Your hair smells good."

"Uh, thanks."

"So does the rest of you." His voice was too close. He was too close. She gave the paper one more gentle tug and pulled it free. She quickly stood, trying to put some space between them.

"What does it say?" Jake asked, setting the table back on the floor.

"There isn't much writing, but I think it's Italian. The paper has been here a while. The ink is faded."

Jake studied it with her. "Do you think it's connected to the box?"

"I don't know. I'm not getting anything."

"Paranormal juice dried up?"

She frowned. He was probably right. All this activity was draining her.

"You can study it. I'm going to get some sleep. We have a lot of work to do tonight." He took out his gun and a knife and put them on the floor beside his boots. Then he unbuckled his pants and let them drop.

Double holy mackerel.

He dropped onto the bed, lay back, and closed his eyes.

"How can you sleep? Raphael might come back with a whole tribe of guards and kill us."

"He wouldn't need a tribe to kill us. But the door's locked." He adjusted his pillow, which made an interesting play of muscles across his abs. "He doesn't want us dead. At least not yet."

"Yet?"

"First he needs to find out where you got the cross."

"Then he'll kill us?"

"We'll be gone before he has the chance." Jake wiggled his shoulders, getting comfortable, creating more muscle play to tempt her. "In the meantime, I need rest in case I have to rescue you."

"Do you have to be so insulting?"

"Not if you weren't so obstinate. Come on. We both need sleep. It's gonna be a long night. God knows where this box is."

"You can have the bed. I'll…" She looked around the room. There was nowhere else to sleep. Unless she sat in the chair.

"Don't be a prude. I'm not going to attack you."

"I don't know how you can sleep," she grumbled, although she was exhausted.

"You close your eyes, clear your mind, and ignore any distractions." One eye opened and he gave her a withering one-eyed stare before closing it again. "Then you go to sleep."

Kendall wasn't ready to crawl in bed next to Jake Stone in all his masculine glory just yet. She made another sweep of the room, dragging her fingers over surfaces hoping to find something else that would give her some idea who these people were and where they might be keeping the box. But she got nothing more.

"Are you coming to bed?"

"With you in your underwear?"

"I can take it off if it bothers you."

She cursed him under her breath and flung back the covers on her side. She climbed into the bed, fully clothed, and lay stiffly, so close to the edge that if she sneezed she would roll off. Something was digging into her shoulder. She rolled onto her back, but she had to keep her arms stiff to keep from touching Jake. Touching Jake would be a bad idea, because her girl parts wanted it too much. Her brain, on the other hand, said, "Run."

The mattress squeaked and Jake's upper body loomed over her. "Are you gonna toss all night?"

She shrank back into the mattress. "This bed's uncomfortable and I'm cold." She regretted the words as soon as the wicked grin formed on his lips.

"Bet I could warm you up."

She'd bet he could too. The sound of his voice was already making her hot. And he was close enough that she knew he had removed the key from his underwear. She put her hand on his chest. Firm. Warm. Male..."Down, boy," she said and pushed him away. She rolled closer to the edge again. He chuckled and the mattress dipped as he lay back on his side of the bed.

"Sleep tight, Legs."

"You too, jackass."

Minutes later he was asleep. It took her longer. She wasn't used to sleeping next to a male. Other than her father or Adam on a dig, she could count on half a hand the number of times she'd woken up with a man. Jake was nothing like her father. And Adam hadn't gotten the chance to become a man.

She listened to the steady breathing and occasional mutter that everyone makes, even a big, tough bodyguard like Jake. She drifted off listening to him breathe and didn't wake until the ghost came.

CHAPTER SIX

H E STOOD BY THE BED, A SHADOWY FIGURE IN A DARK garment, his head covered by a cowl. At first she thought it was Raphael, until her eyes adjusted to the soft glow cast by the lantern and she noticed that she could see through him to the wall. She lay there, frozen, while he stared at her. She could feel waves of sadness rolling off him even though she couldn't see his face. She reached back for Jake, but he didn't wake.

The ghost turned from her and began to pace the floor, head lowered. Every now and then he would look back at the bed. Then he turned suddenly and vanished into the wall. She sat up. "Jake," she whispered. "Wake up."

He didn't wake, so she shook him. He still didn't move, so she shook him harder, and when that didn't work, she slapped him. Then she became alarmed. Jake was too alert to sleep through a beating. She pulled the covers down and put her ear against his chest. It was warm and his heartbeat was strong. What was wrong with him? Had he been drugged? They hadn't eaten or drunk anything from the castle. She had to get help.

She started to the door, and then remembered the key. She knew it wasn't in his underwear, so she checked under his pillow and found it there. She hurried to the door and unlocked it, but it still wouldn't open. She yanked on the knob and then the door in vain. They were prisoners.

She looked back at the wall where the ghost had disappeared. Maybe that was why he came. To show her a way out.

Her heart pounding, she slipped on her shoes, and since the room was chilly, she pulled a jacket from her bag and put it on over her shirt. After picking up her backpack, she leaned over Jake once more and touched his face.

"Jake. If you can hear me, I'm going for help." God knew where she'd find it. Not from Raphael. He must have been the one who'd locked them inside the tower and somehow drugged Jake.

Using the lantern, she examined the wall where the figure had disappeared and found a notch in one of the stones. She pushed it and heard a click. A section of the wall swung open. She called to Jake once more, but he didn't wake. She checked her watch. Midnight. She would follow this entrance. Maybe the monk would lead her outside the castle.

She grabbed her flashlight and stepped inside the secret door. It smelled musty and stale. The passageway was narrow, but she was used to tight spaces. She'd spent more time inside pyramids and tombs than most kids had spent in a sandbox. A set of steep, curved steps led down. Keeping the light low so as not to startle the ghost in case he was interactive and not a residual haunting, she followed the narrow stairs. At the bottom the passage opened slightly. This must be the third floor. She didn't see the monk, but he must have come this way.

Idiot. He doesn't need an exit. He can walk through walls. You're the one who'll probably get trapped.

It was so quiet she could hear her own breath echoing. Then another noise. Singing. Like she and Jake had heard earlier. If there was someone else here, perhaps he would help Jake. Unless he was the one who'd drugged him, not Raphael. She tried to pinpoint the sound, but it was too muffled through thick walls. She found a small doorway a few feet away. She opened it and peered inside. This was a part of the castle they hadn't seen. There were two doors, one on either side of the hallway. The soft singing sounded louder here, but she couldn't tell if it was English. Someone else must be here, or Raphael was listening to music.

Even if Raphael hadn't drugged Jake, if he caught Kendall here, he'd probably kill her. If she could get to the main part of the castle, surely there was some kind of phone. Considering the lack of electricity, that might not be the case. If she couldn't find a phone, she would have to get somewhere with a cell signal so she could call Nathan.

From the corner of her eye, she glimpsed a robe. She followed the shadow down two more sets of winding stone stairs. At the bottom, she stopped to get her bearings. This must be the first floor. The passageway began to slant downward, changing from stone to dirt. The air was different here, not as dank. The path ended at a set of stairs leading up to a wooden wall. There must be a way out. Using her light, she found a circle like the one on the wall surrounding the castle. She pushed and the wall opened into a space the size of a closet. There was another door in front of her, but no knob or motif. She put both hands on the door and pushed it open. A rush of fresh air lifted her hair as she stepped out. She was in a graveyard. Looking back, she saw that she had stepped out of a massive tree.

For a minute, concern over both Jake and the monk faded into the background as she studied the graveyard. Its pull was powerful. The moon was full, so she didn't need her flashlight. The graveyard was small, perhaps a few dozen graves in all, and edged by the same woods that surrounded the castle. The headstones varied in shapes and sizes, but they were all old, some leaning, others fallen. A breeze stirred, rustling the leaves, and the whispers came, teasing with their secrets, pulling at her to enter the woods. Why?

She moved to the edge and saw a stone building that looked like a chapel. Someone had taken pains to hide it from view. Just like the castle. Beyond it was another statue. They must surround the entire place. She looked around for the monk, but he was nowhere to be found. Maybe he was the one pulling her toward the woods.

She looked back at the castle and remembered the darkness she'd seen, the danger, the blood and bones. This could be a trap. But the whispers calling her were too urgent to deny. She found a path at the edge of the graveyard. Turning on her flashlight, she followed the crumbling stones through the thick woods. The chapel was old but well tended. The windows were intact, showing beautiful scenes in stained glass. The door was made of thick wood. Her senses started tingling. That was the only way she could describe it. Sometimes it was in her fingers, sometimes her body, sometimes her head. She touched the handle and had a vision of a bright light. There were voices, a boy and a girl, but she couldn't hear what they were saying. Her head felt as if it were wrapped in gauze.

She tried to open the door, but it was locked. The nearest window had a clear section in the stained glass, so she used her flashlight to look inside. There weren't any pews. At the front of the chapel there was some sort of altar; a large flat rock, and behind it, three tall, rectangular stones that looked out of place inside a building. There was writing on the stones and on the altar, but she couldn't read the words from a distance. The wall surrounding the altar was decorated with friezes. She wanted to look closer, but she had to get Jake out of the tower. And Raphael would probably kill her with that big dagger if he found her trespassing. *Trespassing.* The image came again, a boy and girl, and the whispers grew frantic. Memories pounded her head with so much force that she knew if she didn't turn them off she would end up with a migraine.

She backed away from the window and distanced her mind, though her heart still raced. She backtracked to the graveyard, wondering if her preoccupation with the chapel had caused her to lose the monk. But there he was waiting for her, standing in the moonlight near the edge of the graveyard. He looked back at her, his face still hidden by the cowl, and then he started walking again.

She didn't know where he was going but assumed he knew the area better than she did. She hurried through the gravestones, and when she reached the place where he had stood, she saw two square stones stuck in the ground. If these were graves, they must be unconsecrated—that, or they were some kind of monument. She touched one of the stones and felt a rush of grief so strong her legs trembled. She dropped to the ground as a vision came.

The robed procession moved silently through the trees, a dozen men—three on each side of the casket, six walking behind—their lanterns swaying with each step as they neared the waiting grave.

She pulled herself from the vision, her chest empty, like it had felt when she found out her father and Adam were dead. Whose funeral had she seen? And where were the other men now? She looked at the other stone and wondered whose body lay underneath. She felt the shadow of evil a moment before something dropped over her head, plunging her into darkness. Grief turned to panic as she clawed at the cloth covering her mouth and nose. Her captor grabbed her arms and pinned them roughly to her sides. She heard voices. *American,* she thought through her panic. But none belonging to Jake.

She struggled, twisting her body, kicking and yelling, her cries muffled by the cloth. Her captor was strong, and struggling just made it more difficult to breathe.

Someone cursed. "Did you see that?"

"Yeah. What was it?" a second man asked.

"I don't know. Where'd he go?"

"He disappeared, just like that." The man's voice was shaky. "I told you I thought I saw something a few minutes ago. I've heard stories about this place. I'm getting out of here."

"What about her?" asked the first voice.

"Thomas is on his way. Let him get her."

ANITA CLENNEY

The arms released her and she stumbled to the ground. She yanked the bag off her head and sat up. She heard the men running through the bushes, back toward the castle. Without waiting to see what had startled them, she took off in the opposite direction, where she'd last seen the monk. She thought she saw him, but realized it was a tall stone. When she drew closer, she counted seven stone pillars, taller than the ones in the chapel, all arranged in a circle. Beyond the pillars, she saw more statues, spaced every few hundred yards. She felt a vibration in her bones as she ran. Ducking behind the closest stone, she waited, trying to catch her breath as she listened for her pursuers. Raphael's voice wasn't there. Had he drugged Jake and sent the men to take her necklace? One of them mentioned Thomas. The same Thomas from the hotel?

She didn't dare turn on her flashlight, so she studied the formation by moonlight. One of the pillars was turned at an angle. She felt it pushing her away, like an opposing magnetic field. Her curiosity was almost as strong as her fear that the men would come back. She ran her hand over the surface and her arm began to tingle. She felt a rush of sensations: danger, protection, power. The stones were old. And they didn't want her here. She felt something near the base, a change in texture. It was hard to see with just the moonlight, so she flicked on the light, and she saw the circle motif. Intrigued, she pushed and heard a grinding noise. The pillar started to move and the ground disappeared under her feet.

He saw the torn, raw ground and his feet froze. His mouth went dry but he forced himself closer to the hole, knowing what he would find.

He woke from the dream disoriented. It took him a few seconds to realize he'd been drugged and that Kendall was gone.

88

He hadn't had any food or drink except the water he'd used to brush his teeth. Water Kendall had given him. But he knew her well enough by now to know that she wouldn't drug him so that she could start searching for the box. She'd just go off and do it. She must have mistakenly given him one of the bottles Raphael brought.

Jake stumbled out of bed too quickly and had to sit for a second until his head stopped spinning. Still unsteady, he checked the bathroom—garderobe—opening the door without knocking. She wasn't there. He went to the door and saw the key sticking out of the lock. He turned the knob but the door wouldn't open. It was locked from outside. Raphael had trapped them in here. Jake had a few seconds of panic, thinking about how Raphael had looked at Kendall's cross and what he feared Raphael would do to get it, but Raphael couldn't have gotten past the inside lock. Either Kendall had climbed out a window and gone exploring or there must be another entrance to the room and Raphael had used it to kidnap her.

Jake went back and touched Kendall's side of the bed. It still held a little warmth. She hadn't been gone long. Then he noticed her backpack and phone were missing. A kidnapper wasn't likely to let her gather her things. He threw on clothes and boots. Since the door was locked from the other side, picking it was out of the question. He gave it a shove with his shoulder, testing. No give. It was too thick to break down, and chopping through it would be too noisy and take more time than he had. That left the bedroom window or the garderobe. He chose the window.

It opened onto a small ledge, but it was a good eighty feet off the ground. Raphael had locked them in a tower, just like Rapunzel. Jake didn't have hair long enough to reach the ground, but he had the coil of rope in his pack that he hadn't told Kendall about. A pale flash in the woods caught his eye. Someone was out there, and she had blonde hair. What was Kendall up to now? Did she want the box for herself? Maybe she *had* drugged him. Didn't matter what her motives were. He had to get her back before she got hurt. Nathan would hold him responsible.

He took the rope from his pack and checked the length. Not quite long enough, but he could jump the last twenty feet. After testing the ledge to be sure it was safe, he tied the rope to the heavy bed and gathered his things. He put his knife inside his boot, tucked his gun into a holster and slipped his pack through the window. Standing on the ledge, he checked the drop again and made sure he hadn't been spotted. The moon was bright and he didn't want an unpleasant surprise halfway down.

He slung his pack over his shoulders and slipped on gloves so he wouldn't shred his hands. Wrapping the rope around his ass, he dropped over the edge, planted his feet against the tower wall, and then started lowering himself down. When his rope ran out, he found a thick vine and used it to get the rest of the way down. He dropped to the ground. Ducking low, he sprinted toward the trees. He searched the ground. No tracks. He was certain he'd seen her from the window, but how had she gotten here? And where did she go? She couldn't have vanished into thin air.

He found the first footprint in front of a huge tree near an old graveyard. She was alone. Raphael hadn't taken her. Dammit, she *was* after the box. All this psychic crap must be a ruse. The box had to be valuable if both she and Nathan were so desperate to find it. She probably wrote the note at the hotel and then claimed it was the man in the elevator just to throw him off. Hell, she was probably working with the man. That would explain why she'd been watching his room and his surprise when he saw them in the elevator. It pissed him off to think that he'd misjudged her. Even though she drove him insane, deep down he'd trusted her. He looked around the graveyard. Did she believe the box was buried here?

He studied the footprints again. They appeared out of nowhere. After a few minutes he found the door in the tree. There was just enough room to stand inside. On the back wall, there was another door that opened to stairs that led to a tunnel, and probably to their room.

That explained how she'd gotten here, but not why she'd left. He tracked her through the graveyard, trying not to think of all the bones that lay under his feet. Every now and then he glimpsed another statue. The whole place seemed to be surrounded by them. Outside the graveyard, two more sets of footprints fell in behind hers. A cold finger ran down his spine.

She was being followed.

He found the place where the tracks came together. Smeared footprints, trampled grass and moss—evidence of a struggle. His stomach felt like mush. Had they killed her? The two larger sets of prints broke away and went back into the woods the way they'd come. It looked like they'd been running, while Kendall's tracks continued toward a circle of tall stones. The air felt heavier, as if he were trudging through mud. He pushed forward and saw the footsteps stopped here. He bent to examine them and saw a circle on one of the stones, like the one that had opened the hidden door in the castle wall. He pushed it and the stone began to slide forward. He jumped clear as a set of worn stairs were revealed.

Kendall lay on her back, gasping for air. The beam from her flashlight speared the darkness, showing the stone stairs where she'd fallen. It felt like she'd hit every step coming down. When she could finally breathe, she made a quick check for broken bones. Her hip was numb, her foot throbbed and she was missing a shoe, but there were no serious injuries as far as she could tell. Her backpack had probably protected her spine. She sat up and reached for her flashlight, lying a few feet away.

She was in some kind of underground room. The walls reminded her of the Egyptian tombs her father had excavated. An arched door with mosaic tiles along the edges led farther into the tunnel. She wanted to explore, but this wasn't the time. Rising, she collected her shoe, readjusted her backpack, and started back up the stairs. She heard a scraping sound above her. They had followed her. She slipped off her shoes and ran for the arched doorway. If this didn't lead to an exit, she was screwed. Jake could be too.

From the position of the steps, she thought the passage might lead back to the castle. She dreaded the thought of running into Raphael, but she had to help Jake. She looked around, hoping to see the ghost monk. She'd followed him here. Maybe she could follow him out. Unless it had been a trap all along.

The floors and walls were the same here—stone and mosaic tiles. Her breath echoed, an eerie sound, and she shivered, wishing she'd brought a heavier coat. A noise sounded behind her. They were inside. Her flashlight flickered once and went black. She banged it against the heel of her hand to no avail. She removed her pack and felt around inside for extra batteries. Changing them didn't help. The fall must have broken it, and she didn't have another flashlight. She couldn't move quietly if she couldn't see where she was going, and there was no telling what nightmares this place held.

She found a recess in the wall and crouched in the darkness, waiting. She saw a flash from the corner of her eye. A light. She watched it moving steadily toward her, the beam widening. Then the light vanished. Had he left? She pressed her back against the wall and tried to listen, but the blood rushed past her ears so hard she couldn't hear. The air stirred and the hairs rose on the back of her neck. Eyes straining at the darkness, she gripped the flashlight, ready to use it as a weapon, when a light struck her full in the face. She swung the flashlight and heard a curse.

"Kendall?"

"Jake?" Her body flooded with relief. She launched herself into his arms and held on tight until her aches forced her to let go. "I'm glad to see you."

"That's why you just bludgeoned me with a flashlight."

"I thought you were one of my attackers."

"I saw where they grabbed you. What happened?"

"They ran away. I think the ghost scared them off."

"Ghost?"

"I followed him from our room through a secret passageway."

"You're out here chasing ghosts?" He gave her a God-help-me look and aimed the flashlight deeper inside the tunnel. "I thought we agreed that you wouldn't run off alone."

"I was trying to get help. I couldn't wake you, and I was afraid you'd been drugged."

"I was."

"But neither of us ate or drank anything."

"I think it was in the water you gave me to brush my teeth."

"You think I drugged you?" Kendall asked.

"I don't think you're that desperate. Must have been Raphael. You probably gave me one of the bottles he brought us. It's the same brand as the bottles we bought."

"No, this one was in the bottom of my backpack. It came from the inn."

"Then someone at the inn tried to drug me."

"You mean tried to drug me," Kendall said. "It was my bottle of water. Someone must have followed us to the inn. The thieves said Thomas was on the way, that he would handle me."

"Thomas. Bet that's not a coincidence."

"I didn't see him at the inn."

"If you're good, your target won't see you." Jake tilted her chin, shining the light over her face. He brushed a thumb underneath a tender spot on her cheek. "Did they do this?" His voice sounded tight.

"No. I fell down the steps. I didn't step back quick enough when the stone pillar moved. I guess Jill *did* fall first."

Jake ran the flashlight over the rest of her, checking her out. "Are you OK?"

"Stiff," she said, "but I'll live. I've had worse falls."

"Let's get out of here before Thomas shows up. We can't go back that way."

Kendall touched her hip and winced. "I think the castle is ahead of us. These places always have secret entrances. Surely we'll run into a dungeon or something."

"Are you sure you're OK to walk?"

"Unless you want to carry me. I'm kidding." They started walking away from the entrance. "Why would Raphael lock us in the room?"

"We're trespassing. He wants your necklace. That makes two good reasons. You went into his library when he as good as told you to keep out. That's three. If I think long enough I can probably come up with a couple more. That's why I said, 'Don't go anywhere alone.' Remember that conversation?"

"Are you forgetting that I tried to wake you up?" Kendall asked.

Jake moved his light closer to the wall as they walked. "How hard did you try? I feel like I've been hit in the face."

"I didn't hit you. Tapped maybe. How did you find the secret passageway?"

"I didn't. I went out the window."

"Of the tower? My God. That's three stories high."

"You can thank me later for playing Knight in Shining Armor."

"What are you doing?" she asked, watching him run his light over the wall.

"I saw something."

She leaned closer, looking at the stone illuminated by his flashlight. "It's the circle motif." She stared at the mark. It looked familiar. She had a feeling she'd seen it somewhere besides on the boundary wall and the pillars. "Maybe the box is hidden here. Try pushing the mark."

He did, but nothing happened. "Hold on…" He reached into his pocket and pulled out a knife. He ran the blade along a crack in the mortar and a seam appeared in the wall.

"What is it?"

"That, Legs, is a door." Using his knife, Jake cleared a section with an outline six feet high and three feet wide. It looked heavy and old.

"Can you get it open?" she asked.

"I haven't met *anything* I couldn't open yet." Her gave her a cocky grin and pushed the motif again. Nothing. He put his shoulder to the door but it still didn't budge.

"Looks like you've lost your technique, stud." She elbowed him aside. "Let me try."

"You gonna try abracadabra?" He fluttered his fingers in the air.

"Maybe it slides open." Kendall put her hands on the door and a force slammed into her, knocking her into Jake. He grunted and caught her in his arms. She held on to him as the images rushed through her head. Piles of bones. And underneath them, Nathan's box. "It's here."

"The box?"

She nodded. "We have to find it fast. We're in danger."

Jake examined the motif again. "It looks like there's something inside the circle." He scratched at it with his knife. "There's a small hole. I think it's a lock."

Kendall peered over his shoulder at the small opening he'd revealed. "Since we don't have the key, do you think you can kick it down?"

"I'm not Superman. That's solid stone, probably two feet thick." A slow smile started across his face, and his flashlight dropped to her chest.

She crossed her arms over her breasts. "Is now really the time?"

He grabbed the cross dangling from her neck and turned it around, pointing to the etching on the back. "Look at this. Remind you of anything?"

"It looks similar to the motif," she said, looking at the mark. It was faded, but she could make out a circle. "I guess that's why it seemed familiar when I saw it on the boundary wall."

"Uh…do you feel that?" Jake asked.

"It's humming." A low sound resonated through the cross. "I don't think it's just a cross. I think it's a key." She slipped the cross over her head and stuck the end inside the slit. Light flashed inside the opening, spilling out of the hole. There was a click and a section of the door retracted.

Kendall took a step back. "Did you see that?"

"It *is* a damned key," Jake said, his breath warm at her ear.

Kendall studied the door, and the cross sticking out of the lock. "If it's a key…" She turned the cross in the hole and a grinding sound echoed in the tunnel as the door began to open.

"Damn."

When it was open, Kendall tried to look inside, but Jake threw out an arm stopping her. "Wait. Make sure it's not a trap."

"I'm not going in. I just wanted a peek."

"There could be a blade waiting to decapitate us. You have a great body, but it wouldn't look as good without your head." When he saw that the door stayed open, he took out his knife and, holding it in front of him, eased it into the passage. Nothing happened. "It didn't set off any alarms or traps. Try the lock again."

She put the cross in the lock and turned it. The door started to close. "It works."

But he still wasn't satisfied. "We need to make sure the cross will open the door from the other side."

"You'd make a good archaeologist. How did you get to be so skeptical?"

"You don't want to know."

She probably didn't. Still, she'd spent enough time exploring dangerous places to know they had to move cautiously. "We need something to block the door in case it doesn't work. I don't want to have to rescue you if you get stuck in there."

He gave her half a smile. "I don't see anything here strong enough to block it. It would crush our packs. I'll have to risk it."

"So you can take risks but I can't?"

"Give me the cross."

She gave him the cross and he stepped inside. He used the flashlight to find the lock, and then inserted the key. The grinding noise sounded again and the door started to move. He tossed her the light. Chivalrous.

Just before it closed, she threw her backpack between the wall and the closing door. It hit the bag and slowed, grinding to a stop.

"I appreciate you sacrificing your makeup for me, but I don't think I could squeeze through this hole," Jake said, looking at her through the six-inch crack.

"I can pass food to you and keep you from starving to death."

"Let's cross our fingers and hope you don't have to." He turned the cross in the keyhole and the door started to open again. "At least we know we won't get trapped in here."

"Then why don't you look more pleased?"

"It's not exactly my kind of place. But I think it's yours." He moved aside and she stepped in. The air was musty and dank. He flashed his light around the dark interior, and she saw the walls were lined with bones.

"Catacombs," she said, her voice breathless with awe.

CHAPTER SEVEN

B ONES. THEY WERE EVERYWHERE. GRAVES HAD BEEN CUT into the walls, some holding entire skeletons, while others had been disturbed, with pieces littering the floor.

"This is amazing."

Jake grunted. "Maybe for someone who grew up poking around tombs."

"You don't like catacombs?"

"I don't like bones. Watch it. You're about to kick a skull."

Kendall looked down and stopped.

"I think the head belongs to him," Jake said, pointing to a headless skeleton lying in one of the niches in the wall. "Maybe he's your ghost." He hoped a joke would ease the tightening in his throat.

She reached down and picked up the skull, her hands cradling each side as she stared into the hollow eye sockets. Her lips thinned and she stepped toward the grave, carefully placing the head back with its body. "It's not him." She turned abruptly and walked away.

He looked back at the skeleton, wondering what she had seen. She started walking and he stayed close, sharing his light. The beam revealed centuries of cobwebs and dust as they moved deeper into the catacombs. In addition to the skeletons, there were coffins against the walls and in private alcoves barred with iron doors.

She seemed right at home here. He'd rather be locked in a morgue.

The air grew colder as Kendall moved through the warren of tombs. She stopped suddenly and bent over.

"Feeling claustrophobic?" He sure as hell was.

She shook her head and pointed to a coffin in one of the alcoves. "There."

He considered asking how she knew, but didn't bother.

"We need to open it," she said.

That was what he figured she'd say. The lock on the door was old and rusty. Jake set down his pack and took out a small bolt cutter. He cut through the lock and pushed on the door. It creaked opened, doing nothing to settle his nerves. He didn't like this, and it wasn't just because of the bones. They stepped inside and he felt the floor give. A scraping noise was all the warning they got.

Kendall yelled, "Look out!" at the same time Jake tackled her, knocking them clear as a stone crashed from the ceiling, landing where they had stood seconds before. They lay sprawled on the floor, him on top of her, not exactly what he'd had in mind when he wanted to get her underneath him.

He got up and helped Kendall to her feet. "Holy moly, that was close," she said, brushing herself off. The fallen stone was the size of a tire. Big enough to have crushed their skulls.

"Our first booby trap. Don't move until I make sure it's safe." Jake pointed his flashlight at the ceiling to see where the stone had come from. There was a large ledge above them. "The floor in front of the coffin must have been the trigger that tilted the ledge, releasing the stone."

"I wonder how long that's been waiting for some unsuspecting thief."

"Not long enough," Jake muttered. He picked up his pack and threw it in front of the coffin. Nothing. "I think it's OK, but let me go first." He climbed over the deadly rock and checked the area to make sure there wasn't a second trap. "Stay there until I open the coffin, just in case we missed one."

"We should draw straws," Kendall said. And the damned thing was that she was serious.

"I'll test it," Jake said. "If a rock hits me in the head, you can rescue me or bury me. If a rock hits you in the head, I'm dead anyway."

"Nathan's not that harsh," Kendall said.

She didn't know the Nathan he knew. But she was smart enough to know that one of them needed to stay clear until they were sure the coffin didn't have another trap. Two dead relic hunters wouldn't do anyone any good.

She didn't join him until after he opened the lid. There was nothing left of the body but bones swathed in a dark robe. They moved closer, standing side by side, the only two creatures breathing in this place of death. At least on two legs, he thought, as something squeaked past his boot.

"Is this it?" he asked, looking at the empty sockets and mocking grin. All skeletons looked the same. Like they were laughing at death.

The monk's hands were crossed over his abdomen. Time had eased its grip on the bones. One white finger protruded from the sleeve of his robe.

Kendall nodded but didn't speak. Her hands hovered over the monk. "It's here," she said.

Jake heard a tiny noise behind them and pulled out his gun. He had a knot in his gut now that definitely wasn't caused by bones. "Hurry." Whoever attacked her would eventually come back.

Kendall gently pulled back the sleeve of the robe. Underneath the monk's hands, hidden in the folds of his robe, was a box like the one in Nathan's drawing. She'd found it.

"You ever play the lottery?"

"A few times," she said. "That's not how my gift works."

He put his gun back and opened his pack, pulling out a shirt to wrap the box in. When he reached for it, Kendall grabbed his hand.

"No. Something's wrong."

"'Course it is. We're disturbing the dead." Jake reached for the box again and heard a click behind them.

"Don't touch that."

He spun, reaching for his gun, and a beam of light hit him in the eyes, blinding him.

"Touch the gun, Jake, and she dies," a voice said.

He eased his hand away from the gun, surprised. The man knew his name. He must be Thomas. When the light lowered, Jake saw three men dressed in monk's robes, their faces covered by hoods. They were all armed. He could probably take them, but he couldn't risk Kendall getting caught in the cross fire. He would have to get her to safety first.

One of the thieves pointed his gun at Kendall's chest. "Drop your flashlight and gun and move away from her. Play the hero, and I'll have to kill her." It was the one who'd called him Jake.

"Now, move away from the coffin. Over there, outside the alcove."

Jake kept Kendall behind him as they moved. "When I give the word, find someplace to hide," he whispered.

"Give me your necklace," the thief demanded, reaching for it.

Kendall clutched her cross. "Why?"

"You know why. Give it to me now."

Kendall took off the necklace and handed it to the man. The thief lifted it to examine it, and the beam from his light fell on his face. Jake was sure he'd seen the man before. Thomas? He didn't have a beard, but Thomas's could have been fake.

Jake was waiting for them to go for the box. Once they were distracted he'd make his move.

The thief stuck the cross in a leather bag and one of the others reached for the box, dislodging the corpse's hands. Jake started to move when a whirring noise filled the catacombs. Kendall shoved him out of the way as a barrage of rocks shot over the coffin like cannonballs. Flashlight beams danced around the catacombs like strobe lights on a disco floor. Judging by the yelps of pain, a few of the stones must have hit their mark. Kendall had warned Jake just in time.

When the assault stopped, Jake pushed Kendall aside. "Now."

Before the thieves could retrieve their fallen flashlights, he dropped to the floor, kicking the legs of the man who was still standing. One of the others grabbed his flashlight but Jake kicked it out of his hand, and then added a kick to the man's ribs. He grunted and Jake hurried to the spot where he'd pushed Kendall. A shot rang out before he could get to her and she screamed. Was she hurt?

"Bitch! She bit me."

He had two choices: kill the thieves now, or take advantage of the darkness and get Kendall to safety. Only one of the men posed a real threat—the one who knew him. Jake decided to play it safe and get Kendall out of harm's way. He found her by scent and grabbed her.

"It's me," he whispered. He pulled her into the small space behind a nearby coffin. "Don't make a sound." He lay down in front of her, shielding her as the men cursed and scrambled for their flashlights.

"Where'd they go?" the first thief asked, shining his light close to their hiding place.

"Who cares? Let's get out of here. I'm bleeding. One of those damned rocks nearly took off my ear."

"But we're supposed to—"

"He'll never know."

"Then take their flashlights and gun. Let the catacombs kill them."

There was a rush of feet and the lights disappeared, leaving the night cold and still. Jake lay there a second longer until he was sure they were gone.

"Stay here. I'm going after them. I'll come back for you when it's safe."

"You're not leaving me here."

He didn't blame her. He'd risk getting shot rather than stay in here with all these bones.

"Besides, you can't go after them alone," Kendall said. "That's three against one."

He wasn't worried about the odds. He just needed her out of the way.

"If you leave me here, I'll follow you," she added, and he knew she would.

He climbed out of the hiding place and then helped her out. "Then be quiet and come on. We have to hurry before they get away."

"I can't see anything," Kendall said.

"I think there's another light in my pack. I put it down when we found the box." Jake stooped and fumbled in the darkness, trying to hurry before the men got away with the key. If they didn't get it back, he and Kendall would become two more sets of bones for the tomb's collection. He found his second flashlight in an inside pocket. He turned it on and the light flashed over Kendall. She looked like she'd been rolling on the floor. "Let's go. We have to move fast."

"What are we going to do when we catch them?"

"I'm going to sneak up on them."

He was disgusted that he'd let them get the drop on him, all because he was worried about Kendall and a bunch of dried bones. This was the last time he was going on a job with a woman. If Nathan didn't understand, he'd just have to send Jake back.

He reached the closed door to the catacombs but they were too late.

"We're trapped." Kendall moved up beside him, studying the door. "Do you think you can open it with your knife?"

"I doubt it." He tried his knife and some other tools from his pack, but nothing worked.

"Maybe Raphael will discover us missing and come looking for us," Kendall said.

"I don't think we want him to find us here."

Kendall hugged her arms. "If we don't report in, I guess Nathan will start searching for us eventually. He must know where the castle is located by now."

Eventually might not be soon enough. And he wasn't sure he trusted the Almighty Nathan, not after that thief recognized him. It raised a hell of a lot of questions that couldn't possibly have good answers. And the only connection was Nathan.

"He won't come looking for us just yet." But when he did, he'd better have some answers. Jake swung his light into the catacomb. "Come on. There must be another way out."

The catacombs had hundreds of residents. They searched for a couple of hours, digging through nooks and crannies, shoving aside coffins and desecrating bones, always watching for booby traps. There was no way out.

"I think we're stuck here for the night," Jake said, dropping his pack near a small recess in the wall. "We can bed down here." The small space would conserve body heat, keeping the wall at their backs and a line of sight to the main corridor.

"I hope there aren't any more booby traps," Kendall said.

"They're probably limited to the area around the box. How'd you know what that last one was?"

"We ran into a similar one in Egypt. A slingshot device with a wire attached to a sarcophagus."

"Did you get hurt?"

"One of my friends cut his arm."

His? "What kind of friend?"

"He was an archaeologist."

"Did you kiss his injury and make it better?"

"You're impossible." Kendall pulled her jacket tighter around her. "Is your thermal blanket in there?" she asked, looking at his pack.

She wouldn't have known about it if she hadn't snooped in his pack. He pulled out the thin blanket and spread it on the floor.

"Do you have another one?"

"No. You should've packed a blanket instead of a makeup kit." He was only partially teasing. He'd looked in her bag and knew she carried some makeup. She didn't need it. "I'm surprised that a woman who's used to sleeping under the desert stars doesn't have something to keep her warm."

"I lost mine, along with my spare flashlight. I didn't have a chance to replace them. This trip was unexpected. I should have thought about it when we stopped for supplies." She plunked down on the blanket. "What if the thieves come back?"

"I don't think they will. They got what they wanted."

"We have to get the box back."

"Thanks for warning me not to touch it. Guess I owe you one."

"I think we're even. It wasn't just the trap. That box scares me. I don't know what's in it, but it's powerful."

"Evil?"

"I don't know, but we have to find it."

"You're starting to sound like Nathan." Which made Jake wonder what the hell was in the box. "After we've rested, we'll find a way out. Whoever made that fancy door must have built another entrance. They might have an opening in the top to let in light and air. You get some sleep. You got pretty banged up in that fall. I'll keep watch."

She lay down on the blanket. "We don't have enough food and water to last very long."

"We have protein bars. And if we get desperate, we can drink urine." He sat down and leaned against the wall, positioning himself so he could see if anyone came from either direction.

"I'd rather die of thirst."

"Then you've never been really thirsty." He turned the flashlight off to conserve batteries.

"Have you?" Her voice was soft in the darkness.

"Yes."

"When?"

"I've spent time in the desert too. I got stuck there once. It wasn't fun."

"Drinking urine is beyond gross."

"It's better than dying."

He felt her eyes on him in the dark.

"Whose urine?" she asked.

"Mine."

"What were you doing in the desert?"

"On assignment."

"For Nathan?"

"No. That was before I met him."

"What kind of assignment was it?"

"We were looking for some buried coins. Aren't you tired?"

"Why do you hate talking about yourself?"

"I'm not that interesting."

"When it comes to privacy, you're as bad as Nathan. Are you sure you aren't tired?"

"I'm fine." He spoiled it by yawning.

"Liar." He heard shuffling and saw the dim glow of her watch. "It's two in the morning," she said. "You should get some sleep too."

"You just want my body heat."

She snorted. "I don't need it. I have your blanket."

But Kendall was right. He was tired and the thieves were probably long gone. He lay down beside her, close enough that they could share heat, yet not so close that she would think he was taking advantage of her. Then he decided that she could use some distraction from the thought of thieves, booby traps, and those damned grinning skulls. He let his leg touch hers. She jerked like he'd poked her with a hot iron. Before she could speak, he rolled over and faced her. "It's going to get colder. We'll need each other's heat. Scoot to the edge and turn around." When she did, he pulled the excess blanket over both of them, trying not to press closer, which is what he wanted to do. He adjusted his arm and his hand brushed her breast. "Sorry."

"Was that an accident?"

"If I'd done it on purpose, you would have known."

"Do it again and you'll be carrying your balls home in your backpack." The harsh words lacked punch, and he noticed she didn't move away.

They lay in silence for several minutes. He could almost hear Kendall's wheels turning as fast as his own. "Why do you hate bones?" she asked.

"It's a long story." One he didn't want to tell.

After a minute, she spoke. "I was trapped in a tomb once. One of the boards fell, blocking the entrance. I was terrified."

"How'd you get out?" he asked, pressing a little closer, not because he wanted to—though he did—but because she was still shivering.

"Adam found me."

"Adam?"

"He was my best friend."

"Where's Adam now?"

"He died in a plane crash when he was twelve."

Jake felt a hand squeeze his gut, but he refused to let the memory in now. The past was done. He had to make sure Kendall had a future.

"What if we don't get out?" she said.

"We will."

"Promise?" Her voice was a whisper.

"I promise."

The catacombs got chillier and they snuggled closer as he listened to the stillness of night. It always amazed him how many sounds could be heard in a place where there was silence. The sound of her breathing. His own breath. Tiny scurrying sounds, an occasional bone being dislodged, hopefully by the scurrying critters and not the bone's owner. Even the air seemed to have a voice, tired and weary, clothed with centuries of death.

Death.

As hard as he'd tried to keep it out, the memory slipped in.

He forced himself closer to the hole, knowing what he would find. His knees dropped from under him and he sank to the ground, staring at the locks of blonde hair and bleached bones against the dark soil.

CHAPTER EIGHT

K ENDALL WOKE TO ABSOLUTE DARKNESS, HEART POUNDING with fear, but it wasn't her fear. What was she sensing? Was it Jake? She could feel him behind her, breathing harsh, his hand gripping hers. He must be dreaming.

He'd scooted closer in his sleep. The move wasn't a come-on but the need for warmth and human contact in a place of death. Ordinarily, she didn't mind tombs. She'd spent a large part of her childhood crawling through them. It was different when the tomb might be hers.

Jake's breathing was calmer now, and she let the sound soothe her. His hand had relaxed, resting over her stomach. She could smell him, warm and male. Part of her wanted to snuggle tighter and another part wanted to roll over and wake him up so they could forget about danger and death and bad dreams, at least for a while. She wondered if anyone had ever had sex in catacombs. She snuggled deeper into his warmth until her eyelids grew heavy. When she woke again, she was cold and alone.

She sat up, looking at her watch: four thirty in the morning. "Jake," she whispered, eyes straining in the darkness. Farther down the catacombs, she saw a light moving toward her. She couldn't tell if it was Jake or if the thieves had come back to make sure they didn't escape. It could be Raphael. He must have played some part in this. A shadow moved in front of her. A monk in a cowl. The thieves had come back. She gripped the blanket and pressed her body as far into the alcove as she could. The monk turned and faced her. She froze. Had he seen her?

He started walking toward her, but there was nowhere for her to escape. He moved closer and closer and she couldn't help but cry out, expecting an attack. She felt a rush of air and he disappeared.

She jumped up and turned, staring at the wall where the apparition had disappeared. Just as silently as the ghost had moved, Jake appeared behind her. "What's wrong?"

"I just saw the monk."

He turned off his flashlight and pushed her against the wall, putting himself in front of her. "Where?" he whispered.

"Not the thieves, the ghost. He walked right through this wall."

"Here?" Jake turned the flashlight on and aimed it at the wall. "Sure you weren't dreaming?"

"I wasn't dreaming. It was the same ghost I saw in the bedroom."

"How do you know?"

"I could tell from his memories."

"You read memories?"

"Sometimes."

"So much for personal privacy."

The very reason she didn't have a husband or boyfriend. "Where were you?"

"Looking for a way out."

"Alone? You could have run into another trap."

"I found a lantern," he said, cutting off her reproach.

"Does it work?"

"I was about to find out when you called my name." He led her to a group of coffins housed behind an iron grille. "Look up there." He swung his light up and she saw an old lantern hanging from the wall. "Hold the flashlight."

She held the light while he got the lantern down. He gently shook it. "It's full. And someone left matches. I guess Raphael comes down here to check on the box."

"Too bad he didn't leave a map." There was a flicker, and soft light filled the catacombs. He handed the lantern to Kendall. "I know it's all in my head, but I feel warmer already," she said.

"There's another one on the other side." After he lit the second lantern, he turned off the flashlight and stuck it in his pocket. "We'll save the batteries in case we need them later."

In case they were trapped down here for good.

"Now we can see to find our way out of this hellhole," he said, moving back toward their blanket. He held the lantern close to the wall.

"What are you looking for?"

"You said your ghost walked through the wall in the bedroom where there was a secret door. Maybe there's a secret door here."

"I got the feeling you didn't believe in ghosts."

"I don't. But I'm starting to believe in your visions."

That was a start, Kendall thought. "Haven't you ever felt a presence, like someone was with you, but when you turned around, he wasn't there?" In the flickering light of the lantern, she saw a haunted look cross his face and knew he had his own ghosts, whether he believed in them or not.

"So you're a ghost expert too?"

"No, but I've encountered a few."

They both systematically searched the alcove, running their hands over the rough stone. Kendall's fingertips brushed over a notch that didn't feel natural. "I think I found something."

Jake scraped at the notch with his knife, uncovering the motif. "I've never been so glad to see a circle. There must be a door here."

"But we don't have the cross to open it."

"I don't see anything that looks like a lock on this one." He pushed the mark and they felt the wall give.

"Push harder," Kendall said.

He grimaced, shoving against the wall with his shoulder. Kendall started pushing with him, and the wall opened several inches.

"Another secret tunnel," Jake said.

"We were in front of the door all along."

"That explained why the recess looked like a doorway. I'll check it out first. We don't want to stick our heads inside a trap." He used the lantern to inspect the other side of the door before climbing through. "This is going to be a tight squeeze."

After Jake made sure it wasn't booby-trapped, Kendall climbed through, holding her lantern in front of her. "Yikes, this is cramped." It was nothing like the tunnel on the other end of the catacombs. This one was just tall enough to clear Jake's head, and barely wide enough for his shoulders.

"At least there aren't any bones here," he said after they had walked for a few minutes.

"You sound relieved."

"Told you, I don't like bones."

She did, but right now she needed daylight and fresh air. And a bathroom. "Do you see an end?"

"Not yet. Don't panic on me."

They walked on in silence broken only by the occasional scrape of feet. "How did you meet Nathan?" she asked.

"It's a long story," he said.

"It's not like either of us is going anywhere."

"It's complicated."

"Just say you don't want to tell me, for goodness' sake."

"I don't want to tell you."

"You're as bad as him, with all these secrets." She wished she had a bottle of water.

"Men don't blab everything like women do."

"We don't blab."

"Yes you do."

"How would you know? Have you ever been married?"

"No."

"Have you ever wanted to get married?"

He hesitated. "No."

"Good. You're not marriage material."

He grunted. "What about you? Any husbands hanging around?"

"No." What man wanted someone who might see inside his head? Even though she usually couldn't, there was always the threat. She would pick up an object belonging to him and inadvertently blurt out something she wasn't supposed to know. That kind of thing tended to freak people out. It didn't take long to get a reputation as a wacko. Or a witch.

Adam was the only one who had understood. An image flashed through her head. A boy with rumpled, sun-bleached hair and tanned skin, holding up his latest treasure, his face split into a grin. Her heart gave one soft squeeze and the face faded back into the place where she kept it. "Where the hell is the end of this tunnel?" Her voice echoed strangely in the small confines.

"What about sex?"

Kendall stopped. "Sex?"

Jake kept walking. "You don't strike me as a total prude. You're probably—what—twenty-five? I doubt you're a virgin."

"I'm twenty-eight and my virginity or lack thereof is none of your concern."

He stopped suddenly. "There." His lantern showed a set of steps leading up to a stone door.

"I hope we don't need the key."

They climbed the narrow staircase and she waited while he searched for a way out. The space was so tight there was barely room for one person. "Here we go." He pushed something and a door opened in the wall, amazingly quietly for stone. He put his hand over the lantern, keeping the light low. He stuck his head out and looked around before motioning for her to join him.

She followed, scraping her body through the doorway. Kendall looked around in surprise. "We're inside the entryway of the castle." The tunnel door was inside one of the stone columns. This place was full of secrets.

"Quiet," Jake whispered. "Raphael may be here. I don't know how he's involved, but we don't want to announce our presence…" He stopped. Raphael lay on the floor behind the column, the light obscene on his dead, amber eyes.

"Oh my God. They killed him too."

Jake kneeled and touched Raphael's chest. "He's been dead for about four hours."

"You can tell how long he's been dead?"

"I can tell from his body temperature. The thieves must have killed him." He pointed to the tracks leading to and from the body. "The footprints match the ones where you were attacked."

"If they weren't working for Raphael, then who?"

"I don't know. See if you can pick up anything from him."

"Touch him?" She didn't mind bodies that had been dead for a long time. That was history. But fresh death was disturbing. Swallowing, she knelt beside Jake and stretched out her hand. A ripple moved over her skin and she hesitated. There was some kind of weird energy surrounding Raphael. Jake put his hand on her shoulder in encouragement. She closed her eyes and touched Raphael's chest.

A blinding light flashed as screams filled the air. Men were running from the light, eyes wide with terror, swords and shields dangling uselessly. Protect it. He must protect it.

Kendall yanked her hand back.

"What the hell was that?" Jake asked.

"I don't know. You saw it?" She'd never had anyone else share her visions. Except Adam.

Jake looked shaken. "Were those Raphael's memories? How old is he? I saw men in armor holding swords and shields."

"Maybe they're someone else's memories, someone connected to him." Otherwise, Raphael was really old. Or he had been.

Jake shook his head and stood. "Let's just get out of here before the trail gets colder. What are you doing now?"

"Look at this..." She lifted a cross from Raphael's neck.

"It looks a lot like yours. Bring it. If it's also a key, we might need it yet."

"You take it."

Jake pulled the cross over Raphael's head and stuck it in his pocket. "Let's go."

"I want to get the piece of letter I found under the desk. It's still in the tower room."

"Hurry. There could be more of those thieves. I need to get you someplace safe."

"Should we call the police?"

"No."

"Why not? There's a dead guy here."

"You want the cops to pull us aside for questioning while the thieves get farther away? They've already got a head start. No cops."

"I feel like we should do something," she said, looking at Raphael again. Even in death he looked fierce. Kendall felt a wave of sadness at such a needless loss.

Jake nudged her toward the stairs. "Nathan can have his people take care of it later."

"The one guy knew you. He said your name."

"Must have been Thomas."

She hadn't seen his face clearly, so she couldn't say, but Jake obviously had. Why else would he have acted so surprised?

They hurried to the tower and found a metal bar in front of the door to their room. "We really were prisoners," Kendall said. "How did we not see this when he brought us here?"

After lifting the bar so Kendall could get inside, Jake examined the mechanism while she retrieved the scrap of paper. "The bar was hidden along the doorjamb," he said, when she returned.

Kendall put the paper in her bag. "We need to find whoever was singing. They might be prisoners here too. Or whoever killed Raphael could have found them."

Jake wasn't pleased, but they made a quick search on all three floors, checking the rooms with unlocked doors. Jake even picked a couple of locks, but they didn't find anyone else. They discovered bedrooms in every size, sitting rooms, parlors, and libraries, all modernized with electricity and indoor plumbing. At one time this must have housed a large group. Where were they now?

"Three floors of nice rooms, and he sticks us in the tower," Kendall said.

"Prisoners don't get the good rooms. Raphael put us in the tower for a reason."

And now they would never know why. They hurried back down to the first floor. They were both silent as they passed Raphael's body. Jake stopped at an open door they hadn't seen when Raphael showed them around.

"He must have stayed here," Kendall said. The room had a small bed and a few pieces of furniture, including a desk with books, papers, and pens. A window overlooked the statues and underneath, a table held a glass of wine that Raphael would never finish.

"Stay close," Jake whispered.

They stepped outside and he grabbed her hand, tugging her toward the statues. Kendall felt a vibration deep in her bones, like a warning. They had almost reached the statues when Jake stopped. Two dark shapes lay on the ground.

"What is that?" Kendall asked. When they got closer she saw two of the thieves, their robes twisted about their bodies, faces covered by hoods. Jake kneeled beside them and pulled one hood back to check for a pulse. The dead man's eyes were solid black.

"What happened to their eyes?" she asked.

"Hell if I know." He checked the other thief. "Neither of these is Thomas. He must be the third thief." Jake started searching the corpses. The vibration got stronger, along with Kendall's sense of dread.

"What are you doing?" she asked.

"Looking for the box. Maybe we'll get lucky." But they didn't. "Thomas must have it. Let's see if we can find him." He stood and started to take a step.

"Stop!" She grabbed Jake's arm. "The statue...It's humming. Don't touch it!"

He picked up a rock and threw it at the statue. There was a hissing noise and a blinding flash of light as the rock fell.

Jake shaded his eyes. "What the hell!"

"They are sentinels, just like in the vision."

"I guess we know what happened to thief one and thief two," Jake said, studying the statues. "Maybe if we don't touch them." He picked up another rock and tossed it between the statues. The wall of light flashed again. Jake moved back beside her and cursed. "It's like some kind of electric fence."

"How did we get through before?" she asked. "Maybe it only comes on at night."

Jake stuck his hands in his pocket. "Or Raphael turns it on when there's a threat, like having two strangers show up out of the blue."

"We could wait until daylight to find out. It's almost five thirty."

"There's gotta be a switch that controls it. Or at least another way out. No one's gonna hike that far for a gallon of milk. This would be a good time for your sixth sense to kick in."

"I can't make it happen. It works when it wants to."

"Can't you take some kind of classes to learn how to control this gift?"

"I wish."

"Raphael must have some kind of control on him." Jake frowned and pulled the cross out of his pocket. "It's humming too." He looked at the statues and then at the cross again. "I have an idea. Stand back." He nudged Kendall backward several feet.

"What are you doing?"

"Testing something." He walked toward the statues.

"And if it fails?"

"Cremate me and spread my ashes over Lake Watauga in Tennessee."

"Are you crazy?"

Holding the cross by the tip, he stretched out his hand. The humming was almost deafening now.

"Jake, stop! Please!"

Slowly, he let the tip of the cross move even with the statues. He stretched his hand farther, until the cross was between the statues. Nothing happened. He followed with his fingertips, his hand, his wrist, and then his entire arm. He jerked his arm back and grinned. "It works."

Kendall let out a pent-up gasp. That was the bravest thing she'd seen since Adam jerked that snake away just before it bit her. "What made you think it would work?"

"It was humming in my pocket, like the statues. Almost as if they were talking to each other."

"And it hummed in the catacombs too."

Jake nodded. "I figured if it was the key to the catacombs, it must be some sort of key here."

That was pretty darned brilliant, she thought. Not to mention courageous.

"I'll go first to make sure it works," Jake said. "Then I'll toss the cross back to you."

She wanted to close her eyes but she couldn't. He approached the statues and slowly walked between them. She kept her eyes on him, willing him to be safe. When he made it across, she finally drew a breath.

He turned, flashed her a grin and threw the cross back through the statues. "Heads up."

She caught it against her chest and held it close, trembling. Jake stood on the other side of the statues waiting. His eyes met hers through the darkness. He stretched out his Cringing, she focused on Jake and approached the statue. All sounds seemed to stop, as if she were caught in a bubble, but she could still feel the vibrations surrounding her. It felt like minutes had passed, yet it could only have been seconds. When she was safely through, Jake grabbed her and pulled her farther away from the statues. She wrapped her arms around his waist and leaned against him.

With his arms still wrapped around her, they both turned back and looked at the statues. Jake squeezed her arm. "Let's get out of here."

"How are we going to find the box?" she asked. "We have no idea where Thomas is."

"Nathan's checking his background. We'll find him."

Even with a flashlight, it wasn't easy to find the opening in the wall. When they located the motif, she pressed her palm against the mark and the door opened, allowing them to step through.

The trail had been challenging in daylight; in the dark it was a nightmare. Her muscles ached from her fall, and she was tired and thirsty. The trip back across the bridge was the worst. Jake tied off the rope and went first. This time he made it across without any mishaps. When he reached the other side, he tied his end of the rope to a tree, and Kendall looped her end around her waist. After she made it across, they quickly coiled up the rope and continued walking. They came to a clearing and Kendall rested against a scrawny tree.

"I have to stop." Her throat was so parched she started to understand how a person could drink urine to stay alive.

"We can't stop."

"I'm ready to collapse…" Something whizzed past her face and a chunk splintered from the tree. Jake shoved her to the ground, covering her body with his. "What was that?"

"A bullet."

"Someone's shooting at us? What next?"

Jake lifted his head, scanning the direction of the bullet. "We get out without getting shot."

"How? I can't even see."

"We crawl."

They crawled on hands and knees, sometimes on their stomachs, until they reached the next wooded area. Jake pushed her behind a small bush and into a cave.

"How did you know this was here?"

"I saw it on the hike in."

Kendall rubbed her arms against the October morning chill. "The shooter must be Thomas. The other two thieves are already dead."

"We'll wait here and see if he moves on." Jake's whisper came from different locations. Kendall knew he was checking out the cave.

She couldn't see anything. She reached out and touched a wall. Cold. "What if he doesn't leave? I'm so tired I could drop, and my throat is parched." She rubbed her arms against the chill. Jake sat down next to her and put his arm around her shoulder. She could feel the heat coming off his body and gratefully leaned into the warmth. "You've done this before, haven't you?" she asked, and she felt him nod. "I've encountered ghosts and booby traps, but being shot at and nearly electrocuted are new to me."

He gave her a gentle nudge. "Stop talking," he whispered. "You'll give our position away."

They sat in silence for several minutes. She could tell he was listening. She couldn't hear anything, not even Jake breathing. The silence stretched painfully long. "How long do we have to wait?" she asked in a small voice.

"I have to go out there and see if he's gone. I need you to stay inside." She felt his breath warm on her face. "Please."

She touched his hand. "Hurry."

He left and she felt the immediate loss of body heat and comfort. She loved caves and exploring, but after almost being killed the cave felt as bad as the catacombs.

He was back in minutes. "Let's go. Slowly, no noise."

She followed his lead as they moved out of the cave and onto the trail. There weren't any more shots. When they drew near the place where they had left the car, dawn was breaking. She thought she saw a flash of red and then she spotted the car. Her steps quickened.

"Wait. I found footprints." Jake bent and studied the ground. "Thomas's, I think. What's this?"

Kendall looked back and saw him pick something up, his brows pulled into a frown. "There weren't any tracks leading from the castle," she said. "How did he get here? Fly?" She kept moving toward the car. "Hurry, we're almost there."

She was twenty feet from the car when Jake tackled her to the ground. She lay there stunned, her face pressed into the dirt, his weight holding her down. Her ribs felt like they had cracked. She sucked in her first breath to verbally blast him when the car exploded.

CHAPTER NINE

A BALL OF FLAME ROLLED OVER HER HEAD. SHE SCREAMED and tried to get away, but she couldn't move with Jake's weight crushing her. She pushed and shoved until she finally shifted him off her. He didn't move. His eyes were closed.

She knelt beside him. "Jake!" He didn't respond. Blood trickled down his face from a gash on his head. Another noise caught her attention over the roar of flames: a car engine. The shooter. They had to hide. "Jake, wake up!" He still didn't move. She grabbed him under the arms and tried to pull him toward the tree line a few yards away, but it was like dragging a log. Before she could get him hidden, a vehicle stopped on the road. It was a blue car, like one she had seen at the inn. The door opened and Brandi jumped out. She ran toward the car, holding an arm up to protect her face. "Are you OK?" she yelled.

"Jake is hurt."

"Jake?"

Kendall had forgotten their aliases. "I need to get him to a hospital," she said. She didn't question what Brandi was doing here, or the coincidence that a nurse would come along when Kendall needed one most. There was time for that later.

The women flinched from the heat and knelt beside Jake. "His pulse is good," Brandi said. "He's taken a hit to the head."

"A hit?" A bullet? Had the shooter fired as the car exploded?

"Debris from the car, most likely. How did it explode?"

"I don't know. Where's the nearest hospital? We need to hurry."

"I saw a hospital sign a couple of miles from the inn."

Together the two women got Jake in the car. Kendall sat in the back, supporting his weight. She looked back at the burning car and put her hand over Jake's chest, needing to feel his heartbeat. He'd sacrificed himself to save her, again.

Brandi tossed their backpacks on the passenger side before climbing in the driver's seat. She brushed a strand of hair from her face. She looked like she'd been sweating.

"What are you doing here?" Kendall asked, fumbling in her backpack for a bandage.

"I was looking for you and…Jason. Roberto was worried when you didn't come back last night. He was afraid you'd tried to find some castle he told you about. I had to run an errand in this direction, so he asked me to look for your car."

Kendall covered Jake's wound as best she could. His eyes were still closed. If Brandi hadn't come along, there was no telling what might have happened to Jake. Or to her. There was no cell phone signal in the area and no help anywhere for miles, and a crazed killer was running loose. "Thank you," she said and meant it. Whatever Brandi's reason for being here, she may have saved Jake's and Kendall's lives.

"Did you find the castle?" Brandi asked.

"No. We were just…hiking. It got late so we decided to camp for the night." A horn honked, startling her, and a luxury car flashed by.

"Slow down, this isn't a racetrack," Brandi muttered. "These rich guys think they own the road."

"Kendall!" Jake jerked upright, startled by the horn.

"Lie still," Kendall said, gently trying to push him back down. "You were hit on the head. You need to see a doctor. We're on the way to the hospital."

He pulled away and sat up. "No hospital." He slumped back against the seat, letting some of his weight rest against her. "Too dangerous," he muttered.

Kendall met Brandi's worried gaze in the rearview mirror but Brandi quickly looked away. "You're a nurse. Can you take a look at him?"

Brandi's hands were clenched on the wheel. "Sure. Back to the inn, then?"

"Yes." And pray that whoever tried to kill them wasn't following.

One hour earlier...

Nathan pulled up to the inn around six in the morning. There were a few cars in the parking lot. The place looked quiet. Everyone was probably still asleep. He parked and walked toward the front door, his gut tense. He should have told Kendall and Jake everything, but it was too risky. There were some things he couldn't let anyone know. As he walked through the lobby, a dark-haired man at the front desk looked up, his face worried. His expression eased when he saw Nathan, giving him a long, appreciative look.

"Hello, how can I help you?"

"I'm looking for my...sister. I think she's staying here. Kara Monroe." He knew the names they were using. He knew every place they'd been.

The man frowned. "She isn't here. She and Jason went out. I'm worried that they might have run into trouble."

"Trouble?"

"They asked about a castle nearby. I shouldn't have told them where it was, but I didn't think they would actually go."

"Why shouldn't they go to the castle?"

"It's not a good place." He looked over his shoulder, as if someone might be listening. "They say it's cursed."

"Cursed?"

"I'm sorry." He frowned. "I'm Roberto, the innkeeper. You are?"

"Uh, Nick. So this castle is supposed to be cursed?"

"That's what everyone says."

"How long have they been gone?"

"Since yesterday afternoon. They should have been back by now." He shrugged his shoulders. "They're honeymooners. Maybe they got distracted."

Honeymooners?

"They're such a lovely couple. I would hate for them to get hurt."

"Tell me where this castle is. I'll go look for them."

After Roberto gave him directions, Nathan walked outside. He had just gotten in his car when he noticed a man standing behind some bushes watching the inn. He had brown hair and wore dark clothes. Was he looking for Kendall and Jake? A moment later, another man came around the side of the inn and started down the lane toward town. This man was young and had a beard. He wore a ball cap pulled low over his eyes, and a leather bag hung from his shoulder. He kept his head down, as if he didn't want to be noticed. Every few seconds, he glanced behind him. The watcher stayed hidden until the young man was halfway up the lane, and then he followed.

Curious, Nathan waited a minute. Then he started his car and went after them. The town was quiet at this early hour. Not many people moved about. The men knew their surroundings better than Nathan did, and in the time it took him to park they had darted down a side street near a small church. He hurried after them, but they had vanished. A moment later he heard a soft cry in the graveyard behind the church.

Keeping to the shadows, he eased inside the graveyard, his senses on alert. Something was wrong here. He felt it in his bones, that deep ache that sometimes accompanied the other anomaly.

A creaking sound came from deeper in the graveyard. He crept closer and saw an iron gate closing. He started to turn back when the metallic scent of blood flooded his nostrils. He looked around and saw a freshly dug grave close by. The ache got stronger as he approached the hole. The young man lay sprawled at the bottom of the grave.

Nathan jumped inside the hole and checked for a pulse. The man wasn't dead yet but would be soon. He'd lost too much blood. Nathan was surprised when the man gripped his hand.

"Stop him. Can't let him find it."

Nathan bent closer. "Who?"

"Imposter. They're in danger." He gripped Nathan's hand harder, panic rising in his face as he fought death.

He wouldn't win. The man's beard was coming loose. Was he the imposter? "Tell me your name."

He yanked something from his chest and pressed it into Nathan's hand. "Tell her I love her. Tell her..." He pulled in a quick, shallow breath. "I'm sorry..."

He was dead.

Nathan pulled his hand from the dead man's and turned it over, looking at the object resting on his palm. His heart sank. It was the cross he'd given Kendall. They must mean Kendall and Jake. What had he done? Adrenaline surged through his body, but he pushed it back. He couldn't let it happen here. He had to stay calm.

He slipped the cross in his pocket and put on driving gloves. He searched the man's pockets for ID. There was none. He picked up the leather bag. Whatever had been in it was gone. Then he felt a thin book at the bottom of the bag. He pulled it out and saw that it was a journal. The shocking thing was that it was exactly like the one in his dream. He couldn't explain why, but he brought it to his nose, inhaling the familiar smell of the leather. He flipped it open and saw sketches and words written in code. Flashes shot through his head and for a moment he saw a man's face, then a girl's, neither of them clear. Flipping through the pages, he noticed one had been torn out.

Voices sounded on the street. He had to leave before he was seen. He stuck the journal in his pocket and hurried from the graveyard, escaping by the same gate the murderer had used. Someone else would have to call the police. The dead man was beyond help, but if he didn't hurry, Kendall might be next. Nathan prayed it wasn't already too late.

It took him half an hour to find Jake and Kendall's car. Even though it was still burning, enough remained of the vehicle that he recognized the BMW Jake had rented after exchanging the Maserati. He tried to get closer—dreading, desperate—to see if they were inside, but the fire was too hot. He lost control then. He threw his head back and roared with rage until he was numb. He threw his fist, and heard a tree splinter. Why had he sent them? This wasn't like the other hunts. He'd known that from the start. His desperation for the box had cost her life. Now, he'd lost her and the box. Without both, he might as well be dead. He sat down and leaned against a tree, his body numb as he stared helplessly at the flames.

He would have to deal with the authorities. Money would make things go smoothly. The only family Kendall had left was her aunt. Her father was dead. Had been for a long time. Jake… He had no one. Just like Nathan. He had Fergus, but not flesh and blood. All three of them were alone. Now only he was left. Along with Fergus, they had been the closest thing he had to a family. He rubbed his hands over his face. They would have probably been shocked to hear it. Especially Jake.

When the flames had lessened and his blood had calmed, he clenched his jaw and moved closer to the car, steeling himself for what he would find. It was still too hot to get close, but it was clear that there were no bodies inside. They couldn't have been in the car when it exploded. Relief made him feel weightless.

Then where were they? If they left the car, they must be on foot. He heard a noise behind him and saw someone dart into the trees. "Kendall?"

There was no answer, so he took off in pursuit, following the moving leaves. Whoever was running away may have witnessed the blast. Or set the explosive device. He heard a scraping sound and the trail ended at a large rock as tall as a man. On closer examination, he noticed a mark etched into the stone in the shape of a circle. Like the one on the back of the cross. This place must belong to the secret order. Kendall and Jake had done it. They'd found the group. A faint line edged the mark. A button? Nathan pushed and the rock started to move with the same scraping sound he'd heard a minute ago. Light spilled out from the opening. Nathan crept forward and saw that steps had been cut into the rock. Cautiously, he descended and found himself in a lighted tunnel.

There were two sets of railroad tracks. An old railcar with a hand pump waited on one of the lines. He could hear something moving in the tunnel ahead of him. He put his hand on the rails and felt the tremor. Whoever was running from him had taken the other railcar.

He climbed inside and pumped the handle. It started moving, slowly at first, but quickly gained speed. The tunnel appeared to start out as a cave. Then it changed to dirt walls reinforced by wood and stone. Drips of moisture on the walls indicated a spring nearby. Within minutes, he reached the end of the line. The second car was there.

Nearby was a small wooden door in the wall. It wasn't locked. Pulling a knife from his pocket, he eased the door open and peered inside. A small hallway led to another door, also unlocked. He opened it and stepped into a room. The early morning light came through the windows that stretched from the first floor to the second, showing ancient weapons and paintings on the walls. This must be the castle. A door closed somewhere above him and he thought he heard singing. He started to turn when he caught sight of a statue outside. He moved toward the window in a daze. It couldn't be. He heard the singing again, closer now, and whirled. An old man stood at the top of the stairs, wearing a brown robe like a monk's. White hair framed a face that looked ancient, but his eyes were bright. He smiled.

"You're here."

"Let's do this quietly," Kendall said. It was after seven o'clock. She hoped everyone was still asleep. She and Brandi got Jake out of the car, balancing him between them. He was half-unconscious and still fussing about the hospital.

"Shhh, we're not going to the hospital," Kendall promised.

They eased inside, moving as quietly as they could across the lobby. Together, they propped Jake against a wall, with Kendall supporting him while Brandi checked to see if the coast was clear. Her understanding of their wish for secrecy was as confusing as her showing up at the exact moment they needed a ride, like some kind of fairy godmother.

Brandi peered around the corner. "Come on." They got three steps up the stairs and Jake started wobbling between them. They had to stop before all three of them fell.

"I'm losing him," Kendall said. "Hold on a second." She readjusted her hold, getting a better grip on him. "You push him from behind."

Brandi moved into place, making sure he didn't fall backward. They got to the top of the stairs with Jake slouched over on Kendall, and Brandi prodding and supporting from behind.

"We made it," Kendall said.

A door opened and Loretta's head popped out, her hair wrapped in curlers. "Good Lord. Is Jason drunk?"

Brandi started to speak, but Kendall quickly interrupted. "He fell and hit his head."

"On his honeymoon, poor thing," Loretta said. "Gilbert, come quick. Jason needs help." She raised enough commotion that the entire floor gathered in the hallway before Kendall and Brandi got Jake to the door.

Roberto came up the stairs, wearing striped pajamas, his face aghast. "You went to that place? I knew it. What happened? You look like you've been rolling in dirt."

"We went camping," Kendall said. "He fell while we were hiking."

"What happened to you?" he asked.

"I had to rescue him."

"By yourself?" Roberto sniffed. "Is his hair singed?"

"We had a campfire."

"We were worried when you didn't come back." Roberto said. "I thought something horrible had happened."

"The car broke down. It wouldn't start."

Brandi gave Kendall a sharp glance but didn't contradict her. She helped Kendall maneuver Jake toward the bedroom, while Roberto, Gilbert, and Loretta called out directions as if they were moving a grand piano. He was nearly as heavy. "Open the bedroom door," Kendall said, panting.

"Where is the key?" Roberto asked.

"It's in my bag. Here, you take this side." She exchanged places with Roberto and dug in her bag for her room key. Jake opened his eyes, looked at Roberto and tried to pull free.

"Hold on," Kendall said. "We're almost there." Jake had already slumped again, dead weight.

"I can't hold him," Roberto groaned, sagging lower.

Gilbert moved around to help, and Roberto shifted in front of Jake to keep him from toppling over. Loretta grabbed him by the back of the belt as Kendall opened the door. They all staggered across the room and Jake fell across the bed, landing on Roberto.

After they dug the innkeeper out from under Jake, they stood around the bed.

"You think he'll be OK?" Loretta asked. One curler was dangling over her ear.

"He could have a concussion," Brandi said. "I'll get my medical bag. Roberto, get some ice." She hurried from the room.

Roberto frowned, straightening his pajamas. "Shouldn't he see a doctor?"

"He doesn't like doctors," Kendall said.

Kendall was a little leery about letting Brandi check Jake out, but she was a nurse, supposedly, and she had rescued them. If she had wanted to hurt them, she would have done it without a roomful of witnesses.

Roberto went for ice and Brandi returned with a bag. She took out a small light and gently patted Jake's cheek until he opened his eyes. He tried to get up.

Kendall leaned over him, putting her hands on his shoulders. "It's OK," she whispered.

His eyes locked on hers and he lifted his hand to her face. He looked dazed, but he lay back and let Brandi check him.

"I don't think he has a concussion," she said. "He must have a tough skull." She removed the bandage Kendall had put on and inspected the wound. "It isn't too deep. He could get sutures, but most men wouldn't bother. I'll clean it and put ice on it. When was his last tetanus shot?"

"Uh…" A wife should know this. "I can't remember."

"When he wakes, ask him."

"Good thing we have a nurse here," Loretta said.

When Brandi was finished, she handed Kendall four pills. "Give him two of these for pain. You take two as well. You look like you need them."

"We should get him out of those clothes before they ruin the covers," Roberto said, looking at Jake as if he wouldn't mind the task.

"Ke…Kara can take care of that." Brandi glanced at her watch, as she'd done several times since they arrived. She seemed anxious to leave. "Let's go so they can rest. I'll stop by and check on him later. Keep him in bed."

Brandi gathered her things and left. The others reluctantly followed. Kendall stood by the bed watching Jake. He looked vulnerable with his head bandaged and his face and hands dirty against the white sheet. He'd taken the brunt of the blast to protect her. Her eyes started to sting. She touched his dirty hand. "Thank you," she whispered.

He gently squeezed her fingers.

"Jake, are you awake? We need to get you out of these clothes."

He didn't answer with a smart remark or even open his eyes, so she knew he'd drifted off. Jake wouldn't have missed an opportunity like that. She sighed and considered where to start undressing him.

She started at the safest place, his boots. After she'd removed them, she reached for his shirt, which smelled burnt. Getting it over his broad shoulders wasn't easy. For one thing, she had to touch all that masculine skin. His chest was intimidating, damned near perfect. She swallowed and looked at his jeans, dreading this part. She didn't know why she was so bothered. She'd already seen everything. Maybe that was why; she knew what was underneath. She unbuckled and unzipped him. Holding his underwear in place with one hand, she pulled and tugged—forced to touch areas way too intimate for her to be touching—until the jeans were off. She could only imagine what he would say if he were awake.

She got a cloth from the bathroom and cleaned his face and hands. He'd sacrificed himself to save her. There was more to Jake Stone than just a smart-ass flirt. It made her wonder if he had always been this tough. What his childhood was like. If she looked deep enough, she might find out for herself, but she tried not to read lives if she could help it. It was like stealing. She usually limited her prying to objects…when it was within her control.

She tucked the covers around him and went to close the curtains, so the daylight wouldn't disturb his sleep. Through the window, she saw Brandi hurrying up to the inn with a big tote over her shoulder. She'd certainly left quickly. She had seemed distracted.

Puzzling over the nurse, Kendall went to bathroom to clean up. Her reflection in the mirror told her that she looked worse than Jake. There was a spot of red on her cheek. Blood? She leaned closer and swiped it off with her finger. Her head started buzzing.

They ran through the woods. Some of the girls were crying. She was whispering to them to be quiet, but it wasn't her voice. It was a man's. Shouts came from behind them and everyone started to scream. They'd been caught. She looked back and saw a man raise a gun. She heard a blast and felt the bullet pierce her body as blackness fell.

The vision left as quickly as it came. She was herself again, if a little jarred. Jake's blood must have been triggered one of his memories. What had happened to him? She couldn't explain why she'd had the vision now and not earlier when she was bandaging his wound and cleaning him up. Another quirk of her frustrating gift.

The bathtub tempted Kendall from the corner, yet energy from the past hovered over it like a cloud. She started toward the shower, frustrated that she couldn't take a blasted bath because of all these memories that weren't even hers. It wasn't fair. After a moment, she turned from the shower and instead reached for the faucet on the bathtub and cranked on the water. Someone had died in there, but she was alive and she was dirty.

Stripping, she eased into the hot water. The bruises were starting to show. She blanked out the whispers from the past and let the warmth soak into aching muscles. She was about to get out when the door opened and Jake stepped in. They were both surprised. She covered herself with her hands and he looked away.

"Didn't know you were in here." He looked so lousy she knew it wasn't an act.

"I thought I locked the door," she said, slipping lower in the water. "Are you OK?"

He leaned against the counter. "I need a shower. Feels like I'm covered in bones."

"I'll get out and help you."

He attempted a weak leer but gave up. "What about you?" he asked. "You've got some bad bruises."

She nodded, embarrassed that he'd seen them.

"You could've been killed," he said.

"I wasn't, thanks to you."

"That's what I'm here for. To guard your body. If you're done, I'm going to start the shower so it's hot." He walked past her, but had to stop after a few feet. He sat on the toilet and rested his head in his hands. "Maybe not."

"You shouldn't be out of bed."

"I'll get back in after I shower. Uh, did you undress me?"

"Yes. I didn't want to ruin the sheets. Why?"

"Just wanted to make sure it wasn't Roberto."

Kendall smiled. "Are you going to leave so I can get out?"

"I'd rather sit here. I won't look. Promise."

She reached for a towel and held it as a cover as she stood. True to his word, he didn't lift his head. She started to think he'd fallen asleep when he spoke.

"You decent?" His voice was muffled.

She wrapped the towel around her and let the water out of the tub. "Sort of," she said, moving toward the door.

He stood and winced.

"You should see a doctor, and that cut needs to be stitched or it'll scar."

"Chicks dig scars, right?"

It would be a shame to mar that beautiful forehead, she thought, even though he had other scars—little ones here and there: in front of his ear, at the top of his thumb. Maybe it added character, but one that size could easily get infected.

"If you're so worried about it leaving a scar, fix it yourself."

"Sew up that cut? I don't think so."

"Don't need to sew it. I have superglue in my pack."

She'd used it on cuts, but that was in the desert when the closest doctor was over one hundred miles away.

Jake reached for the shower and turned it on.

"Maybe you should take a bath instead. You don't look very steady."

"I've been hurt worse than this. I think I can manage a shower."

"You'll probably drown."

"Then you'll be rid of me," he said, stripping off his underwear.

She hurried out and quickly got dressed, listening for any crashes coming from the bathroom, but all was quiet. His backpack was on a chair. The first-aid kit was tucked in a side pocket. She pulled it out and saw a piece of paper behind it. It must be the warning note that Thomas had written at the hotel.

"Find what you were looking for?" Jake stepped into the room wearing his usual towel.

"Sorry, I was getting the superglue." She held it up. "See."

Frowning, he walked to the bed and sat down. His eyes looked tired.

Kendall put his backpack on the floor and moved the chair closer to the bed. "You look rotten."

"You don't." He leaned back against the pillows. "You going to read a book to me?"

"I'm going to fix your cut." She sat down and opened the kit. It had bandages, antiseptic, thread, needles, and superglue. She took a breath and hoped touching his injury now wouldn't have the same effect his blood had had in the bathroom. She pulled the old bandage off. Not much blood now anyway, but it must still hurt. "I'm sorry about your head."

"How sorry?" He lifted one sexy brow—the one near the cut—and winced.

"Not that sorry." Kendall gently pushed the edges of the wound together, cleaned off the new blood and applied the superglue without a single foreign memory rushing through her head. There seemed to be no rhyme or reason to her sixth sense. After the glue dried, she covered it with a bandage. "Brandi left some Tylenol, but I don't trust her completely. She rescued us, but someone here must've drugged my bottle of water. My money's on her. She's a nurse and could easily acquire medications."

"It's possible. Her legs look familiar."

"What?"

"When we were leaving the hotel, you said you felt like someone was watching us. There was a woman there. I couldn't see her face, but I saw her legs. I think it was Brandi."

Kendall shook her head. "You really have a thing for legs, don't you?"

"Has nothing to do with appreciation. That was all I could see. You should be proud of me for IDing her just by her legs."

"Forgive me if I seem less than enthusiastic. Why didn't you mention it before?"

"I wasn't sure then. I'm still not, but she's definitely acting strange."

"Assuming she was the one who drugged the water, she was probably trying to keep me from finding the box. But why help us get back here? Why not just leave us there?"

"Maybe she doesn't want us dead, just out of the way."

Kendall gave him some of her own Tylenol and a bottle of water that had been left on the dresser, compliments of the inn. "You need to eat."

"I need a steak."

"It's breakfast and we're in Italy. How about pastry or some fruit?"

He wrinkled his nose. "Let me get dressed and we'll go downstairs."

"You need rest. I'll run down and bring something back."

"I don't want you to go alone."

"I'll be fine. If Brandi wanted to hurt me, she would have already done it. I'll go straight there and back."

Loretta was in the dining room looking over a table filled with assorted pastries, cheese, fruit, juices, and coffee. Her curls looked like cabbage rolls today. "I'm starving to death. I haven't eaten since yesterday afternoon. I went to bed and slept like the dead. I think I got some bad pizza." She picked up some kind of pastry and sighed. "I miss bacon and eggs." She put the pastry on her plate and found a seat. "How's the patient?"

"He's resting. I came to get some food."

"Poor thing, falling on his honeymoon. I hope it doesn't interfere with the...you know...activities."

Kendall felt herself blush. "I'm sure it'll be fine."

"You think he'll feel well enough for the tour? There's a haunted graveyard."

"We'll see." Kendall prepared a breakfast tray and started upstairs. When she reached the landing, she saw Brandi's door cracked. She was talking to someone. Kendall eased closer, trying to listen.

"Why haven't you called? I'm getting worried."

Kendall's tray bumped the door. She cursed under her breath and turned to go but before she got to her room, Brandi stepped out. "Ke...Kara? Is Jason OK?"

Kendall put on a smile. "Yes. He's resting. Sorry, I was bringing his breakfast when I saw your door open." Kendall moved closer, trying to see inside Brandi's room. "I wanted to thank you again for helping us out, but I didn't realize you were on the phone. I don't know what we could have done if you hadn't shown up. It was almost...miraculous."

Brandi stood in the door, making it hard for Kendall to see past her. "You're welcome. I'm glad I was there." Brandi's bottom lip was red, as if she'd been biting it.

"You seem worried. I couldn't help but overhear part of your conversation. Is everything OK?"

Brandi straightened her shoulders. "It's fine. I just have a… patient who's not doing well."

She was lying. The emotion was genuine, but not its source. "I'm sorry. If I can help, just let me know. Even if you want to talk."

Because I sure as heck want to know what you're up to.

"The best thing you can do is keep Jason in bed." Brandi put on a smile as fake as Kendall's. "One less patient to worry about."

"Right." Kendall went back to her room. Jake was sitting on the edge of the bed staring at his cell phone. He was still in his towel. She placed the tray on the table near him. "I thought you were resting. What are you doing?"

"Phone's fried."

"Maybe it's the battery," Kendall suggested.

"I put a new one in." Jake tossed the phone on the bed and picked up a bottle of water. He frowned and exchanged it for a cup of coffee. "Those statues must have destroyed it."

"You don't trust the water?"

"Do you?"

"I suppose not. We know someone here must have drugged the bottle I took to the castle. I assumed Thomas followed us here, but what if Thomas had an accomplice? I just overheard Brandi leaving a message for someone. She said she hadn't heard from the person and was getting worried."

"It's possible." He rubbed his head. "We need to find a new place to stay."

"You can't leave. You can barely stand up."

Jake touched his forehead. "If she's working with Thomas, I want you out of here. That might explain what she was doing at the car."

"She said she was running an errand nearby. Roberto asked her to keep an eye out for us."

"She could have been waiting to give Thomas a ride. Maybe they planned to take the box and run away."

"Then where is Thomas now?"

"I wish I knew." Jake took a bite of pastry. "Did anyone else see us sneak in?"

"A couple of people."

"We'll get some sleep, and then leave."

"And go where? We don't know where the box is."

"Isn't that what you do, find things?"

"Sometimes, but I can't always control it. Finding relics is one thing. We have people trying to kill us. We need to call Nathan and let him know what's going on."

"Do you want to tell him we lost the box?"

"No, but we need to let someone know about Raphael. Nathan can call the police."

"Raphael's dead. We can't help him. I don't want the police involved yet. Nathan might feel compelled to tell them."

"He's not going to be happy."

"Nathan's never happy."

He wasn't, Kendall thought. He was too serious, too stressed. He'd never offered to discuss his personal life with her, and she didn't feel like their relationship was such that she could ask. She wasn't the only one who worried about him. Fergus watched over him like a mother hen.

"Why aren't you eating?" Jake asked.

"I'll get something in a minute. Do you think Thomas was the shooter?"

"Seems like a long time to hang around and wait to ambush us when he didn't know if we would escape the catacombs. Not to mention there was a car bomb waiting."

"Maybe it was the goat herder. I would suggest Brandi, but why would she shoot at us and then give us a ride?"

Jake shook his head and took another sip of coffee. "Unless she was trying to scare us off. If she wanted to kill us, she had the perfect opportunity. She wouldn't take us from the secluded woods to a crowded inn so she could knock us off."

Kendall studied his posture: the way he didn't quite look at her, the set of his shoulders. "You don't believe the person who shot at us set the bomb."

"Are you using your mind tricks on me?"

"I can tell from your body language. You think there's more than one person after us?"

Jake sighed and set the cup down. "It would seem that way, but maybe they were just being very thorough."

"If the killer finds the car he'll know we made it out."

"Let's hope he didn't go back to check it out."

"How did you know the car was going to blow up?"

"I saw tracks and a cigarette butt. Then I spotted the wires."

"How did they time it to go off just as we got there?"

"Might have been watching. Might have been a coincidence. Damn, I can't keep my eyes open."

"Sleep for a couple of hours. We can't really leave anyway since we're playing dead."

"A few hours' rest, and then we'll plan our next step." He lay back on the bed and pulled the covers over him.

"Do you want to put on something besides a towel?"

He shook his head, his eyes already closed. "Don't leave the room. And eat something."

For several minutes, she watched his chest rise and fall, the pulse ticking at his throat, and knew he was asleep. His face didn't relax. He looked just as alert as when he was awake. His hair was still wet, and there was a spot of shampoo he'd missed above one ear. She dabbed it off and he flinched. She wondered if he was reliving the bomb.

She was tired, but too tense to sleep. And her body ached. That fall down the steps in the catacombs hadn't helped. She tried a couple of bites of pastry but had no appetite. She took two Tylenol, and then found the scrap of paper from the old desk in the castle. She sat on the sofa and studied it, but didn't get any further impressions. She'd have Roberto look at it later. Maybe he could tell her what it said.

She made a list of things they did know. The castle...rumored to be cursed—definitely haunted. They had found the box in the catacombs and lost it, probably to Thomas, yet still didn't know what it contained or why Nathan was so determined to find it. Obviously, he wasn't the only one. The cross...a key posing as a necklace. She hadn't imagined that light flashing when she put it in the lock. Raphael...She had no idea what Raphael was or what his part was in this. But he was dead now. The statues...like some kind of laser fence. The ghost...Where did he fit in?

Jake shifted beneath the covers and Kendall watched him for a moment. He was a stranger, yet he didn't feel strange. Then again, she'd spent more time in bed with him than she had with any other man in years. He rolled over, exposing a muscular arm with a tan line revealing his preference for T-shirts. He was good looking—gorgeous even—but he wasn't any happier than Nathan. That shouldn't have troubled her, but it did. She rubbed her head, which was starting to feel like a ball of cotton, and then gave up and climbed in bed beside Jake, clothes and all.

"No," he muttered.

Did he want the whole bed for himself?

His breathing quickened. "No," he said again.

She rolled over and saw that his eyes were closed, his brow furrowed. Kendall put her hand on his shoulder. His skin was firm and warm. "Jake? You're dreaming."

He rolled toward her, too close, and she tried to ease away. "Don't leave."

If it had been a demand, she would have moved, but it was a plea and it nailed her to the spot. She turned over and relaxed against him, feeling his heart beating strong and steady against her back. But it was Adam she dreamed of when she slept.

"Who are you?" Nathan asked.

The old man walked slowly down the steps, his gaze moving over every contour of Nathan's face. "I'm Marco. I've been waiting for you." He smiled. His white hair was wild, and he had a long white beard that made him look like Moses. His robe, similar to a monk's, was covered in dirt and something else. Blood?

"Do you live here?" Nathan asked.

"Yes."

"You are Italian?"

He studied Nathan again, his eyes intelligent in spite of his appearance. "We are from all places. You are from America?"

"Yes. Are you alone here?"

"No. Raphael is here."

"Raphael? Who is he?"

"A guard."

"He's your bodyguard?"

"No, just a guard."

"What does he guard?"

The old man looked confused. He frowned. "The treasure. Raphael guards the treasure. And me."

Nathan's adrenaline started to spike and his skin warmed, but he controlled the urge. The last thing he wanted was to scare this old man to death. He might be the only link to Kendall and Jake's location. "Where is the treasure?"

"It's hidden."

"Do you know where?"

Marco frowned and scratched his bearded chin. "I don't remember where we put it."

The old man must be senile. "What kind of treasure do you have?"

"Many things. Important things. We have to protect them."

"Money?" A box? Had Jake and Kendall found it?

"There are coins." He sat on a chair and scratched his chin again. "Jewels and gold, I think." He nodded as if he had done something good. "Yes, and objects. Lots of objects."

"Can you take me to Raphael?"

"I think he's dead. Like the others. The statues killed them."

Nathan's heart lodged in his throat. Kendall and Jake? "There are others here?"

"The strangers. Raphael said not to let them see me."

"Can you take me to them?" If it was Kendall and Jake, someone must have killed them here and then burned the car.

The old man nodded and started toward the door. He looked back to see if Nathan was following. The old man led him through the castle and they stepped outside. He could see the statue more clearly now. Farther away, he could see another one and another, just like in his dreams. He glanced back and saw the castle was camouflaged by vines.

"There." The man pointed to two lumps on the ground, and Nathan's chest filled with dread. It took all his strength to keep his adrenaline under control. He swallowed and started toward them, his feet like lead. When he got closer, he saw the bodies were covered by robes similar to Marco's. Shoes stuck out from under the edge of one robe. A man's shoes. Jake? He turned to the other body. It was completely covered. Impossible to tell if it was a man or a woman. He knelt beside it, heart clawing at his throat as he reached for the hood. He pulled back the cowl with a trembling hand, and he saw a man's blackened eyes.

It wasn't her. His relief faded as quickly as it had come.

But it could have been her. Just because there were no bodies didn't mean she hadn't been in the car. Someone could have pulled her out and taken her to the hospital. She could be lying in a morgue. "Did you see a man and a woman here?"

Marco shook his head, but Nathan's relief was cut short. "I heard them," the old man said. "Arguing."

"Did you hear their names?"

"No. But they were looking for something. The man didn't trust Raphael."

Mistrustful. Sounded like Jake. "Do you know where they are now?"

"They left." The old man's eyes grew bright for a moment, and Nathan could sense the wisdom and intelligence that had once been there. "They're in trouble. We need to warn them."

"How do you know they're in trouble?" Nathan asked.

"I know things. Where is your father?"

He must be confusing him with someone else. "My father is dead."

"Yes. I'm sorry. I forget things sometimes."

"Show me where you last saw Raphael."

The old man led him back inside to a spot in the foyer near huge columns. There was a pool of dried blood, but no body.

"Did you bring the key?" Marco asked.

"What key?"

"To the box."

CHAPTER TEN

D O YOU HAVE THE BOX?" THE REAPER ASKED.
"We had it, but it's been stolen," his guide said.

"Stolen?" he roared. "I must have that box."

"I understand. I'm searching for it now."

"Jake must have taken it. Get Thomas to help you find it. He knows him."

"I'm sorry, Thomas is dead. All your men are."

"Jake. Damn him. I knew he was trouble. I should have killed him before."

"I don't think Jake stole the box. I think Thomas took it. He was a traitor. I overheard him talking to someone about destroying the box."

"Thomas? He's been with me for two years," the Reaper said.

"Then with all due respect, I would be wary of any information he was privy to."

"And you didn't tell me this before?" The Reaper's voice was low, menacing.

The guide shivered. He had to tread carefully. He had been hired to find the box, but what he was doing was very dangerous. The Reaper was not a man to be crossed unless the reward was so large it made the risk worthwhile. He wasn't even sure he was a man. But greed was stronger motivation than fear. "I wanted to make sure before I told you."

"Who do you think has my box?"

"I believe Thomas gave it to someone else before he died." The guide had killed Thomas too soon, thinking the box was in his leather bag. Now he had to find it again. "I have an idea where it may be."

"Maybe Thomas was working with Kendall and Jake. I'll send others to help you retrieve it."

"No. This is delicate and needs to be handled with discretion." The guide couldn't steal the box for himself if others were there. Thomas's betrayal had played nicely into his hands. If this plan worked, only the highest bidder would know the box had been found.

Kendall woke, her head thick with dreams, and with Jake wrapped around her like a blanket. His arm was slung over her waist, his leg covering her thigh, and at some point he'd lost the towel. She pondered whether to move or stay. She wanted to stay, but that wouldn't be wise.

Why not? He wouldn't expect anything in return. No complications. Just a detour on her road to...where? She wasn't sure where she was going. Nothing in her life had been normal up to this point. No reason to believe it would start now. What man would shackle himself to her, knowing about her *gift*? She might as well have buckteeth and a face full of warts.

"How did you sleep, my beautiful bride?"

Kendall jumped in surprise, accidentally elbowing Jake in the face. He cursed. She scrambled away and faced him. He was holding his head. He moved his hand and she could see fresh blood seeping through the bandage.

"You're not much fun on a honeymoon."

"I'm sorry. You startled me. How long have you been awake?" Could he have known what she was thinking? It was hard to remember that others couldn't do what she sometimes could. She wished she couldn't either. Life would be much simpler.

"Not long. Why? Were you trying to seduce me in my sleep?"

Kendall shook her head and stood up. "What time is it?" she asked, stretching.

Jake looked at his watch. "Damn. It's seven thirty *at night*. We rested all day." He sat up and the sheet slipped low on his stomach.

Kendall looked away. "We needed the rest. What does it matter since we're trying to stay hidden?"

"We have work to do before the trail gets cold. How about tossing me some underwear before you fix my head. Unless you want me to get them."

"I'll get them." She grabbed underwear from his duffel bag, and found a bandage and superglue. She dropped everything on the bed and sat on the edge. "Why am I doing this? You can change your own bandage."

"You hit me. It's the least you could do." He leaned back and watched her as she worked. It was unnerving being so close to him. The gray in his eyes darkened until they looked like a stormy sea. "You could do more than bandage my head." His gaze was steady, not leering, a heavy look that made her feel as if she were caught in a hurricane. She was tempted to forget about caution and just see what would happen.

He must have seen it in her eyes. He lifted a hand to her face, running his thumb over her lips. His breathing changed, and she saw he was getting hard. There was a knock at the door and the moment broke. Kendall jumped, knocking the tube of superglue on the floor. "I'll get that."

It was Brandi. "How's Jake?" She looked past Kendall to where Jake lay, hands over his lap.

"Good. But I was about to change the bandage, if you want to take a look."

"Sure." Brandi approached the bed. "You look better than you did earlier," she said to Jake. "How on earth did the car explode?"

Jake shrugged. "I'm not sure. Faulty wires…"

"You were hiking there?"

"Yes," Jake said. "It's a good thing you came along."

"Both of you were very lucky," Brandi said. "You could have been killed." She glanced at Kendall. "I'm surprised your injuries aren't worse."

"He threw himself over me just before the blast."

"What a gentleman. When was your last tetanus shot?"

"Last year."

Brandi took out a flashlight and checked his eyes again. "Looks good." Her hands weren't as steady as they had been this morning. Something had her so tense she was ready to crack. She flicked off the light. "But no more hiking. You both need rest. Lots of it. Nurse's orders." She removed the old bandage and looked at his cut. "Superglue. Innovative."

"It works," Jake said, "until your bride gives you a good head butt and rips it open."

"Don't tell me the honeymoon is over," Brandi said.

"She's a messy sleeper. Throws her elbows around."

"Can you stitch it?" Kendall asked, wishing she had one of those bones he'd hated from the catacombs. She'd hit him on the good side of his forehead.

"I don't have sutures with me." Brandi applied more glue and quickly bandaged Jake's head. "Off your feet. Stay in bed and rest. Things should be quiet. Everyone will be leaving for the tour soon."

Kendall walked her to the door. As soon as it closed, she heard the mattress shift.

"Interesting," Jake said.

She turned and saw Jake pulling on his underwear. She quickly lowered her eyes. "What's interesting? Brandi?" Of course he'd think she was interesting. A hot redhead. All she needed was a short nurse's uniform.

"She called me Jake."

"So did Thomas." She looked up, noting with relief that Jake had on boxer briefs. But Jake in boxers was just about as good as seeing him naked.

His eyes narrowed. "What's that mean?"

"I just think it's strange that he knew your name."

"He probably heard it from you. You can climb like a billy goat but you're loud as hell."

She scowled at him. Adam always said she was loud too. "I slipped and called you Jake in Brandi's car. She probably heard me."

"Then why are you accusing me?"

"You're hiding something."

"Everyone's hiding something." He walked across the room and grabbed a pair of jeans from the duffel bag and pulled them on. "You telling me you don't have secrets?"

"It's too much of a coincidence that she just magically appeared right after a bomb blew up our car. And when we were running from the castle, I thought I saw red hair."

Jake picked up his Dopp kit and headed for the bathroom. "We'll question her, but not until everyone's out of the inn. Maybe during this damned tour Loretta keeps talking about."

"She's not going to admit it if she's involved."

"We can make her talk."

"I think Roberto might object to you torturing his guests."

"I'll see if I can get her to talk without going that far."

"What'll you do? Seduce her?"

"Sometimes it works." He disappeared into the bathroom.

Kendall frowned. How would he know?

When he returned, he picked up his boots and a pair of socks lying on the bed.

"We need to start searching for the box," Kendall said. "We know Thomas left the castle, but he could be anywhere now."

"I'm still waiting for Nathan to get back to me on Thomas's ID. With his resources, they should know something soon. That may help us track him down. In the meantime, think you can do anything with this?" Jake picked up a jacket lying over a chair and pulled something from the pocket. It was a cigarette butt.

"Is this what you found near the car when you saw the tracks?"

He nodded. "It must have belonged to whoever set the bomb."

"And one would assume that would be one of the thieves. Unless you're right and there's someone else involved."

"Or the goat herder was smoking." He handed her the burnt stub.

She smelled it first. Sometimes one of her five senses could open the door to the sixth. Smell was the strongest. The butt smelled disgusting, like old cigarettes always did. She saw eyes but not their color, only the greed behind them. "He's greedy. And desperate."

"That's all you're getting? Greedy and desperate?"

"What do you want? His name? Maybe a street address?"

"It'd be nice."

"I've told you, it doesn't work like that."

"How does it work? You knew Thomas wrote the note."

Her gift seemed to work however and whenever it wanted. Sometimes it felt like having a person with a twisted sense of humor living inside her. Often when she was sure she would get something, she didn't. Other times she would get glimpses when she was least expecting them. Her father had warned her that it wasn't an easy gift to have. He was right.

"It's complicated. I can try it again later and see if I pick up anything else." She sighed. "This is the first time anyone's tried to kill me. I don't like it."

"It doesn't get easier the second or third time."

"I keep thinking about Raphael's face when he saw my necklace. He looked like he was going to have a heart attack. What happened to his cross?"

"I have it in my pack."

"We need to find out where Nathan got his cross. Obviously it's connected with this secret order, since Raphael had one."

"You've seen his collection. Wasn't it there?"

"No. But I haven't seen everything he has." Jake raised an eyebrow. "You know what I mean. I hadn't seen this cross until he gave it to me at his house." Yet she felt like she had. "Nathan doesn't show me everything…I'm going to hit you if you don't stop doing that."

"You sure he didn't hire you to handle more than just his relics?"

"Not everyone thinks with their…" She waved her hands at his crotch.

He grinned and started pulling on a sock. "Your eyes are greener when you're pissed. I like it."

"We need to call Nathan."

His grin faded. "Not yet."

"Why are you being so pigheaded about this?"

"We'll call him when we find the box. Trust me, it's better that way."

"I'd trust you more if you would tell me what he's holding over your head."

He paused, one sock on, one off. "What makes you think he's holding something over my head?"

"You don't like taking orders. It galls you to do what he says."

He yanked on the other sock. "Your *gift* tell you that?"

"A blind person could see that."

He shoved his feet into boots and started lacing them up. "I owe him something."

"What?"

"That's between him and me." He stood and walked to the door. His mood had soured.

"Where are you going?"

"To get us some food. Do I need your approval for that?"

"Brandi said you should rest."

"I don't care what Brandi said. I have too many people giving me orders already. Don't leave the room."

He left the room without even asking what she wanted to eat. He didn't like taking orders but he loved throwing them out. Kendall got the torn piece of letter from her bag. Roberto would know what it said. That made her think about the note Thomas had written. Maybe she could pick up something new that would help them find him. She found Jake's pack beside the bed and unzipped it. The note was still in the side pocket. She removed it and saw that it wasn't the note from the hotel. This paper had been ripped from a notebook or journal. Someone had sketched one of the statues. Jake must have done it. When? She turned it over and saw more sketches. There were four objects, including a dagger, or was it a sword?

A noise sounded in the hallway. Thinking it was Jake, she quickly dropped the paper and stood. She heard Brandi's door shut. Kendall peeked out and saw Brandi heading downstairs. This could be the perfect opportunity...Kendall checked the hallway, and then crept to Brandi's door. Locked of course.

Kendall wasn't any good with locks, but she could climb like a monkey, and she had noticed Brandi's window was partially open when she brought them to the inn. Luckily, Brandi's room was located right next to Kendall and Jake's. Kendall raised her window and looked outside. All clear. She climbed out and balanced on the ledge. The trellis was between the two rooms. She stretched out her hand and tested the boards. Sturdy. She swung one leg over and got a foothold before following with the other. Brandi's window was still open. It was a stretch, but she got the window opened enough to slip inside.

Brandi's room was smaller than Kendall and Jake's. And it was neat. Kendall hated rifling through someone's drawers, but she had to know if Brandi had the box. Kendall searched the entire room, carefully leaving no trace of her presence. If there was a box here, it was invisible. She was about to close the last drawer when she noticed the silver locket in the corner.

She picked it up, almost immediately dropping it again at the rush of emotion. *Anger and heartache.* Holding it lightly to lessen the effect, she opened the locket and saw a picture of a family: mother and father and two young children, a boy and a girl who looked about the same age Kendall had been when she lost her father. Even from such a small picture, the hair and clothing suggested wealth, and the styles weren't recent. This must be Brandi as a child. Whatever had happened had broken her heart.

Kendall heard voices approaching the door. It was Brandi and Jake.

Kendall hurried to the window. Thank God it was getting dark. She slipped out onto the trellis. The tour group was just leaving. She hoped their eyesight was too poor to see her clinging to the side of the inn. She peeked inside and saw Jake and Brandi entering the room. Had he decided to go for seduction rather than torture without even telling her, when she was supposed to be his wife?

She clung to the trellis, trying to decide what to do. Go back to her room? Wait it out? She chose to wait. After what seemed like an eternity, she couldn't stand it anymore. She couldn't hear any sounds coming from Brandi's room. Kissing wasn't loud. Sex could be, but not necessarily. Kendall peeked inside. Brandi was lying on the bed and Jake was hovering over her. Kendall's mouth dropped open. She stood on her tiptoes to see better. Her foot slipped and she banged into the wall.

Jake replaced the telephone in the library, feeling a little better about what he had to do. He had a buddy on assignment in Italy who had agreed to keep an eye on Kendall until Nathan got there. His next call would be to Nathan, telling him to come get her. He wouldn't be happy that Jake was going off without Kendall, but time was running out. Two thieves were already dead. Thomas must have the box. Who knew what he'd done with it. Sold it. Destroyed it. Jake didn't really care. He wanted Thomas.

After Nathan found out how close Kendall had come to dying, it wouldn't be hard to convince him to collect his relic expert and take her someplace safe. Kendall was the one who was really going to be pissed. But it would be for her own good.

He started for the stairs and met Brandi. She seemed startled to see him. "How are you feeling?" she asked.

A lightbulb went off in his head. "Actually, my cut's bothering me. Could I get you to take a look at it? Make sure it's not infected?"

She looked like a rabbit searching for an escape, but she was a nurse and he was injured, so that didn't leave her much choice. "Sure." She started toward Jake's room.

"Kara's resting. Could we do it in yours?"

"Uh...OK." She was nervous now. She opened the door to let him in. Loretta's door opened. She and Gilbert stepped into the hall. Loretta's eyes widened and her lips pursed.

"Jason...Brandi. Me and Gilbert are leaving for the tour. I hope you'll join us. And Jason, bring your *wife*." Loretta took Gilbert's arm and they left.

Damn.

Brandi stepped inside her room. The minute she turned and closed the door, he hit a pressure point on her neck. He scooped her up as she collapsed and laid her on the bed. Then he went to work. Her room was small and neat. It looked like no one stayed here. He sniffed. Kendall was so stuck in his head, he could smell her even in here. He moved quietly. He didn't want Kendall to hear him and try to help. This was a one-man job. He searched the entire room but couldn't find any sign of the box. He went back to Brandi and bent down to check her breathing. He heard a thump outside the window. Someone was out there. He hurried to the open window and peered over the edge. Kendall was clinging to the trellis, looking at the ground.

Dammit. What was she up to now?

He heard Brandi rousing, so he hurried over and told her she'd fainted. She looked alarmed, and when he insisted that she not worry about checking his forehead after all, she quickly agreed. He went back to his room to yell at Kendall, but she wasn't there. He looked out the window and saw her standing on the ground, her back pressed to the wall. He watched for a second, wondering what she was up to now. She peered around the corner of the inn, and then jumped back out of sight. Brandi was walking through the parking lot, headed for town. The tour group was well ahead of her. Kendall gave Brandi a head start and took off after her. Jake cursed and hurried downstairs. By the time he got outside, Kendall was a good distance ahead of him, walking at a fast pace. Had she seen him in Brandi's room?

She had reached the main street now, darting in and out of the couples and families on their way to dinner, tourists walking stiffly on sore feet and a group of prima donnas prancing around in stilettos. Damn fool things to wear on cobblestones, no matter how good they made a woman's legs look. He wondered if Kendall ever wore stilettos.

The tour group had gathered in front of the church, their lanterns held high. Roberto stood at the front of the group, announcing in a loud voice the first stop; the graveyard, haunted by a man who had been buried alive. Even this far away, Jake could hear Loretta squealing with fright. Brandi put her head down and hurried past the tour group. She darted onto a side street just past the chapel. Kendall quickly took the street on the other side of the chapel, her shoulders set with purpose.

Jake followed, trying to figure out what the hell either one of them was doing. He hadn't gotten far, when he heard a scream.

Kendall cut through the graveyard, hoping she hadn't lost Brandi. She was going to figure out what the nurse was up to if it killed her. She immediately regretted the thought, since dying had been so frequently imminent in the past twenty-four hours. It was time for answers. Like what was Jake doing in her room with Brandi on the bed? Kendall hurried past the headstones. She could hear them calling to her, whispering their stories. A shadow stepped out from behind a grave and a hand closed over her mouth.

CHAPTER ELEVEN

S HE FELT DEATH, GREED, AND DESPERATION IN THE ARMS clamped around her chest. The cigarette smoker. Kendall fought and kicked as her assailant dragged her between the headstones. A mausoleum near the back of the graveyard appeared to be his destination. Kendall knew from the tour map Roberto had given her at the inn that the mausoleum was the entrance to a small catacomb. There was no way she was going to be held prisoner inside a tomb again.

The sound of voices reached her ears, and she saw the flicker of lights approaching from the other side of the graveyard. She recognized Roberto, speaking louder than the others. "They say his spirit still roams at night."

She couldn't move her arms, but she managed to open her mouth enough to bite down on her captor's finger. He swore and let go. She turned and threw a kick that she hoped connected with his groin. Groaning, he doubled over. Kendall screamed at the top of her lungs and shot across the graveyard.

She registered the looks of horror a second before the place erupted into chaos, lights swaying and falling as members of the tour group fled, tripping over headstones and crashing into one another. A hand reached out again, pulling her into the shadows. She screamed, but no one heard her. Everybody else was screaming too.

"It's me."

"Jake. My God. Someone just tried to kidnap me."

"Again?"

"It must have been Thomas. Maybe we can catch him. Do you have your gun?"

A bone-chilling scream sounded nearby and Jake swung his flashlight. Loretta had fallen in an open grave and Gilbert was trying to pull her out.

"It wasn't Thomas," Jake said. The beam from his light dropped behind Loretta to the other occupant of the grave. "That's Thomas." Jake held the light on the face long enough for Kendall to recognize him.

"Oh my God! You killed Thomas."

Jake didn't answer, so Kendall looked at him for an explanation. He was staring at the body, a stunned expression on his face. "His beard is fake."

Kendall looked at Thomas. His beard was coming loose, and his ball cap had fallen off. "Did you do this?"

"I didn't kill him." Jake's voice sounded hollow, a harsh contrast to the chaos surrounding them. "It must have been whoever tried to kidnap you."

"Should we check to see if he has the box?" She hated the thought of searching a dead body, but they had to get the artifact. Two other men had joined Gilbert, and together they were trying to extract Loretta from the grave.

"Stay here." Jake hurried over and jumped down in the grave. He gave Loretta a boost from behind and the four of them managed to free her. While the others pulled her away from the grave, Jake squatted beside Thomas, holding his light close to the body so he didn't draw attention to the fact that he was searching the dead man. Kendall could see from Jake's posture that he was still shocked. What was wrong with him? She would have suspected that he didn't deal well with death—he did have that aversion to bones—but he'd touched Raphael's corpse without any problem.

In less than two minutes, he was back. "Whoever killed him must have taken it." His voice was still flat. "He had that leather bag with him in the catacombs. That's what he put the necklace in. I would guess it held the box also. It's empty now."

"How long has he been dead?" Kendall asked. "Maybe it's just been stolen."

"Hours. The body is stiff."

"So the killer is probably long gone. Then who tried to grab me?"

"He could have come back to hide the body."

Guilt mixed with her grief at the loss of human life, even a thief's. It was probably hitting her hard because she had known he was going to die. Should she have warned him? Would it have made any difference? "I wonder who Thomas was pretending to be."

"Come on. The police are arriving." Jake nudged her out from behind the tombstone where he had pulled her. Roberto was calling out to the group, trying to gather them in one place. A few onlookers circled around Loretta, who was lying prone on the ground, while others moved toward the grave. There was confusion as to whether the ruckus was real or staged.

As they left, Kendall saw red hair and a pallid face at the back of the confused crowd, staring in shock at the grave. Jake took Kendall's hand and they slipped through the crowd, joining the onlookers on the streets who had gathered to see what all the commotion was about. Jake put his arm around Kendall's shoulders and pulled her close, as if they were tourists, yet she could feel the conflicting emotions in his body. He was still angry at her for leaving the inn, and he was also confused by whatever had happened back there at the grave.

"I told you not to leave," he said.

"I wanted to see where Brandi was going."

"And it almost got you killed. How long before you learn?" He pulled her into the cover of bushes near the lane leading to the inn. It looked deserted. Only a couple of lights were on inside. "Be quiet and follow me." They approached from the side, slipping past the trellis to the back entrance. They made it upstairs unseen. Everyone else must still be at the graveyard.

"Wait here while I check the room." He unlocked the door and walked inside. He left the door open, and she could see him moving around the room. She dreaded the lecture she knew was coming. A couple of minutes later, he motioned her inside. "It's clear." He stopped her when she reached for the light. "Don't." He crept to the window and looked out.

"You think he's watching?"

"If he's smart." Jake rubbed the back of his neck. "What were you thinking, leaving like that? You climbed down the damned trellis. What the hell am I going to do with you?"

"I'm sorry. I'm not used to having a handler. You seem to think it's hunky-dory to do whatever you want without telling me. I saw you go into Brandi's room."

"You're jealous?" he said in disbelief.

"The fact that you would have sex with anything that moves is none of my concern, but you seem to think you can do whatever you like, while I have to report to you like a kindergartner."

"Your devotion overwhelms me." He moved close, causing her to take a step back. "I wasn't screwing Brandi, I was searching her room."

"I saw you with her on the bed."

"You saw me checking on her after I knocked her out," Jake hissed.

"You knocked her out?"

"How else was I supposed to look for the box? The only *thing* I want to have sex with is you." He stepped even closer and she could feel frustration and heat rolling off him. "I don't even know why. You won't follow orders. You take risks. And you get under my skin like an itch. Sometimes I just want to...Ah, hell." He yanked her to him and kissed her. It was an angry kiss, as much teeth as lips. His hand moved up to grip her hair, pulling her head back. A soft rumble escaped his throat and the kiss softened, but his breath came harder, tangling with hers. His hands slid down her back, pulling her tighter against him. His hips nudged hers and she felt her insides flip. She didn't even realize they'd moved until her thighs bumped the bed. He gently pushed her down and moved over her, his hard body pressing against hers, his mouth and tongue making mush of her common sense. His groan melted with hers as one large hand slipped under her shirt.

Without warning, he lifted his head. One second he was doing things to her mouth she'd never felt before, the next he whispered "Hide" and moved like a jungle cat toward the door.

Kendall sat up, dazed. She saw the knob turning and heard the soft sounds of someone picking the lock. She slid off the bed and hurried toward the closet. The door eased open and a shadowy figure stepped inside. All hell broke loose. There were slams and thumps and grunts as shapes flew across the room. Something crashed into the bed, slamming it against the wall. She jumped up to help, but it was too dark to tell which shadow was Jake. Dodging the grunts and growls—growls?—she flipped on the light. She squinted at the brightness and then blinked in shock. Jake and Nathan were in the middle of the room, bodies locked in combat. They jumped apart, and lowered their fists. Nathan shielded his eyes.

The two men appeared equally stunned to see each other. Nathan scrubbed a knuckle over a split lip and stared at Kendall with eyes that were strangely bright. Then he did something he'd never done. He crossed the room and hugged her. "I thought I'd lost you," he whispered so low she almost didn't hear him.

At first she was too stunned to react, but then she hugged him back, wrapping her hands around his waist, feeling his heart pounding against her cheek. There was something different about him. Not just the fact that they were hugging, whereas he'd rarely touched her before. He felt strange, not himself. Her skin started tingling and she became light-headed. Sensations and smells started pulling together and forming…

"If this lovefest is over, I'd like some answers. For starters, why are you breaking into our room?"

At the sound of Jake's scathing voice, Nathan let go of Kendall, breaking the spell. Jake watched them, his jaw clenched, forehead bleeding again, and the beginnings of a black eye to match Nathan's split lip. Both men were bruised and disheveled, their clothes torn. Nathan wasn't wearing his usual suit but jeans and a black shirt, which was gaping where buttons had been ripped.

"You didn't check in so I came to find you," Nathan said. "What happened to the car?"

"How do you know about that?" Kendall asked.

"He knows every step we've taken. He has a tracking device hidden in our duffel bags." Jake looked at Nathan and raised an eyebrow. "What? You didn't think I knew? You've tracked me on every assignment."

"You've been tracking us?" Kendall said.

Nathan's jaw clenched. "If you get in trouble, I know where to send help. What happened?"

Jake gave a rude laugh. "We've been imprisoned in a tower, almost killed by booby traps, left to starve to death in the catacombs, shot at, our car was blown up, and Kendall's almost been kidnapped twice. We barely made it out of that castle alive. Hell, we were almost electrocuted by giant statues. What were you thinking, sending her into a death trap? You might not give a damn about me, but think about her."

A muscle worked in Nathan's jaw. "You think I knew all that would happen?"

"You knew more than you told us."

"It's over now. I'm calling off the search."

Jake shook his head. "I'm not calling anything off. Someone tried to kill us. I'm not letting that go."

"I'm not letting this go either. I'll handle it."

"What? Send in your goons?"

"What do you think *you* are?" Kendall asked, regretting it when she saw Jake's frown. He was far more than a goon. She turned to Nathan. She could see disappointment in the set of his shoulders. "But what about the box? And your cross? They stole it too."

"We'll have to find them later," Nathan said. "Who were the thieves? I don't suppose you got any names?"

"You sure you don't already know?" Jake said, earning a surprised look from Kendall and Nathan.

"How would I know?"

"One of them was the guy from the hotel, Thomas Little. The one you were checking out. The interesting thing about Thomas is that I've seen him before. In *Iraq*."

Kendall pulled her jaw back into place. "You knew Thomas before? Why didn't you tell me?"

"I didn't recognize him at the hotel. I didn't see his face clearly with that beard."

"Then why didn't you tell me in the catacombs?"

"There wasn't time to explain."

"We had all night," Kendall said, exasperated. "You're one to talk about keeping secrets."

"I don't know who Thomas is, but he doesn't work for me," Nathan said. "We ran his ID. He didn't exist until five years ago. We're still checking him out."

"Who he really *was*," Kendall said. "He's dead now. Someone stabbed him and took the box. Now all three thieves are dead and we have no idea who has the box."

"Maybe you have it," Jake said to Nathan. "You could have had Thomas follow us and steal the box and then had him killed.

Perfect plan. No one would know you had the relic. We would think it was stolen. The men who knew the truth would be dead."

"Are you bloody insane? I'm going to pretend you haven't just accused me of murder; that you're sleep deprived or someone hit you on the head."

"He did get hit on the head when the car exploded," Kendall said.

Jake frowned at her. "I want answers."

"Well, accusing Nathan isn't getting us anywhere. Maybe you made a mistake about seeing Thomas in Iraq."

"I'm not mistaken. I saw him only a couple of times there, but it's him. You heard him say my name."

"That's true," Kendall said.

"He must have recognized me at the hotel. That's why he looked shocked when he saw us in the elevator and what he meant when we overheard him saying he'd seen a ghost. He was talking about me, not you as I'd thought."

"Another thing you forgot to share," Kendall said. Did either of them ever tell her the whole truth? "What was he doing in Iraq?"

"Trying to foul up an assignment, as far as I can tell, and now he shows up here doing the same damned thing. There must be a connection. Looks like a setup to me."

Nathan frowned. "Why the bloody hell would I set you up?"

"To keep an eye on me? To ease your boredom? Who knows what makes you rich boys tick."

"I don't know anything about your assignment in Iraq."

Kendall didn't know exactly what they were referring to, but she knew Nathan was lying. Not from reading him, but from knowing him. Now wasn't the time to confront him. If she told Jake, there would be all-out war. "Are you military?"

"Not exactly."

"His team contracted their services to the highest bidder," Nathan said.

"You're a mercenary?"

"No. We do what you do. Find things."

"Hidden treasure or hidden terrorists," Nathan said, his tone unusually sarcastic.

Jake scowled but didn't reply.

"What was your assignment?" Kendall asked. "Maybe there's a link."

"We were hired to get inside the palace of a prince who was supposed to be supplying terrorists with weapons and information."

"Was he?" Kendall asked.

"We never found out. The mission failed." Jake put on his blank mask again.

"I don't see how a prince supplying weapons to a terrorist could be linked to this," Kendall said. "Another loose thread." They had a whole tapestry of them. Just like the one in the castle. "Maybe a little time away from the situation wouldn't hurt. Then we can figure out who Thomas is."

"The trail will get cold," Jake insisted. "I'm going to keep searching. You go home. You might have climbed a few pyramids and opened some tombs, but this is no place to play Indiana Jones."

"You really are a jackass!"

There was a tap on the door. "Kara, Jason? Is everything all right?"

"It's Roberto," Kendall whispered. "Stay out of sight so he can't see you've been fighting." She rose and went to the door, opening it just a crack. "Sorry for the noise. We have company."

Roberto's frown lightened. "Your brother. *Merda*! I forgot to tell you he stopped by early this morning."

Brother?

"Is Nick staying tonight? I don't have another room available. Could he sleep on the pull-out sofa?"

Nick? Pull-out sofa?

165

"Good idea. I'll let him know. Oh, do you suppose I could get some ice? For drinks."

"I will bring some up in a moment."

"Thank you, Roberto." She closed the door and turned to Nathan and Jake.

Nathan's nostrils flared. "You've been sleeping in the same bed?"

"We didn't know there was a pull-out," Kendall said.

Jake gave a nonchalant shrug. "We're posing as newlyweds. Why would we need it?"

"I trusted you," Nathan said to Jake.

"We didn't have sex," Jake said, giving Nathan a cold stare. "Not that it's any of your business if we did. She doesn't belong to you, no matter what your dick thinks."

A low rumble came from Nathan's throat.

"Stop it! Both of you! I'll take the sofa. You two can have the bed."

"You take the bed," Nathan said. "Jake and I will flip for the sofa."

"This honeymoon's going downhill fast," Jake muttered.

While they waited for the ice, Kendall explained to Nathan in more detail about the events at the castle, including Raphael. She'd just finished when there was a tap on the door, and Roberto called out that he'd brought the ice. Kendall got rid of him as quickly as she could.

"You two need to clean up. You both look like hell." She didn't wait for a reply but went into the bathroom and got clean washcloths and towels. When she started back, they were talking in hushed voices.

"...her away from here," Jake was saying. She stood inside the door, listening. They were obviously talking about her. "It's too dangerous for her. I was going to call you so you could put her someplace safe."

"And how were you planning to get away from her?" Nathan asked, his expression doubtful.

"I was going to get a friend to keep an eye on her until you showed up."

"Keep her prisoner?"

Kendall stepped into the room. Nathan and Jake turned, both looking guilty.

Kendall glared at Jake. "You were going to sneak out and keep me prisoner here. You're unbelievable."

Jake rubbed his forehead. "It's not safe for you to keep searching for this box."

"He's right, Kendall."

Now they were on the same side. "Well, you're not putting me anywhere. I'll decide when I stay and when I leave." She threw a washcloth at each man. "Sometimes you both act like I don't have a brain."

"This has nothing to do with intelligence," Nathan said, holding the washcloth he'd caught. "I'm sending you home because I don't want you hurt. I want you both back in Virginia. Take a few days and relax. You've earned it."

Jake's eyes were hard. "What if we don't want to leave?"

"You don't have a choice."

"She can go back," Jake said. "But I'm not leaving."

"If you know what's best, you will."

Even Kendall could hear the hidden threat. Jake looked like he wanted to kill Nathan.

"Stop arguing and ice your injuries," Kendall said, handing them each another washcloth filled with ice. "And for goodness sake, sit down. You're both pacing like panthers." And all that maleness was shrinking the room.

Nathan chose a chair and Jake sat on the bed, both scowling as they cleaned up and put ice on their cuts and bruises.

"We need to focus," Kendall said. "I know Brandi is involved in this. We should confront her."

"I'll do it," Jake said. "You don't confront anybody." He pulled a chain out of his pocket. "I found this in the graveyard where Thomas was killed. The killer must have dropped it."

"It's the chain that held my cross…I mean Nathan's cross," Kendall said, reaching for the chain. "Everyone seems to want the cross. Raphael, the thieves. When I asked the thief why, he said, 'You know why.' I guess they knew it was safe passage past the statues."

"If Thomas knew, he didn't share the information with his fellow thieves," Jake said.

"Where did you get the cross?" Kendall asked Nathan.

"It was part of a collection I've had for a long time."

"I don't know why you even bothered to ask," Jake scoffed. "You knew he wouldn't tell you."

"Don't worry about the cross," Nathan said. "We'll figure it out later."

Kendall put the chain on a nearby table. "What about Raphael? Someone needs to remove his body."

"No one is there," Nathan said.

"How do you know?"

"After I found the car, I saw someone disappear through the trees. I followed him to an old underground railroad that led to the castle."

"I knew they had a way to get in and out without climbing bridges and passing those damned statues," Jake grumbled. "Where was it?"

"Not far from the road. There was an old man in the castle. His mind seems to come and go."

"It must have been him that we heard singing," Kendall said. "Did he know anything about the box?"

Nathan looked down at his hands, something Kendall had noticed he did when he didn't want her to see his eyes. It didn't matter. She couldn't read him anyway. "He mumbled something about treasure."

"Treasure?" Jake said.

Nathan shrugged, still not meeting Kendall's eyes. "I think at one time the order protected some kind of treasure. Relics, maybe some other things."

"Where is the old man?" Kendall asked. "Could we talk to him?"

Nathan pressed the cloth to his lip. "Later. He's safe now."

"Maybe the old man moved Raphael's body." She didn't mention the vision she'd seen because she didn't know how to explain her suspicion about Raphael. It didn't matter now. He was dead.

"I don't know," Nathan said. "But he seems confused."

Jake touched his eye, which was already blackening. "We need to stay here tonight. The killer is probably watching this place, and if we leave the same night the body is found, the police might get suspicious."

Nathan nodded in agreement. "I'll call and have the jet waiting tomorrow."

"Are you coming with us?" Kendall asked.

"No. I have some things to take care of."

"We don't even know who's trying to kill us," Kendall said.

Jake gave Nathan a hard stare. "I bet he does."

Nathan blew out a resigned sigh. "I think it's the man I told you about, the Reaper."

"All this to sell a box on the black market," Kendall said. "It must be rare."

"It's rare."

"You can't find this guy, even with your resources?" Jake asked.

Nathan rubbed his eyes. "Every time I think I have a lead, it disappears. I'm not even sure he's real."

"Those thieves were real. Someone hired them and then killed them. And he's still after Kendall."

"Why would he want me if he already has the box?" Kendall asked.

"Maybe he wants more relics," Jake said.

A flash of fear crossed Nathan's eyes. "Rumors are that he's searching for unusual pieces." He looked like he wanted to say more.

"What aren't you telling us?" Kendall asked.

Nathan gave a humorless laugh. "You wouldn't believe me if I told you."

"Try us," Jake said.

"I've heard he's searching for the Fountain of Youth."

"You gotta be kidding," Jake said.

"I told you," Nathan said, his voice dry.

"That's fairy-tale stuff," Jake said. He cocked his head and studied Nathan.

Kendall wasn't sure what she thought about that. She had come across all kinds of things she couldn't explain, like her gift. "You think there could be a Fountain of Youth?"

Nathan shrugged. "I don't know. But if someone believed it was real, I imagine he'd do anything to get it."

"Don't tell me that's what we've been chasing," Jake said.

Nathan shook his head. "It's not the Fountain of Youth. I think the box contains a spear."

"A spear," Jake said. "We nearly died over a spear? I think I'd feel better if it was the Fountain of Youth."

"This isn't an ordinary spear."

"A spear's a spear." Jake grunted.

Kendall pulled in a quick breath and touched her side. "Not if it's the Spear of Destiny."

Jake gave her a startled look. "That's what was on the tapestry at the castle."

"There's a tapestry in the castle library depicting the Crucifixion," she told Nathan, leaving out the part about the pain she'd felt. She needn't have bothered. Jake filled in the details she hadn't wanted to share.

"When she touched the tapestry she doubled over in pain."

Even Nathan seemed surprised. "You actually *felt* the spear?"

"I felt something. If this is the Spear of Destiny, no wonder those thieves were so desperate."

"I suspected that was what was in the box, but I wasn't sure until now."

"Isn't the spear supposed to be in the Vatican?" Jake asked.

"The Vatican has one spear," Kendall said. "And another is in Austria. No one knows which is real. Some people believe they're both fakes."

"Fakes." Jake frowned. "At Saint Peter's Square you said something about a fake. Is that what you meant?"

"I don't even recall saying it. Maybe my sixth sense was trying to tell me something."

She was sure Jake would have rolled his eyes, but one was starting to swell and must have hurt. "You have a strange gift."

"You should experience it from this side," she muttered.

"So the pope has a fake spear and we found the real thing," Jake said.

"There are all kinds of myths and conspiracy theories," Kendall said. "Hitler had the spear at one point. He was obsessed with relics he believed would bring him power."

"And the Spear of Destiny has long been thought to possess power," Nathan added. "Some say it was behind Alexander the Great's victories."

"I thought Hitler committed suicide," Jake said. "Doesn't sound like the spear worked for him."

"He committed suicide *after* he lost the spear," Kendall said. "Although in reality Hitler's decline began earlier. But that's how the myth goes. You have the Spear of Destiny, you rule. You lose it, you die."

Nathan nodded. "I don't know if the box holds the real thing or not, but someone thinks it's authentic."

"Authentic enough to kill for." Jake touched his swelling eye. "Assuming it's real, how did the Protettori get it?"

"One of the theories is that Hitler hid the real spear before he died," Kendall said.

"I doubt he hid it here," Jake said.

"If this box contains the real spear," Kendall said, "then the Protettori must have switched it and someone has figured it out."

Jake shook his head. "Just what the world needs, another Hitler."

"If we're dealing with the person I think we're dealing with, he's probably the most dangerous individual either of you've encountered. I can't let you go after him," Nathan said.

"Let's rest tonight. In the morning we can figure things out," Kendall said quickly, trying to divert another confrontation. "Are you staying?"

Nathan glanced at Jake sitting on the bed. Kendall hoped her boss wouldn't notice the rumpled covers. "Until morning. I'll have the jet waiting at noon."

"Did you bring a suitcase?" Kendall asked Nathan.

"No. I didn't plan on sleeping here."

"What about a car, or did you sprout wings?" Jake asked.

Nathan gave Jake a look he might have given an annoying dog. "I left it in town when I saw the crowd." He stood, hands in his pockets. "Can you give us a second? I need to talk to Kendall. Alone."

Jake wasn't pleased, but he rose from the bed. "I'll go see if Brandi is here. We can make her talk." As Jake walked past Kendall, he trailed his fingers over her arm. "Don't get too cozy with my *wife* while I'm gone."

When the door closed, Nathan glanced at the bed, and then at Kendall's mouth. Could he tell she'd been kissed? Almost more than kissed. She didn't know what to do with that. It hadn't been awful, like some kisses were, with the guy's entire life in his lips. Jake's kiss had set her body on fire, in a good way, making her want things she knew she shouldn't. If Nathan hadn't showed up when he did, she and Jake would probably still be in bed. Not sleeping.

"If he's bothering you, I'll fire him." Nathan moved closer.

Kendall stood, facing Nathan. She'd never noticed how big he was. Maybe because he didn't usually stand so close. "He's just being Jake, and he did save my life. More than once."

"Maybe I'll keep him around for a while longer." A grin played at his lips and it was hard not to stare. She'd never seen him grin. And he still hadn't shaved. She'd never seen him this disheveled. The look was very sexy. He winced and touched his tongue to the cut on his lip.

"That's going to hurt tomorrow," she said.

"It hurts now." He looked down at her lips and she wondered what he was thinking. If Jake had been standing there with a cut lip, he would have suggested she kiss it better. But not Nathan. "You'll tell me if he gets out of line?" Nathan's gaze moved from her lips to her eyes.

She held his gaze, refusing to glance toward the bed. Was it out of line if she wanted what Jake was offering too? But she nodded and Nathan's eyes grew serious.

"I'm sorry I got you into this mess."

"You don't have to apologize. If someone's trying to use this box for evil, we have to stop them."

"It's not worth you getting hurt." He took her hand in his, and his eyes flashed with something that gave her a weightless sensation in the pit of her stomach. "When I saw that car burning, I thought you were dead." He'd never made a move toward her and at times even seemed to be avoiding her, but there was something simmering between them that neither of them had addressed. She looked at his hand, just touching hers, and noticed the scrapes on his knuckles.

"Good grief. Did you do this fighting Jake?"

"No. I did it earlier." He started to pull his hand back when Jake walked in the door.

"I knew I couldn't trust you to keep your hands off my *wife*," he mocked.

Nathan frowned at Jake. "I'm beginning to wonder why I ever hired you."

"That makes two of us. When you want to tell me the real reason, let me know. Brandi's not here."

"I'll track her down," Nathan said. He walked to the window and made a call.

"Thought you said there wasn't anything between you two," Jake said, slipping up behind Kendall.

She turned and faced him. "There isn't."

"I'm not blind."

"It's not what you think. Have you eaten?"

"You're not going to distract me with food." He put his hand over his stomach and she heard a growl.

Nathan came back and saw the two of them standing close. His eyes narrowed.

This was not going to be a fun night. "Have you had dinner?" she asked Nathan.

He shook his head.

"Then we should get something to eat. Roberto has probably told everyone you're here. I'll go down and try to make it look reasonable that my brother has joined me on my honeymoon."

"You're not going anywhere alone," Jake said.

"You two can't go down there," Kendall said. "You've got a swollen eye and he has a split lip."

Jake touched his eye. "I got it when I fell down the hill on our camping trip and you had to rescue me. Remember? The black eye's just a late bloomer."

"What about Nathan's lip?"

"I ran into the door earlier today," Nathan said.

Kendall rolled her eyes and sighed. "Maybe it's best if you do put in an appearance. Behave and act normal," she warned. As normal as one could with a fake husband and a fake brother.

There were several people in the dining room, where Loretta was holding court in curlers and her muumuu, retelling her harrowing experience over a plate of spaghetti. "And there I was right in the grave with him. I thought they'd never get me out."

Kendall was glad the inn supplied American food in addition to Italian. After seeing Thomas dead and wondering if she should have warned him, she didn't have much of an appetite. She chose a plain sandwich and a soda—she still didn't trust the water—then she took a seat at Loretta's table, hoping the woman's presence would dictate that Jake and Nathan sat elsewhere, giving her room to breathe.

They didn't. They both grabbed a plate of food and plunked down on either side of her.

"I've never been that close to a corpse. Rigor mortis, and all that blood." Loretta shuddered and took a bite of spaghetti. "Boy, Jason, you got a real shiner. I didn't notice it before."

"Just noticed it myself," Jake said, digging into his food. "Late bloomer."

Loretta looked at Nathan's split lip. "What happened to you, Nick?"

"I ran into a door."

Loretta shook her head. "I declare, this place must be cursed. Dead bodies and open graves, people falling down hills. And on their honeymoon, no less."

"Don't say that," Roberto whispered, joining them. He smiled at Nathan, who gave Roberto his reclusive billionaire smile and then concentrated on his food.

"Well, it's true," Loretta said. "I've never seen so much bad stuff happening. I hate to think what would have happened if Brandi hadn't insisted on going to find Kara and Jason."

Kendall put her sandwich down. "I thought Roberto sent Brandi to find us. She said she had an errand to run and he asked her to look for us."

Roberto frowned. "I was worried, but it was her idea to look for you."

Why would she lie?

"Even with the dead body, this is the best tour I've ever been on," Loretta said. "Everybody says so. Even Gilbert."

"What was the grave doing there?" Kendall asked.

"An old woman in town died yesterday," Roberto said. "I'm sure it was for her."

"I don't think I'd want a used grave," Loretta said, adjusting her waistband.

"Did the police say who the man was?" Kendall asked, curious who Thomas was pretending to be.

"I heard someone say his name was Thomas Little. He was a tourist." Roberto shook his head. "So sad."

So the dead man was using the same alias from the hotel.

"I thought I saw you and Jason when they were pulling me out of the grave," Loretta said.

Kendall took a small bite of her sandwich. "We'd changed our minds and decided to join the tour after all."

"Has anyone seen Brandi?" Loretta asked. "I might get her to look at my foot. I think I sprained a toe."

"I saw her at the back of the crowd," Roberto said. "She didn't look well. I haven't seen her since. She seemed worried today."

"Well, enough of this depressing talk. What a nice surprise, Kara, having your *brother* show up on your *honeymoon*."

"He's always wanted to see Italy," Jake said. "He doesn't get out much. He's kind of…backward."

"We'll take him under our wings. He'll be hootin' and hollerin' in no time. Roberto will show him around, won't you?"

"It would be my greatest honor," Roberto said. "There's a cozy little trattoria a couple of miles away with a bar. They have music and dancing."

Loretta clapped her hands. "We can all go. Gilbert's quite the dancer. You should see him clog. And the honeymooners need some fun after all this bad luck," she said to Nathan, who made a movement with his lips that didn't come close to resembling a smile. Loretta didn't notice. "Though they spend most of their time up in that room, so I'm sure they're managing to have some fun."

Jake kissed Kendall's cheek. "That's what we're supposed to do." He smiled at Nathan, who looked like he wanted to scalp Jake with his butter knife.

"Where's Gilbert?" Kendall asked, wishing she'd never suggested coming downstairs in the first place. How the hell would Jake and Nathan sleep in the same room without killing each other?

"He pulled his back getting me out of that grave. Darn, I forgot. I guess he won't be doing any dancing. There's Brandi now." Loretta motioned to the door of the dining room. "Oh my, she doesn't look well."

Brandi looked terrible. Her face was blotchy, eyes strained.

"We did just see a dead body," Roberto said.

Loretta belched behind her napkin. "You'd think a nurse would be used to dead bodies."

Just then, Brandi glanced at their table and the color drained from her face. Kendall studied the nurse, trying to read her shock, and slowly became aware of Loretta talking.

"I bet you've heard it a thousand times," Loretta was saying.

"I'm sorry, what did you say?" Kendall asked.

"I said all the girls must envy you, having such a handsome husband and brother. I bet you and Jason will have beautiful children."

Kendall looked back at the door, but Brandi had disappeared. Kendall stared at the empty doorway wondering why Brandi had looked so shocked to see Nathan.

"Call it," Kendall said, holding the coin.

"Heads," Jake said, pissed. He hated this whole mess. He didn't know what was up between her and Nathan, but he'd never seen his boss touch anyone, let alone hug them.

"Tails," Kendall said. "Nathan gets the sofa."

Nathan didn't bother to gloat. He went to the sofa and started to unfold it. Jake was glad they hadn't known it made a bed. He liked sleeping with Kendall, even if sleeping was all they did. He watched Kendall carry the sheets she'd found over to Nathan and help him make up the pull-out.

"If you want to take a shower, I'm sure Jake could lend you some clothes. You're about the same size."

"He's not wearing my underwear," Jake said.

"Doesn't matter," Nathan said. "I'm leaving first thing in the morning."

When Kendall finished helping Nathan make up his bed, she gave Jake a warning look, grabbed her pajamas and headed to the bathroom.

For the hell of it, Jake pulled a blanket from the bed and put it on the floor right beside Kendall's bed.

Nathan scowled at him. "What are you doing?"

"Making a bed." Jake grabbed a pillow and threw it down on the blanket. Pissing Nathan off wasn't smart since he had the power to make his life hell, but Jake didn't care. He was pissed too. Nathan had put them all in danger without even bothering to tell them what they were getting mixed up in. Kendall could have died. Nathan wasn't calling anything off. Jake was going to find out who was behind this and stop them. And he was going to find out what Thomas had been doing here and who he was working for.

He turned off all but one light, took off his shirt and pants and climbed into his makeshift bed, fuming. If Nathan hadn't arrived, Jake would probably be in bed with Kendall doing a hell of a lot more than sleeping.

Across the room, Nathan removed his shirt and slid into bed, still wearing his jeans. His eyes met Jake's across the room, and Jake felt something cold settle in his spine, as if he were looking at something not human. Then Kendall came out of the bathroom and tripped over him, accidentally kicking him in the ribs, and all he could think about was breathing.

"What are you doing down there?" she asked, rubbing her foot.

"Trying to sleep," he wheezed. "Right now, I'd settle for breathing."

Without even checking to see if he was OK, she stepped over him and got in bed. He listened to the covers rustling as she settled. He looked across the room at Nathan and saw he was watching Kendall. One big damned pajama party without any of the fun. Jake punched his pillow into obedience and closed his eyes, shutting out the smell drifting down from the bed.

He woke to heavy breathing. His imagination got the best of him for a minute, until he saw Nathan tossing and turning on the pull-out bed. Must be having a nightmare. He knew about those. Nathan's breathing came faster and he shot up in bed. Jake pretended to sleep and watched through the slits between his lashes. Nathan jumped to his feet and threw on his shirt. He was moving strangely. He started toward the door, and then bent down. Jake could hear noises, like cloth moving around, but he couldn't see over the bed to take in what Nathan was doing without being spotted. After a second, Nathan stood and hurried to the door. He paused once and looked back at the bed where Kendall slept.

Jake blinked. For a second it looked like Nathan's eyes were glowing.

The minute the door shut, Jake rolled to his feet and pulled on his jeans and boots. He grabbed the keys and slipped into the hallway, still putting on his shirt. Why would Nathan leave without a note? If not for him, at least for Kendall. There was some kind of connection between them. It might not be lust, but it was strong. He crept downstairs. The inn was quiet. Everyone must be asleep. Jake hurried outside into the cool night air. It had rained and the grass was wet. Something streaked across the yard and Jake followed. He was fast, the fastest on his team. And his team had been the best, yet he couldn't keep up. Nathan—it must be Nathan—moved like light.

Jake followed him into town and found the spot where Nathan had parked his car, a dry patch protected from the night's rain. The only sign that he'd been there. What the hell was he up to?

He went back inside the inn and started up the stairs. When he reached the landing, he saw a man entering a room at the end of the hall. The lights were dim, so he couldn't see the man's face. Jake unlocked his door and stepped inside. He locked the door again, shucked his pants and boots, and started to climb in bed next to Kendall when he saw something lying on the floor. He bent and picked it up. It was the cross the thief had stolen from Kendall. How had it gotten inside their room?

Rome, Italy

Nathan sat in one of his offices, staring at the papers scattered across his desk, not really seeing them. Kendall must think he was a bastard, rushing out like that. She probably already thought he was one. He was distant, always on guard. He had to be or she might discover his secret. If he'd stayed in that room with her and Jake any longer, the whole bloody inn might have found out. It was getting worse, harder to control. The damned thing was that he didn't know what *it* was. Whatever it was, he sure as hell didn't want it.

He blew out a sigh and looked at the security report in front of him. There had been another attempt to break into his network. And one of his guards who'd gone on vacation had turned up dead. He had to get Kendall and Jake out of here, and then he needed to ask Jake some questions. Starting with where he'd gotten the sketches. Nathan picked up the piece of paper he'd taken from Jake's pack. Four objects drawn on one side, and a statue on the other. He'd never seen this paper in his life, but the things sketched there had haunted his dreams for as long as he could remember. All these years, he thought the images were only dreams. If the statues were real, maybe the other things were too.

He opened the journal and put the piece of paper inside, matching the torn edges. He rubbed his hands over his neck, trying to loosen the knots. He hadn't hired Jake just because he was the best in his field; Nathan also wanted to know what he was really doing in the Middle East. After a few assignments, testing him, he'd decided Jake was merely a pawn in Iraq. In spite of his rebel attitude, Jake was trustworthy enough to send with Kendall. Now Nathan was worried that he'd put her in the lion's den.

He put the journal down on top of the papers littering his desk, not really seeing the names at the top. Fergus's soft tap sounded on the door. "Come in."

Fergus stepped inside. His clothes were impeccable and his hair was in place, even though he'd traveled all night to get here.

"How was your trip?" Nathan asked.

"Fine." Fergus glanced at the papers on the table, his eyes going to the names on the reports. "Did Kendall and Jake agree to leave?"

Nathan put the papers in a pile and stuck them in a folder. He trusted Fergus more than anyone else. He'd been like a father to him, but he didn't want to share this information, at least not yet. "They don't have a choice. I'm sending them home on the jet. Call ahead and tell the guards to keep Kendall and Jake at the mansion. But keep them apart."

"You don't want her with Jake?" Fergus frowned. "He's kept her safe so far. Quite impressive considering the lack of information they were given." Fergus gave him a disapproving glare.

"Just do it, please." Nathan rubbed his eyes. "I need you do to something else. Have the research team look into this foundation." He picked up a card on which he'd written the name of the foundation that was linked to the castle. He needed to investigate deeper, but he didn't have the time. He looked up to see Fergus still frowning at him. "What's wrong?"

"You need to see a doctor?"

"No I don't."

Fergus's chin jutted out. "It's getting worse."

"And you think doctors can help?" He gave a raw laugh.

"But how do we know they can't? You're basing your belief on a dream about two men discussing a curse."

"I don't think it was a dream. I didn't see the men's faces, but one of them was holding a journal." Nathan held up the journal he'd found in Thomas's pocket. "This one."

"Where did you get it?"

"From a dead man."

"Surely you're not robbing graves."

"One of the thieves who stole the box from Kendall and Jake had it." Which made no sense, but this was the right path. It had to be. Nathan closed his eyes. Sometimes they felt like they would explode.

"See," Fergus said. "Even when you're…normal…you still hurt. Why won't you listen to me?"

"I was a boy when my father hired you to take care of me. I'm a man now and I don't need a keeper."

Fergus looked offended. "You're making a mistake, sir. About many things." He took the card from Nathan and turned to go. "For one, your father didn't hire me."

"What do you mean? You've been with me since I was a kid."

"I wasn't hired until after the accident."

"Then who the hell hired you?"

There was knock on the door and Marco stuck his head in. Fergus looked at the man and his mouth dropped open as if he'd seen a ghost. Fergus was never tanned, but he was ashen now. The two men stared at each other, and then Fergus walked out without a backward glance.

CHAPTER TWELVE

KENDALL WOKE UP GROGGY. SHE LOOKED DOWN AT THE ARM around her waist. In the darkened room, she wasn't sure who it belonged to. His scent registered at the same time she noticed the scar at the top of his thumb. How had Jake gotten in bed with her? This would start another war. Irritated, she checked to see if Nathan had seen them, but he wasn't there.

"He's gone," Jake said in her ear. His mouth moved lower, nuzzling her shoulder.

She thought about what happened on this bed last night before Nathan showed up. The kisses, bodies pressing…She tried to move away, but Jake had her pinned with his arm. "When did he leave?"

Jake let one bare foot touch hers. "In the middle of the night."

"Did he say where he was going?"

"No." Jake brushed his lips over her ear, sending tingles to places she didn't need tingles. "Didn't really have time. He snuck out."

Nathan probably left to get the jet ready. "Could you move your arm so I can get up?"

"I don't want to." His hand moved down her stomach.

She sighed and trapped his hand, stopping its descent. "I thought you were sleeping on the floor."

"The floor's no place to sleep on your honeymoon."

183

"I believe you were going to sedate me and sneak out on our *honeymoon*."

"I can make it up to you," he said, pulling his hand free and slipping one finger in the waistband of her pajamas.

She lifted his arm and slid free, turning to face him.

He let his head rest against the pillows, eyes smoldering as he watched her. He looked too darned sexy first thing in the morning.

"Nathan didn't say anything?" she asked.

"No. Didn't even leave a note. What's wrong? You miss him already?"

"What's he holding over you?" she asked, ignoring his jabs.

She thought he was going to refuse to answer, but he looked at the ceiling, his face serious now. "I was in trouble. He helped me out."

"What kind of trouble?"

"I'm tired of talking." He reached for her leg, letting his hand slide up her thigh. "We've seen the merchandise. I think it's time to take it for a test drive."

Kendall moved quickly off the bed. "You need a cold shower."

"Your cold shoulder's doing the trick."

"What time are we leaving? It'll take a couple of hours to get to the jet."

"I'd rather leave while it's still dark. It's six now. Sun rises a little after seven. We need to be out of here by then."

"I'm going to take a shower." Maybe she would take a cold one. "Do you need the bathroom first?"

He got out of bed and walked around to her side. No man had a right to look so good in underwear. He made quick use of the bathroom before Kendall got in the shower. When she came out, he was gone. She packed her things and put the bags near his. He hadn't zipped his pack all the way. She knelt to close it and saw a glint inside. At first she thought it was the chain he'd found near Thomas. Without thinking, she opened the pack and reached for the object. It wasn't the chain. A cross lay on top of a coil of rope. Raphael's? Then she noticed the small differences. Raphael's was wider and the openings smaller than this one. Stunned, she picked it up. It was hers—Nathan's. The one Thomas had stolen in the catacombs. A noise came from Brandi's room, pulling Kendall from her shock. Was Jake searching for the box again? She put the cross back in Jake's pack and went to check.

She opened the door and saw a man entering his room at the end of the hall. She hadn't seen him before. He must be a new guest. He turned the doorknob and Kendall saw a gold ring on his finger. It had a large red jewel. The man turned and spotted Kendall. She wasn't sure if his flinch was physical or if she'd merely sensed it, but it was enough for her to know he recognized her, and that he was shocked to see her there. Or shocked to see her alive?

They had to leave. Now.

She hurried toward the stairs. Jake wasn't in the dining room. She heard a voice in the library and peeked in. Loretta was looking at the shelves, hair in curlers, wearing another muumuu and talking to herself.

"Kara! Oh, you're up early. Are you and Jason going to watch the sunrise?"

"No. Actually, I was looking for him."

A secretive look crossed Loretta's face. "Maybe he's in the dining room with the others. They're going to watch a genuine Italian sunrise outside town. I'm too tired. All night I dreamed about that danged grave. I need something boring to read to get my mind off of dead bodies." Loretta grabbed a book and brought it to the door. She gave Kendall another cryptic look. "You seem worried. Is everything OK with you and Jason?"

"Why do you ask?"

Loretta moved closer, putting on her conspiratorial face. "I didn't want to say anything, but I saw him going into Brandi's room last night before the tour. *With* Brandi."

"I think he wanted her to check the cut on his forehead."

Loretta gave Kendall a knowing look. "Careful that she doesn't *check* something else. I'd keep an eye on that girl. She's got something up her sleeve. I think she put something in my drink that day in the dining room when she went to get us water. I slept like the dead all day and all night." Loretta clapped her hand to her curlers. "You don't think she has designs on Gilbert?"

"No, I don't think so."

"She's sneaky. I've seen her watching you and Jason when you don't know she's looking. She's not the only one. When I started downstairs, that new guest was listening outside your and Brandi's rooms. He's probably a pervert. I never did trust men who wore rings, especially big fancy rings. Other than wedding bands, of course. It seems kind of primpy. I notice you and Jason don't wear them."

"He doesn't like rings and mine is being repaired."

"I see. Jason's definitely not the primpy type, but you might want to consider getting him to wear one. With those looks…" She wiggled her eyebrows. "You just keep an eye on that Brandi, you hear. She's up to something, and I hope it isn't stealing your husband. Anyone could see you two are madly in love."

Madly in love? Her and Jake? A little lust maybe. But love…? Kendall escaped Loretta and started searching for Jake. He wasn't in the dining room or on the patio. Maybe he'd gone back upstairs. She hurried to the room and heard a thump outside the window. She peeked out and saw a man climbing down the trellis. Jake? It was too dark to see. She started to open the window when her door burst open and Brandi stood there, her eyes wide, face pasty white.

"Where is it?"

"Where's what?" Kendall asked.

"My bag. You know what was in it. Where is it?" Up close, Kendall could see Brandi's eyes were swollen.

"I didn't take your bag." Did she mean the box was in it?

"You have no idea what you're doing."

"I swear, I didn't take it," Kendall said, praying that Jake had.

Brandi looked undecided. "It must have been the man you were sitting with in the dining room last night. Who was he?"

"You mean my...brother? Why would he take it?" Surely Nathan hadn't taken it when he slipped out in the night.

Brandi frowned. "He's your brother?"

"I noticed you seemed shocked to see him."

"It wasn't the first time I'd seen him. He was hurrying away from the church yesterday morning when I went to look for you. That was about the time the...the tourist was killed." Her face tightened. "I assumed he must have had something to do with the murder. Where is he?"

"He's gone, but he didn't murder anyone. Are you sure it was him you saw?"

"Unless he has a twin."

"What's wrong?" Loretta asked, popping her head in the door. She had a book clutched in her hand.

"Brandi thinks her bag's been stolen," Kendall said.

Loretta gasped. "Stolen?"

"It's missing," Brandi said, staring at Kendall, her gaze still accusing.

"I bet it's that new guest. I knew there was something wrong with him."

"New guest?" Brandi asked, puzzled. "Kendall's brother?"

"Who's Kendall? Oh, you mean Kara? Lord no, Kara's brother wouldn't steal anything. I mean that strange man at the end of the hall. The one who checked in last night. I told Kara I saw him eavesdropping outside both of your rooms. He's probably a cat burglar. A normal man doesn't wear a big ole ruby ring. I'm going to get Roberto. We'll all need to check our valuables."

Brandi had gone so pale, Kendall though she might collapse. "*He's* here. It must have been him...Oh God. You and Jake have to get out of here now, before it's too late." With a frantic look, she turned and ran from the room. Kendall heard her racing downstairs.

"Wait," Kendall said, starting after her, but Brandi didn't stop. Kendall hurried back to her room and looked out the window. She saw a shadow outside the inn. Jake. She rushed downstairs and out to the patio. She hurried toward the hill, looking for him. Without warning, she was tackled from behind, just like Jake had done before the car blew up. But this wasn't Jake. She could smell the difference. Before she could catch her breath, a dark streak leapt at them, knocking the man off her. They fought for seconds, and then she heard a grunt. One of the men jumped up and fled. Jake hurried over to her. He was holding his side.

"We have to leave," he said. "Now."

"Did you get the box?"

"What box?"

"Nathan's box. Didn't you take it from Brandi's room?"

"No. What are you talking about?"

"Someone was in Brandi's room earlier. She accused me of stealing her bag. I think she had the box in it. I saw a man go down the trellis and thought it was you."

"I was outside checking the perimeter when I saw someone drop down from the trellis. I came around to make sure it wasn't you. Damn. He must have taken it."

Jake looked torn between going after him and staying with Kendall. "Come on. We're leaving." He ushered Kendall back inside the inn and up to their room.

"Who could have taken it?" Kendall asked after the door closed behind them. "Thomas is dead, and Brandi was the victim here."

"Is she still here? I have some questions for her."

"No. She took off when Loretta mentioned the new guest with the ring."

"You mean the man at the end of the hall? I saw him last night."

"Yes. But he couldn't have broken into Brandi's room. He was in the hallway at the same time I heard someone inside her room. And he wasn't the right build as the man who tackled me. But he must be up to no good. Loretta said she saw him listening outside our door and Brandi's."

"Maybe he was an accomplice. Did he see you?"

"Yes. He looked shocked. I think he recognized me."

"Damn. Hurry." He looked inside his pack and frowned. "Did you take a paper out of here?"

"No. Did you kill Thomas and lie about it?"

"Where the hell did that come from?"

"Your pack was open and I saw the cross Thomas stole from me."

"I found it on the floor last night after Nathan left."

"Why didn't you mention it?"

"You were sleeping. I didn't want to wake you. I forgot about it this morning. I was kind of...distracted."

"How did the cross get on our floor? I suppose it could have been the same person who searched Brandi's room. He could have gotten inside ours while we were downstairs last night."

Jake shrugged. "Or it could have been Nathan."

"You think Nathan had the cross?"

"It wouldn't be the first thing he's hidden."

"Brandi said she saw Nathan the morning Thomas died. He was hurrying away from the church. She thought he had something to do with the murder."

"But she didn't tell the authorities. Sounds like a woman with something to hide. Was she sure it was him?"

"Positive, unless he has a twin."

Jake shook his head in disgust. "Dammit. What else is he keeping from us?"

"I think it's time to ask." Kendall scanned the room. "I'm ready if you are. We should tell Roberto we're leaving or he'll have the cops looking for us."

Jake touched his side again. "You go down and check out while I call a taxi."

She found Roberto in the lobby behind his desk.

"Kara. I'm glad you're awake," he said. "I have the keys to your car."

"My car?"

He reached for a set of keys near his computer. "It was delivered earlier. It's parked out front." Roberto must have noticed her puzzled look. "You didn't have it delivered?"

"No. It must be from my brother. He felt bad when he found out about our other car."

Roberto's eyebrows shot up. "Nice brother. You're lucky. Not many rental companies would deliver this early."

"Yes, he's very nice."

Roberto handed her the keys. "The man left this." It was a letter addressed to Kara and Jason. "Is your brother coming down for breakfast?"

"Oh no, he had to leave last night."

Roberto's face fell. "That's too bad. He asked for this." He held up a piece of paper.

"What is it?"

Roberto's voice dropped. "He was asking about that *place*. He wanted to know more about it for some paper he's writing. I didn't know he was a journalist."

She didn't either.

"I remembered there was a historian who claimed to know something about the Protettori. He wrote an article about it several years ago. Your brother asked me to get his name and address."

Kendall looked at the paper. The address was in Rome. Why would Nathan ask for this and then leave in the middle of the night without it? Had he left on his own? Jake obviously had some issues with Nathan. Surely he wouldn't hurt him.

"Could I leave it with you?" Roberto asked.

"Yes. I'll give it to him when I see him. Actually, I came to tell you that Jason and I are leaving too. Something has come up."

His forehead wrinkled in a frown. "Are you leaving because of all the bad things happening? I know it was a terrible honeymoon for you, getting hurt the first day."

"It's not that. We have a family emergency."

"I'm sorry. You will come back another time. Let me make it up to you?"

Kendall assured him they would. "Thank you, Roberto. Well, I should go. Jason is waiting. If you hear from Brandi, would you let me know? I'm…worried about her."

"Of course. I think the murder upset her. Poor man. I heard that a relative identified the body."

Relative? Or *cohort*?

Kendall said good-bye and went up to get Jake. He was in the middle of changing his shirt when she walked in. He kept his back to her, uncharacteristically modest.

"We don't need a taxi," she told him. "Nathan had a car delivered."

"This early?"

"The man who delivered it left a letter." Kendall opened the envelope. It was from Nathan, apologizing for running out without telling them. Something needed his attention and he didn't want to wake them. "He says there are cell phones in the car."

"Nathan's money at work," Jake said, grabbing their bags. "Come on."

Even though the letter was from Nathan, Jake still quickly inspected the Audi, checking underneath the car, in the trunk, and under the hood. When he decided it wasn't rigged with explosives, they drove away from the inn.

"The car is fully equipped, of course," Kendall said, looking at the luxurious seats and control panel.

"And bugged, if I had my guess."

"Did you see a tracking device?"

"Not this time. His guys are probably better at hiding them."

"We need to check in with him," Kendall said. "I want to ask him about the cross."

"You really think he'll tell you the truth?"

Kendall sighed. She wasn't sure. "He wouldn't kill Thomas. I know he wouldn't."

"Who are you trying to convince?" Jake asked. "There's more to Nathan than meets the eye. Even you admit you can't read him."

"But he's not a killer."

"Are you sure?"

"I'm sure."

"Do you think you could try your mojo on the cross again? Maybe you'll get something this time."

"You're just hoping I'll pick up something from Thomas so you'll know what he was doing here." She was curious herself. "I could try. I don't always pick up the same thing each time. But Thomas didn't have the cross in his possession for very long."

"I doubt he had that note at the hotel for very long, but you picked something up on it."

Kendall opened her bag and took out the cross. She let it rest in her hand, trying to feel its history. The sensations she felt were varied. Some were the same as the first time Nathan had given it to her. She caught a thread and isolated it. A little girl giggling. She couldn't see the girl's face but she knew the sound. Then newer sensations took over, but they were jumbled. There was fire, an explosion of some kind. A plane or helicopter, she thought. But it must have been the car bomb. Thomas could have set it.

"I don't know. I sense different things, an explosion, some emotions, but it's just bits and pieces. I'm sorry." She left out the part about the little girl since it didn't seem to fit.

"What kind of explosion?"

"It was just a loud noise and fire. It must have been the car bomb."

"Maybe," he said, softly, wearing his haunted look. "Maybe not."

She knew he didn't want to talk. "We have some time before the jet leaves. Let's try to find this family Roberto told us about. He said it's beyond the hills of the Protettori's castle."

They found the village. It was tiny, a few houses and farms and one Catholic church. It was early, but there was a man near the front of the church.

"Hello," Kendall called.

He turned and his face lit up with a welcoming smile.

"Do you speak English?" she asked.

He nodded and measured with his fingers. "Little." He introduced himself as the parish priest.

"We're trying to locate a family named Romano," Kendall said.

His face grew somber. "Not here. Gone."

"They moved?"

"Dead."

"All of them?"

"Yes. Except the oldest son. Edward was away."

Edward. This must be the right family.

"Makes no sense. Good souls taken and troublemaker left here."

"Edward was a troublemaker?"

"Black sheep, so they say. I don't know him well."

Kendall and Jake exchanged a surprised look. Their Edward?

"How did they die?" Jake asked.

"Fire. House burned. Sad. Whole village mourns."

"What a terrible accident," Kendall said.

"No. Not accident. Arson. Murder."

"Who set the fire?" Jake asked.

"Don't know. Still looking."

"When did this happen?"

"Last month. Did you know them?"

Kendall shook her head. "No, but we wanted to talk to them. We heard that one of their ancestors helped build a castle near here."

"I have not been here that long. I don't know."

They thanked the priest and left. "Edward said that anyone connected to the Protettori ended up dead," Kendall said as they climbed into the car, a bit shocked by what they'd just learned.

"Edward escaped."

"When he said everything was lost in a fire, I didn't think he meant his family."

"Didn't look like he was grieving."

"Maybe he's in denial."

"You didn't read anything on him?"

"No. Sometimes I can't read anything. I never know how it's going to work. It's like being a puppet."

They were both silent as they headed toward Rome. She looked out the window at the scenery zipping past. "The spear is still out there and we're just walking away. It doesn't feel right. I don't like leaving a mystery unsolved."

"Nathan's calling the shots."

She supposed Jake felt like a puppet too. The debt he owed Nathan must be big. Jake didn't make a good puppet.

They arrived in Rome with two hours to spare. It wouldn't take long to reach the airport, so they decided to talk to the historian Roberto had found. The city was bustling, vastly different from the small town and the inn. Kendall found herself missing the quiet countryside. But they weren't here to relax.

Using the directions Roberto had given them, they found the historian's house on a little side street. An elderly man in thick glasses answered their knock. They apologized for visiting so early and explained their request. He led them to a sitting room and gestured for them to take seats.

"Why do you want to know about the Protettori?" he asked, moving to an armchair across the room.

"A friend of ours had heard stories about the group," Kendall said. "Someone told us you might have some information. We were hoping to learn more before we leave."

"You are leaving Italy?"

"Yes."

The historian studied them both for a moment, and then he nodded to himself and leaned back in his chair. "Not much is known about the brotherhood. According to the stories, the Protettori were protectors—as the name says—guardians of a secret treasure. There were rumors of gold and jewels, and even relics. Some of these objects were supposed to have secret powers. There were four that were the most powerful."

"What were they?" Kendall asked.

"No one knows for sure. Many have searched. Some never returned."

Kendall clenched her hands in her lap. "So no one knows where they were hidden?"

"I think if someone found out, they wouldn't have been long for this world. The Protettori were very serious about their duties."

"How old is the order?" Jake asked. His hands rested on his thighs. He looked relaxed, but she had learned to read his body language. He was tense. He had been since they left the inn.

"As old as Christ, I would imagine. I doubt anyone alive knows for sure. They pretended to be monks in order to hide their mission from the world. There were many in the brotherhood at one time, but there was a battle and several of them died."

"What happened?" Jake asked.

"I think only the Protettori could tell you that."

"Are there any Protettori left today?"

"Very few, I would think. But I don't know for certain. No one is allowed near them unless they belong to the order." He studied his hands, and Kendall could see from the pale skin on one finger that he had worn a ring.

"How do you know so much about the Protettori?" she asked.

The historian's eyes grew distant. Kendall almost grasped something swirling in them, but he looked away. "I knew one of the Protettori a long time ago."

"How does someone become part of the order?" Jake asked.

"They were selected from the bravest, the most loyal men, who then made a sacred vow to protect the relics."

Kendall felt her head growing fuzzy and she heard a young boy's voice. The historian's voice intruded and she shook her head, trying to focus. She remembered the torn letter she had found in the tower. She had forgotten to ask Roberto what it said. "Can you tell me anything about this? It's written in Italian."

His veined hands reached for the paper and he studied it. "It's a date. April twentieth. The year is torn off. The only thing legible is "must keep the secret." The historian frowned. "You found this in the castle of the Protettori?"

Kendall squirmed in her chair, but it was too late to pretend she had found it somewhere else. "It was in one of the rooms."

"So someone in the castle was keeping a secret," the historian said.

"Didn't you say you saw a bed with blood?" Jake asked. "Maybe someone gave birth there. Kendall is gifted. She senses things."

Kendall was surprised at the lack of sarcasm in Jake's voice.

The old man leaned forward. "Tell me about your gift. I've always been fascinated by such things."

Again, she started to pick up something in his eyes, and it made her uncomfortable. "Oh, I just get some weird vibes.

Nothing ever pans out." She ignored Jake's frown and rose. "Thank you for your time. We have to be going."

"My pleasure. I hope to run into you both again soon."

After they left, the old man walked to the library and sat down at the desk. The visit hadn't gone as he'd expected. He reached up with now straight fingers and pulled off his gray wig. He removed his thick glasses, and then put on the ring he'd taken off. One of his prized possessions. He didn't like it to leave his finger. Straightening his stooped shoulders, he addressed the body stuffed underneath the desk.

"If they don't have my spear, then who does?"

CHAPTER THIRTEEN

J AKE KEPT AN EYE ON THE REARVIEW MIRROR AS THEY SPED
away from the historian's house. His face was tight.

"Is something wrong?" Kendall asked.

"Just make sure we're not being followed." He glanced at her.
"You're quiet."

"Something's bothering me about the historian."

"You think he's in danger?"

"No. I think he was lying, but I don't know what he was lying
about. Something was…off about him. Maybe your suspicious
nature is rubbing off on me."

Jake navigated his way through traffic. "I think we should
call our friend Edward and see if he knows more than he's saying.
Maybe we should ask him if he misses his family."

They called, but Edward didn't answer, so Kendall left a message asking him to call them back. "We know more about the
secret order, but that doesn't bring us any closer to finding the
box," she said. "I'm almost sure Brandi had it. She wouldn't have
freaked out over her bag otherwise. She said that I knew what
was in it. Who could have taken it?"

"Maybe Nathan came back and took it. It's not our problem
now. We've been told not to find it, remember?" Jake winced and
put his hand over his stomach as he settled back in the seat.

"You must be starving." Neither of them had eaten recently.

"I'd kill for a medium-rare steak and a beer."

"You think about steak a lot."

"Steak and sex."

Sometimes she had a hard time knowing if he was teasing, serious, or trying to distract her. "Forget sex, but I wouldn't say no to a steak. Too bad we aren't here under nicer circumstances. I would love to explore Italy. There's so much to see. The Colosseum and the Pantheon. The Sistine Chapel, Saint Mark's Basilica. And I've love to see Venice. I've never ridden in a gondola."

"We can always come back after we get this mess sorted out."

Did he mean as a couple?

They arrived at the airport where Andy, one of Nathan's closest guards, met them and helped unload Kendall's bags.

"Go ahead to the jet," Jake said. "I need to use the restroom and make a call. I'll meet you there."

No he wouldn't. He was lying to her.

He put his hand on her back, and a sensation shot through her body. She saw three bodies in a room, eyes blacked out like the thieves'. She didn't know who the third body was, but the first two were Nathan and Jake. They were going to die.

Shaken, Kendall managed to keep her voice steady. "OK." She waited until he disappeared and turned to Andy. "I'm not going."

"I beg your pardon," he said.

"I'm staying here."

"I can't let you do that." Andy was tall and strong and more than capable of physically forcing her onto the jet. But he was kind. She'd always gotten along with him.

"Please, Andy. Nathan's in trouble. So is Jake. I can help them."

"I know about your gift, but if you're not on the plane, it could be my job."

"If you make me go, it could be Nathan's life. I know you have to report to Nathan, but just give me a few hours. Please."

After she'd convinced Andy, she hurried outside in time to see Jake getting in the Audi. She hailed the first taxi and opened the door. "I need you to follow that car." She crammed her bags inside and jumped in. "Don't lose him."

The car shot forward, throwing her against the seats. The driver stayed back but kept Jake's Audi in sight. He stopped at a car rental company. He must be switching cars again. Kendall's taxi stayed out of sight, waiting for him to leave. After a few minutes, she heard rumbling, and a dangerous-looking motorcycle pulled out of the parking lot. The rider wore a helmet, so it was impossible to see his face, but she would recognize that body and backpack anywhere.

"Follow that motorcycle." They tailed Jake to a hotel. She had the taxi driver stay back as Jake pulled into the parking garage. He swung a leg over the bike and stood. He pulled off his helmet and turned in her direction, as if he sensed he was being watched, but the taxi was hidden behind several other cars. Carrying the helmet and his pack, he started inside.

She tipped the driver well, took her bags and followed at a distance. When he reached the counter to check in, she swept across the floor toward him. "Hello, darling. Sorry I'm late."

The muscles in his shoulders tensed, and he slowly turned. The look of surprise had faded by the time he fully faced her, but a storm was brewing behind those steel-gray eyes.

She dropped her bags and threw herself into his arms. Standing on tiptoe, she pulled his head down to hers and proceeded to kiss the daylights out of him right there in the lobby. His hand had come up automatically, gripping her arm, and she felt his touch soften. With him sufficiently off-kilter and the clerk certain she belonged here, Kendall moved her mouth close and whispered in Jake's ear. "If you sneak off again, I'll dig inside your head and uncover every underhanded, embarrassing thing you've ever done." She leaned back and gave him a bright smile, and then an even brighter one for the benefit of onlookers.

"Ah, young love," the clerk said, patting his heart.

Jake's answering smile barely lifted one corner of his mouth. He gave her a penetrating stare that would have withered her if she wasn't already so pissed. "There aren't words to express how I feel seeing you here," he said, running his tongue over his bottom lip. He took the key from the clerk and picked up both duffel bags, throwing them over his shoulder. She tried to get hers back, but he brushed her off. He picked up his backpack. With the other hand he grabbed her arm in a pretend lover's grasp and pulled her toward the elevator.

"You're supposed to be on the jet," he hissed, baring his teeth in a fake smile for the benefit of a passing guest.

"So are you. How dare you skip out on me?"

"It's too dangerous for you here. You heard what Nathan said."

"I'm getting sick of you and Nathan telling me what to do. I can think for myself." She stalked along beside him while he found his room.

He shoved the key in the lock and opened the door. "I don't know what the hell you think you're doing," he said, stepping inside. "Do you have any idea how pissed Nathan is going to be?"

"He's not going to be any happier with you."

"You're the one he cares about." Jake dumped the bags on the floor.

"I'm staying. Deal with it."

"You're the most stubborn, irritating woman I've ever met."

"You're a jerk."

He moved around the room, quickly checking under the beds, in the closet, behind the drapes, anyplace a speck of dust might be hiding. When he turned, he moved stiffly. "I'm going to take a shower." He walked into the bathroom and slammed the door.

"Humph," Kendall said to the empty room. She moved the bags out of the way and blew out a sigh. What was she doing here? Jake was right. Nathan was going to be furious. Her head was beginning to ache and she was starving. She picked up the phone and ordered room service. Lasagna and a salad for her, the thickest steak she could get for Jake. Maybe that would soothe his temper. Then they could figure out how to keep Nathan from killing them and figure out what to do next. Including getting her a separate room.

She stared at her phone, wondering if she should just call Nathan and confess. No, she would wait until morning. She lay back on one of the two beds and tried to relive her dream, hoping for some clues as to how she was supposed to save Nathan and Jake. She had no idea what good she would do, but was certain she had to be there. She'd almost dozed off when she heard a tap at the door. She peeked out and saw a bellboy with a tray. She opened the door and he pushed the cart inside. The aroma of food made her mouth water. The bellboy lifted the lid, but it slipped from his hands and clattered onto the tray.

"So sorry…" His apology was cut short when the bathroom door burst open. Jake stood there, holding a gun. He was stark naked. Again.

The bellboy's eyes widened. He yelled and stuck his hands in the air.

Kendall's jaw dropped. It was an impressive sight, in more ways than one. Not the least, the bloody gash on Jake's side.

"You're injured," Kendall said, staring at the blood.

Jake lowered the gun.

The bellboy still had his hands in the air and was gaping at Jake. Jake snatched a jacket from a chair and covered himself while Kendall apologized and escorted the boy to the door, giving him a huge tip. They were going through Nathan's money like water.

"What happened to your side?" Kendall asked.

"It's just a scratch." He walked to the bathroom door and grabbed a towel. He didn't cover himself but dabbed at the cut, which was to the left of his belly button.

"It's not a scratch. Did you get that fighting at the inn?"

"Brandi's thief caught me in the side with his knife when I knocked him off you."

That explained the winces and why he'd changed his shirt. "Do you always get so many injuries?"

"No. I think it comes from being around you."

"Really? How about that scar on your back? I wasn't there for that. Or the one on—"

"My ass?"

Kendall gave him a haughty look. "At least put some clothes on while we try to keep you from bleeding to death."

"I'd planned on staying naked, but if it's getting you hot, I'll put on a towel. Don't know why it matters. You've seen this," he ran his hand over his groin, "as much as some married people I know." He kept his hand there, supposedly covering himself while he reached for the towel, but the gesture made her feel like she needed to stick her head in a freezer.

"You should have left," he said.

"Nathan will die if I do."

"Is this one of your, uh…things?"

"I had a vision."

He finished tucking in the edges of his towel. "And you're willing to risk your life for him."

"Not just him. You're going to die too."

His gaze was steady. "And you think you can save us?"

"I have to try."

"It's too dangerous for you to be here."

"You can't make me leave."

"I can," he said softly, and she knew he could. But he wouldn't. "We'll eat and get some rest, and then figure out what to do in the morning."

"I'll go down and get a room."

"No. As long as you're in Italy, you're sleeping where I can watch you."

She didn't feel like fighting him, and it was safer to be in the same room. Safer in some respects, not others. At least the room had two beds. After that kiss at the inn, it wouldn't be wise to sleep in the same bed. "I don't suppose you're going to have a doctor look at that cut."

"No. I'm going to eat. I smell steak."

She blew out a frustrated sigh. "You're not eating until I look at your injury. Where's the first-aid kit?"

He grimaced. "In my pack."

The cut was surrounded by lots of hot, toned muscles. Far different from bandaging his head. She was feeling warm all over by the time she put the gauze in place. "Where'd you get all these scars?"

A ripple moved across his flesh. "Different places."

There were a couple on his chest, one on his stomach that looked like a bullet wound, and one on his thigh that was visible through the gap in his towel.

"Checking out the package? Figured you'd have it memorized by now."

"I swear, sometimes I want to hit you."

"It's a misplaced sexual urge."

"Why didn't you tell me you'd gotten hurt at the inn?" she asked, ignoring his attempts at distraction.

"I knew you'd never leave if you found out. Can you hurry? My steak's getting cold."

"You need a doctor."

He grinned like a Cheshire cat. "Why see an old man when I can have your hands all over me? It'd be better if you slipped them a few inches lower."

"Give it up. I know you're trying to distract me."

She was learning his tactics. He used flirting to put up a wall and keep her from asking questions. The bad boy wasn't as bad as he seemed. After she finished bandaging his side, she checked his other injuries. His forehead was looking much better, but he still had a black eye from the fight with Nathan. She put the bandages away. "You'll live. You're too ornery not to."

She hoped.

He dressed and they sat down to eat. Kendall tried to plan their next moves, but Jake didn't have much to offer. Strange for someone who was usually so quick. Maybe he was just starving. He was eating with gusto. "You're not very helpful," she said.

"It's been too long since I've had steak." He glanced at the bed. "Not to mention other things." He gave her a look that made her body sizzle again.

"Behave." She grabbed her drink and downed half.

He picked up his beer and studied the liquid, his expression sober now. "Why do you think Nathan's so desperate to get his hands on that spear?"

"It's the Spear of Destiny! Have you seen his relic collection?"

"Some. But he has other relics, objects museums would die for. Hell, he lends stuff to museums. Why is he so desperate for this one? Maybe he believes the rumors and he wants to rule the world."

"Nathan isn't like that."

"How do you know?" He looked irritated. "Don't you think it's strange that you can't read him? He could be evil."

"I can't read lots of people." She didn't tell him she suspected Nathan was blocking her. "But he's not evil. I just...know."

"People are good at hiding what they want kept secret." An edge of bitterness crept into his voice. Jake set down the beer.

"Who betrayed you?"

He frowned at her. "Damn, that's annoying. Don't you get tired of dealing with what's inside everybody else's head, not just your own?"

"You have no idea, but that wasn't my sixth sense. Anyone could connect those dots." She watched him and waited. After a minute of rubbing the scar on his thumb, he spoke.

"I don't know who betrayed me. That's the worst part of it."

"What happened?"

"One of my assignments went bad." He put his elbows on the table and rubbed his temples. "People died."

"I'm sorry. What kind of assignment?"

"The one in Iraq."

"Who hired you? The government?"

"Some rich guy. We never met him. Never knew his name. He worked through a middleman. I figured anything to help counterterrorism was a worthy cause. After a few days, I knew something was wrong. Things weren't adding up. The prince claimed we'd stolen something from him. It was starting to look like our assignment was a cover for something else. I started looking into it, that's when I found them." Jake closed his eyes. "It was the night before we were supposed to fly out."

"Found what?"

He swallowed, and she knew that whatever he was remembering cost him dearly. "The girls." Jake opened his eyes and looked at her. The pain he'd buried had hardened to bitterness. "Young girls. Some not even teenagers. He kept them in a private part of the palace. Locked up like prisoners in two little rooms. The look in their eyes..." His face tightened.

"Oh, Jake."

"He wasn't dealing in weapons, but human trafficking. He was selling sex slaves."

"What did you do?"

"I didn't have much time, but I couldn't leave them there. I got them out and led them away from the palace."

"You got them to safety?"

"I don't know. We were attacked on the way. I got shot."

That's what she must have experienced when she touched the drop of Jake's blood. "Who shot you?"

"Thomas Little."

"Thomas shot you?"

"He was aiming a gun at me, and when I woke up, I had a bullet in me."

"Are you sure it was Thomas?"

Jake nodded. "I only saw him twice before the attack. Both times at the palace. I never talked to him. He looked different then. His hair was longer, and he didn't have the beard. But it was him. I recognized him in the grave, without his hat and beard."

"You didn't see him again?"

Jake shook his head. "When I woke up I was in the palace and the prince was next to me, dead."

"You killed him?"

"I don't know that either. I can't even remember how I got there after the attack. But the Iraqis thought I killed him, that's what counted. And they accused me of stealing."

"Stealing what?"

"Antiques, I think. They kept asking what I'd done with them. I gather the prince collected unusual things."

Like young girls. "What about your team?"

"Killed. They were waiting for me in the helicopter. Someone fired a rocket launcher."

"I'm sorry. At least you got those girls out."

His face lost all expression. "Not all of them." She knew he was finished talking about it.

She didn't blame him. Her memories were haunting enough. She couldn't imagine living with his. She wondered if one of the girls had owned that little wooden doll.

"My God, Jake." That explained so much about him, the protectiveness, not wanting her there in the first place. She gave his shoulder a light squeeze. "I won't hold being a jackass against you anymore."

He almost smiled.

"At least you got out of prison," she said.

"Yeah," he muttered, with a sardonic twist to his mouth. "Since we're baring our souls, tell me one of your secrets."

"I'm in love with a ghost. How's that for a confession?"

Jake stared at her, the look on his face impossible to read. Kendall would have given a lot to know what he was thinking, but this time she drew a blank. He finally looked down at his hands. "Adam?"

She nodded. "I don't know what kind of love it is, but I can't get free of him. The terrible thing is I don't want to be free. I feel like he's alive. I had one boyfriend who accused me of cheating on him. He said he knew there was someone else." Kendall shrugged her shoulders. "I never told him my heart belonged to a dead twelve-year-old."

"Tell me about him?"

"We both lost our mothers when we were young. Our fathers met at a museum. Mine was an archaeologist; Adam's was a rich collector. They were both obsessed with relics, so they started working together. Adam and I went everywhere with them. Museums, fancy parties, but most of the time we lived in deserts and jungles. Maybe that's why we got along so well. We didn't have anyone else. No real friends. Just each other. Sometimes Adam and I helped, sometimes we got in trouble." She smiled. "A lot of trouble. Adam's father had this incredible collection. I never actually saw it. He kept it hidden. Adam and I plotted ways to find it. I think they were moving it when they died. My father had gone with them to help. Adam was supposed to come with me, but at the last minute he went with his father."

"Did you have your sixth sense when you were a kid?"

"A little. It tormented me afterward that I didn't know the accident was going to happen. If I could have just warned them… My abilities became stronger after Adam died. I used to think he must be helping me from the other side. My guardian angel."

"Did he know about your gift?"

"Yes." He was the only one she'd been able to be herself around. Even her father seemed uncomfortable with her sixth sense.

"Where did you live after your father died?"

"I went to live with my aunt Edna. She was kind, but she didn't know what to do with me. I was a mess. I'd lost my entire world. One day Adam and I were exploring, the next everything I knew was gone. Just like that. I didn't even get to say good-bye." Or to apologize to Adam for the fight. "Losing Adam hurt more than losing my father. I always felt guilty about that." Kendall noticed that Jake looked pale. "Are you OK?"

"Death sucks when it takes the young."

Something in his tone caught her. She gave him a sharp glance, but he was staring at the scar on his hand, his face a mask. Maybe he was thinking about the girls the prince had stolen. She started to pry, to see for certain, but that wouldn't be fair. She wouldn't want him digging through her memories of Adam.

Jake blew out a breath. "That's enough of the past. We need to worry about now. Why don't you grab a nap? I'm going to call Roberto and see if he'll give us an update on his guests."

"Turn on the charm," Kendall said with a smile. She repaired the chain that held the cross and slipped it over her head. No rush of memories. No pain this time. She yawned. She was probably too tired to pick up anything. Jake let her choose beds and she lay down, wondering why he wasn't making his usual play.

Finally, she fell asleep. She dreamed of Adam again and the stupid fight. She couldn't remember what it was about. When she tried, the effort made her head throb. She woke up, her pillow damp, and found herself looking around the room, even though she knew she wouldn't see him. It happened a lot, usually when she least expected it. She would be working on a relic and feel him behind her. She would turn, certain she'd see his grin, knowing she couldn't. She'd never had a connection like that to anyone else. She loved her father, and he loved her, but he was busy and always worried about something. Adam was the one who had laughed with her and had taken the time to explain things, to show her a fragment of pottery and explore what it might have held and who might have touched it. When he died, half her heart died with him.

Kendall dried her damp cheeks. She was tired of crying and tired of ghosts. She heard soft breathing from the other bed. Jake lay on his back, legs slightly spread, with one hand underneath his pillow, the other resting on his stomach. She watched him for a minute, watched his chest rising and falling with each breath. Alive. Easing back the covers, she slipped out of her bed and crossed to his, sliding in beside him.

He was on his knees in a flash, his gun pointed at her head.

"Jake! It's me."

He'd already lowered the gun. "Damn. Don't ever do that again," he said, sliding the gun back under the pillow. "What's wrong?" He brushed a thumb over her cheek. "Why are you crying?"

"I had a dream." How pathetic did that sound? Like she was a five-year-old. "I have nightmares."

"I figured you did," he said softly. "Do you want to talk about it?"

"No, but I don't want to sleep alone."

His brows slightly lifted in surprise. "OK."

"If you don't mind."

"You're welcome in my bed anytime." He moved over and lifted the covers, inviting her in.

She crawled in next to him, lying on her back. He was warm, and thankfully, not naked. That was good. Maybe. The mattress moved as he settled his head on the pillow. She could feel him watching her. She stared at the ceiling, wondering if she'd lost her mind.

He stretched out a finger and touched the pulse ticking at the base of her throat. He slowly dragged it over her collarbone, climbing the curve of a breast. "When you say *sleep*, exactly what do you mean?" he asked, his breath warm against her ear.

She turned her head and looked at him. "What do you want it to mean?"

He was on her in a second. His body pressed close to hers, and she could feel his excitement at the prospect of *sleeping*. He balanced on one elbow, chest against hers, one muscular leg wedged between her thighs. His eyes glinted in the dark as his head lowered, his bruised eye making him look like a pirate. His lips touched hers and every nerve in her body electrified. She could feel him, inside and out, taste the frustration and stress and passion, all balled up in his kiss. His mouth was everything: warm and tender and rough.

She ran her hands over the lean muscles of his shoulders and back, desperate to get closer to him, to get inside him, in his head, on his body. She was drowning in his passion. She didn't just feel hers; she could feel his too. He leaned back far enough to slide a hand inside her shirt. Their kisses and hands grew hotter, trying to touch everything at once.

A phone rang, and Jake froze, his mouth still on hers. "Damn." He rolled off her and picked up his phone from the nightstand.

Kendall could still feel his touch all over her body.

"It's Nathan."

"Don't answer. He's going to kill us," she said, feeling a chill douse her passion. She was here because she had seen him and Nathan dying, and she had to do something to stop it. Rolling around in bed with Jake wouldn't help.

Jake put the phone down on the table and sat on the edge of the bed looking at her. He linked his fingers through hers, resting their joined hands against his thigh. "What are we doing?"

"Not sleeping," she said.

He smiled and tucked a strand of hair behind her ear, looking at her with…regret?

"I know. We can't do this," she said, sighing. "It's complicated enough as is."

He climbed back under the covers and pulled her into his arms. He kissed the top of her head and tucked his feet next to hers without speaking.

She lay there, her face against his chest, listening to his heart-beat.

"I have to send you home," he whispered.

"I won't go."

"Yes you will." He dropped another kiss on her head and they were both silent, wrapped in each other's warmth. Kendall wasn't sure what they were doing, or how to stop. It wasn't long until she fell asleep.

Sometime later, a soft noise woke her. A shadow stood by her bed, just like in her dream the first night in Rome. Jake? Before she could say his name, a cloth covered her face, cutting off her air. Instinct took over. She lashed out with a foot and heard a grunt. He straddled her, pushing the cloth tighter over her face. She felt herself slipping into darkness.

CHAPTER FOURTEEN

J AKE'S HEAD WAS SPINNING WHEN HE WOKE. KENDALL! HE looked around and saw he wasn't in the hotel. He was on a cot in a room or two cots and two rooms. Double vision. He struggled to focus. The walls appeared to be concrete, the door metal with a small window. Where was he? Where was Kendall?

He'd no sooner asked himself the question than a guard stepped inside the room. "Come with me."

Jake rose, his head still groggy from the drug. He pulled himself up and stumbled along in front of the guard. He felt a little better after he had managed a few steps. Partway down the corridor, an old man hurried past them. The guard turned back to give the man an irritated look, taking his eyes off Jake long enough for him to hit a pressure point in the back of the guard's neck. He dropped like a rock. Jake checked the doors nearby and found a closet. He dragged the guard inside and shut the door.

There were several doors along the corridor, some with small windows like the one in his room. He ran from door to door, searching for Kendall. He found her in a room around a corner at the end of the corridor. She was lying on a cot with her eyes closed. He stared at her, not daring to breathe, until he saw her chest rise. She was alive. What the hell had Nathan gotten her into? Jake tapped once at the door, but she didn't wake. He couldn't keep knocking or he'd get caught, and he didn't have the strength to deal with several guards at once.

He heard footsteps coming and hid against the wall, waiting. A guard rounded the corner, holding a set of keys. His eyes widened when he saw Jake. Before the guard could react, Jake sidestepped and struck him on the neck, applying the same pressure point move he'd used on the first guard. He took the keys and opened the door. After dragging the guard into the room, Jake closed the door and checked the corridor. Still clear. He hurried over to Kendall.

"Wake up."

Her eyes flew open and she punched him in the chin. It lacked power, but the hit caught him off guard. "What'd you do that for?" he asked, holding his jaw.

She struggled to a sitting position. Her hair was sticking up and she looked like a wild woman. "I'm sorry. I thought you were the kidnapper. Where am I?" She looked around the room, and then back at him, her brow wrinkled.

"I don't know, but we have to get out of here."

"I don't think I can walk. I have too many feet." She studied her fingers, twisting them. "And fingers."

He walked to the door and checked the window. "More guards. They're talking. We'll have to wait until it's clear." He was still too shaky to take them all on. "What's the last thing you remember?"

"I woke up and someone was pressing something over my face. I passed out."

"You didn't see who took you?"

"I think it was him." She pointed at the guard. "I'm going to go kick him." She tried to get up, but Jake knew she wouldn't get far.

He eased her back down. "Don't get up yet. We'll kick him later."

"How'd they get you? You're big and strong. You have lots of muscles. I like muscles." She frowned, as if trying to figure out who was controlling her mouth. She seemed more out of it than he was. They must have given her too much of the drug.

"I didn't see or hear anything. I think they hit me with a tranquilizer gun." He wasn't a heavy sleeper. He doubted anyone could have gotten close enough to administer a drug. He walked back to the door and checked the window. The guards had left. "Come on, let's go. If you get tired, let me know. I'll carry you."

He helped her to her feet and put an arm around her to keep her from falling. She wobbled a little, but she looked a little steadier than she had before.

"You're a good guy, Jake Stone. You pretend you're a jackass but you're a good guy. Sometimes you're a jackass too."

"Thanks, I guess."

"How long have we been here?"

"Several hours."

She stopped. "Who's that?"

A face was peering in the glass at the door. An old man with bright blue eyes and white hair.

"He seems to know you," Jake said.

The old man's gaze was intent on Kendall. A second later, he disappeared.

"That was strange," Kendall said. "You think he's the kidnapper?"

"He doesn't look capable of kidnapping."

"I say Brandi did it."

Footsteps sounded outside in the hallway. More than one person was coming. "We're about to find out."

"We need weapons," Kendall said, looking around the room.

"No. You get on the cot. I'll jump him when he comes in." Jake helped Kendall back to the cot, and then moved to the wall behind the door. There was a click and the door swung open. From her position, Kendall could see the person before Jake did. Her jaw went slack with surprise. Jake stepped out from behind the door, ready to fight his way out. When he saw who the man was, he cursed and pulled back his fist.

"You son of a bitch." Jake threw a punch, but Nathan saw it coming and pulled back. Jake's fist clipped his chin. Nathan shook it off and faced Jake, eyes shooting fire.

Kendall jumped between them before they could throw any more blows. She was still a little wobbly and had to grab hold of their shirts to steady herself. She'd never seen Nathan this mad. His skin was hot with anger. "Stop."

Nathan and Jake each took a step back, still furious. She was angry too. When she got out of here, Nathan could find another relic expert. She was done. "Kidnapping us! Are you crazy?"

"I had no choice." He glanced at his unconscious security guard and turned on Jake. "Are you *trying* to get her killed?"

Jake's fists clenched. "*Me* trying to kill her? You're the one who sent her into a war zone without weapons."

"Don't blame Jake," Kendall said. "He pulled the same crap you did. He left me to board the jet and ditched me."

Nathan looked at Jake, and Kendall felt the gap between them narrow. Not much, but a little.

Nathan blew out a hard breath. His lip had almost completely healed. "You were supposed to leave too," he said to Jake. "You're both in danger here."

"Cut the bull. You don't give a damn about me. You wanted me to make sure your pet got out safe."

Nathan's eyes narrowed to slits. "I gave an order, for good reason—your bloody safety—and I expected it to be carried out."

"Then start explaining things instead of acting like a lovesick prick."

Nathan smashed his fist into the wall. When he pulled it back, Kendall saw there was a hole. He jerked, as if he'd been hit with a cow prod, and hunched over with a loud groan.

A numbing pain shot through Kendall's body at the same time.

The door opened and Fergus appeared, shadowed by three guards. "Nathan, come with me. Now." Fergus pulled at Nathan's arm. He didn't resist but went with the older man. He appeared to be in the grip of some kind of spell.

"What's wrong with him?" she asked.

Fergus pushed him toward the door. "He'll be fine, Miss Kendall. He just needs rest."

The sensation passed as she watched Fergus half-drag Nathan from the room. Nathan's clenched fist was scratched, but it should have been bleeding. One of the guards held a gun on Jake and demanded a set of keys, which Jake grudgingly handed over. The other two guards picked up their unconscious comrade and carried him from the room.

"That was bizarre," Kendall said after the door shut.

Jake's brows drew together. He walked over to the wall and stared at the hole Nathan's fist had left. "More than bizarre. This wall is made of concrete."

Kendall joined him at the wall, staring at the damage. "No wonder he was doubled over in pain."

"His hand should be broken. He wasn't even bleeding. How do you explain that?"

"Adrenaline," Kendall said. "And luck?"

Frowning, Jake walked to the door and inspected the lock. "We've got to get out of here."

"How? There are lots of guards. When Nathan sets his mind to something, he's like a mule, and he thinks he's protecting us by keeping us here."

Jake knelt by the cot.

"You think praying will help?" Kendall asked.

"I'm looking for something I can use to pick the lock."

The door rattled and they both turned. The old man stepped inside the room. Jake scrambled for the door, trying to catch it before it closed, but he was too late.

The old man moved toward Kendall, stopping in front of her. He wore a robe remarkably like her ghost monk's. He searched her face and frowned. "You look different," he said in broken English. He touched a strand of her hair. "But your hair is still the same."

"You know me?"

He nodded, still assessing her. "Your eyes, they have seen much pain." He touched his chest. "And your heart. So much hurt." He looked at Jake. "You too."

"Who are you?" Kendall asked.

"I am Marco." He said it with a grand bow, as if the name should mean something to her. He straightened. "You don't remember me."

"No, I'm sorry."

He sighed and sat on the bed, as if his legs had given out. "No one does."

"How do I know you?" Kendall asked.

He smiled and measured chest high with his hand. "You were this big when you came to the castle."

"You're from the castle...Were you singing?"

"I like to sing."

"I don't remember being at the castle before." Or did she? She had seen the castle and the statues in her vision. Maybe it wasn't a vision but a memory.

"You weren't supposed to be. Women aren't allowed."

"But someone gave birth there. In the tower room."

"There was one before you, but we don't speak of her."

"What was she doing there?"

Marco frowned. "She wanted the treasure, but she fell in love. She became with child. He didn't know and sent her away. She grew ill—she was dying—so she came back to the castle to tell him so that he could protect the child. He kept the secret from the others. The same as I did for him."

"Him?" Kendall asked, confused.

Marco blinked. He appeared to be confused as well. "She gave birth there and died."

"What happened to the child?"

"I don't know."

The secret. Was this what the scrap of letter referred to? "Why was I at the castle?"

"Your father had business there. You wandered away and found our sacred place. Your father was angry," Marco said, shaking his finger, "and rightfully so. It was a serious matter. Could even bring a curse of death."

"What could bring death?"

"Taking the vow. It isn't a game."

Kendall felt her legs sinking under her. The voices of the boy and girl came back to her, the whispered words as light emerged from the stones, swallowing her and Adam.

"Kendall?" Jake crouched in front of her where she sat on the bed.

"I just remembered something." They had been in Egypt when she and Adam noticed their fathers' increasingly strange behavior. There were secret conversations and the relationship seemed strained. When she asked her father what was wrong, he told her they had to go to Italy to clear up a problem. Adam was disappointed that they were leaving Egypt, because he thought he'd found a hidden tomb in a cliff. Other than the statues, she couldn't remember anything of the visit except for Adam, the stones, and a bright light.

"What happened after that?" she asked Marco.

"Everyone was upset. The penalty for breaching the sacred chamber is harsh. I worried what the others might do. I helped your father take you away in the middle of the night."

Adam died right after they visited the castle. So did her father. And Adam's father. Had some kind of curse killed the people she loved? Then why was she still alive? "Why can't I remember?"

"We made you forget. But I believe the memories are coming back. It will be OK now. It will be saved."

219

"What will be saved?"

"The spear." He leaned forward.

"Spear?" Jake asked.

Marco frowned, as if they should know. "The Spear of Destiny."

"Then it *is* real," Kendall said.

"But of course."

"How do you have the real spear?" Kendall asked.

"We switched them."

"When?" Jake asked.

"A long time ago."

"Wasn't that dangerous?" Kendall asked.

"Yes, but it had to be done. Evil men can't be allowed to find these powerful relics."

"There's more than one of these relics?" Jake asked.

"There are many, but these four, they are the most powerful. They must be kept apart."

"Why?" Kendall asked.

"If someone possessed all four there would be no limit to their power."

"Where are the relics?" Jake asked.

"We have them hidden." Marco's eyes dimmed. "There used to be many of us, but there was an attack after you left. Evil tried to destroy us." He frowned. "So much blood and death. But the relics are safe."

The door rattled again and Fergus appeared, his expression alarmed. Two guards stood behind him. "Marco, you mustn't be here."

"I was reacquainting myself with the girl."

"You must come with me, please."

"Then I will say good-bye." He took Kendall's hand and leaned in close. "I'll come back," he whispered. When he stepped away, there was a twinkle in his eye, and Kendall had a flash of a young boy with black hair and an impish grin. "Good-bye." The old man started humming a song as Fergus ushered him out the door.

Jake shook his head. "If he's telling the truth, why reveal all this? What about their secrets? We could be evil."

"He knows we're not," Kendall said.

"I think Marco's missing a few marbles."

"He does seem to come and go. Probably Alzheimer's."

"This just gets stranger. Nathan sends us to this castle to find the Spear of Destiny and now we find out you were there as a child but don't remember it."

"How is it possible that they could block my memories?"

"How is it possible that you can look into someone's eyes or touch an object and read secrets?"

Kendall sighed. "Do you think Nathan knew I'd been there before?"

"Seems a big coincidence if he didn't."

The door opened and five guards came to take Jake away. Even though he was outnumbered and outgunned, they watched him like a fox in a henhouse. They didn't tell Kendall where they were taking him. He paused at the door, pulling free long enough to look back at her. He didn't speak, but the promise in his eyes said he would come back.

———◦———

Other than the dim light coming from the window in the door, it was dark when Kendall heard the rattle. She lay still and watched the sliver of light expand as the door opened. Had Jake escaped? A shadow moved toward her and she didn't know whether to welcome it or scream. A candle flared, and she saw the old man. Kendall sat up as he approached the cot, wondering if Nathan knew Marco was moving in and out of the rooms like Houdini.

Marco stared at her face in the flickering light. "There is something I need to tell you."

"What?"

"Something important." He frowned. "I can't seem to remember. It came to me in a dream and I hurried here before I forgot. My memory isn't what it used to be," he said, waving a gnarled finger in vague circles. "Something about the vow, perhaps." Sighing, he rose. "I'll sleep on it, and when I remember, I will come back."

"Wait. Tell me more about what my father was doing at the castle. You said he had business there."

"It concerned the relics. Ah yes, I remember now why I came. I wanted to apologize."

"For what?"

"For what we did to your father and to you. Our society is ancient and traditions can be unforgiving."

Why apologize for sending them away? Considering the Protettori were a society that didn't allow women on the premises and the penalty for trespassing on sacred grounds could have been death, Marco's actions probably saved them. "Tell me about the society…"

Footsteps sounded in the distance. The old man scurried toward the door with a speed that defied his age. "I must hurry before he comes." He inserted a key in the lock and was out the door before Kendall could get within reach.

A few seconds later, the door rattled again. It opened and this time Fergus appeared with a tray. There weren't any guards. Kendall considered jumping him. If it were Nathan she would have, but she couldn't bring herself to attack Fergus.

He set down the tray and flipped a light switch on the wall. "Here you are, Miss Kendall." The tray held a grilled cheese sandwich and a glass of iced tea. Her favorites.

"Why is he doing this, Fergus? He *kidnapped* us? That's insane."

"I don't agree with his methods, but he had good reasons." Fergus placed a newspaper beside the tray. "Very good ones, I might add."

A commotion sounded in the corridor accompanied by feet pounding, yells, and then there was silence. Before either of them could react, the door opened and Jake appeared, pointing a gun at Fergus's chest. "Don't try to stop us, Fergus. Let's go, Kendall."

"Where are we going?" Kendall asked.

"To find Nathan."

Fergus folded his hands. "Before you do anything rash, and I suspect it's too late for that, I ask you to consider this from Nathan's perspective."

Jake let out a stream of curses. "Nathan's perspective? He kidnapped us and he's holding us as prisoners."

"He brought you here to protect you."

"Protect us?" Jake scoffed.

"He was afraid you were going to die."

Jake snorted. "He doesn't care about anything but her. Although kidnapping's a strange way to show it."

"He cares about you too," Fergus said, drawing his brows into a dignified frown. "You two are like brothers, but you're both too stubborn to see it. Put yourself in his shoes, Jake. If you thought Kendall was going to get hurt, you would do whatever it took to keep her safe, even if it was against her will."

"Like putting me on a jet and sneaking away," Kendall said.

"That's different," Jake said.

"Not much." She thought about Nathan holding her hand in the inn and how worried he'd been. He never hugged her. Maybe Fergus was right. Anyone would do desperate things to protect someone they cared about. Nathan caring about her—that left her with an odd feeling.

"He was desperate," Fergus said. "Someone is trying to destroy him. One of his guards was recently killed. The three of us are the only family he has. He's alone in this world, and that money he has just makes the wall bigger. He can't trust anyone. He keeps everyone at arm's length, except us. Please consider that before you react." Fergus directed this last statement to Jake, and then he frowned. "Are you feeling well, Jake?"

Jake was staring at the picture on the front page of the newspaper. "Look at this."

Kendall knew enough Italian to know that the man in the picture had been murdered. He was a historian in Rome and ironically had the same name as the historian they had visited, but this wasn't the man they'd met. "Oh my God. Who did we meet?"

"The Reaper, I think," Jake said. His face was grim.

"What are you talking about?" Fergus asked.

"We went to meet this historian who knows about the Protettori, the ones who were protecting the box that Nathan wants, but this," she tapped the man's picture, "wasn't the man we met. I kept getting these strange feelings about him."

"He had on thick glasses probably to hide his eyes," Jake said. "He must have known about your abilities."

"If he killed Thomas, he must have the box. Why not just kill us?"

"Either he doesn't have it or he still needs something else. Which means there could be more than one person looking for the box."

Fergus looked alarmed. "We have to tell Nathan."

"Where is he?" Kendall asked.

"He's not here. He left earlier."

Kendall's heart started to thump harder. "For Virginia?"

"No, he went to the castle."

"He can't go to the castle. He'll die." She told Fergus about her vision of Nathan and Jake's death.

He sank onto the cot, the last of his dignified manner gone. "You have to go after him," he said.

"What is he doing?" Jake asked. "Does he think the box is at the castle?"

"He wants the box. He also wants answers. There are things you don't understand."

Jake snorted. "Thanks to Nathan, there are a lot of things we don't understand."

"I can't explain. It will have to come from him, when the time is right."

"He'll be furious to see us there," Kendall said.

Fergus straightened and squared his shoulders. "Better that he's furious than dead."

Jake looked torn. "Personally, I'm considering letting him take his chances with the statues."

"The statues," Kendall said, looking at her watch. "If they're activated at night, Nathan is in trouble."

"He knows about the statues, and he knows another way in—the railroad," Jake said.

"But what other horrible things are there that we don't know about? We need to talk to Marco."

"He won't be coherent," Fergus said. "His medication..."

"We can't leave Nathan there," Kendall said. "I'm mad too. I want to hit him with something, and then resign, and I may do it yet, but I won't let him die."

"I'll find him," Jake said. "You stay here."

"I'm not staying here."

"I can move faster and quieter without you."

"Maybe, but I can sense things you can't, and after that vision I think if I'm not there, you and Nathan will die. So I'm going, with or without you."

Jake glared at her, and then shook his head in defeat. "We'll need a vehicle," he told Fergus. "You don't have a helicopter, do you?"

"It would take too long to get it here. You can take one of Nathan's cars."

"We don't even know where we are," Kendall said.

"You're in Rome at one of Nathan's properties. Please hurry." Fergus led them from the room. Three guards lay in the hall.

"Did you kill them?" Kendall asked.

Jake shook his head. "No. The worst they'll have is a head-ache when they wake up."

"I'll call for more guards," Fergus said. "You'll need help."

"No. We go alone," Jake said. "I don't trust anyone else."

Fergus collected their belongings, and after they had changed and gathered supplies, he led them to a set of stairs. "Go this way so we don't have to explain to the other guards. I'll have a vehicle waiting out front."

"I want mine," Jake said.

Fergus looked surprised but agreed. He hurried off and pulled one of the guards aside as Jake and Kendall hurried up the stairs. They exited the lower level and both of them came to a stop, completely amazed.

"It's the first hotel where we stayed," Kendall said, looking around at the elaborate furnishings. "No wonder they didn't have a problem giving us Thomas's name. Nathan owns the place. That's disturbing."

"I'm more disturbed by the secret compound underneath. Come on." They hurried past the guests milling about the lobby and exited the hotel. "Can you ride?"

"Ride what?"

"That." He nodded toward the motorcycle pulling up out front.

"Crap. We're riding the motorcycle you rented?"

"This will be easier than a car. If we can't find the railroad Nathan mentioned, we can ride this partway up the trail. A dirt bike would be better, but we don't have time to find one."

They took the motorcycle from a sullen guard. "Why not let them help?" she asked.

"I don't trust guards who just kidnapped us. If it wasn't for keeping the spear out of the wrong hands, I'd let Nathan take his chances."

"I think the spear is at the castle."

"Is that one of your *feelings*?"

She nodded.

He looked at his phone. "You have your feelings, I have voice mail." He listened to the message then hung up. "It was Roberto. The mysterious guest checked out the same time we did."

"Did he mention Brandi?"

"She hasn't been back."

Kendall climbed on the bike behind Jake and held on tight as they wound down the narrow streets. The ride to the castle was terrifying. They weaved in and out of traffic, getting so close to cars she could have touched them. The knot she'd gotten in her stomach in Rome was still there when they pulled off the road where their car had exploded.

The car wasn't there now, just singed grass and dirt reminding her that someone wanted them to die. Jake parked close to the area where Nathan had described finding the hidden entrance.

"Watch your leg," Jake warned as she got off the motorcycle. "The exhaust is hot." He helped her off, switched on a flashlight and inspected the area.

She got off the bike and removed the helmet Jake had insisted she buy, shaking out her hair. "Could you have gone any faster? I feel like I've had a face-lift." She was glad the trip hadn't taken long. It gave her less time to worry about Nathan and Jake, but after the motorcycle hit a hundred miles per hour, she started to wonder if they'd reach the castle alive. "If Nathan is here, where's his car?"

"Probably hid it in the trees." Jake already had on his pack and had started searching. "Here. I've found something."

Kendall gathered her backpack and walked over to where he stood in front of a large rock. His light showed the same circle motif. He pushed it and the rock started opening.

"Stand back," he said.

The steps led down into a tunnel with railroad tracks, just as Nathan had said. "I thought he said there were two railcars. I don't see any."

Jake looked around. "That means someone else is here. That's not good. We need to get the bike down here."

"Will it fit down the steps?"

"It'll have to. We don't have time to hike in."

"It's going to be loud."

"There's no other choice." With a lot of grumbling and creative curses, he managed to get the bike down the steps. The roar of the engine was deafening inside the tunnel, which was part cave and part man-made. It took just minutes to reach the end. Two railcars waited. Jake shut off the bike and they climbed off.

"I wonder how many people are here," Kendall whispered.

Jake pulled a gun from his boot. Why didn't she have a gun? She was in danger too. As if her sixth sense could stop a bullet. Of course, she didn't like guns any more than Nathan did, and he knew that.

Following Nathan's directions, they found their way to the first floor of the castle. "I think I hear singing now."

Jake stopped and listened. "That's not singing. That's a scream." A flash of light shot through the windows of the castle.

"The statues." Oh God. Nathan.

Jake took off at a run. The screaming grew louder as they hurried past the columns where Raphael had died. Nathan was right. The body wasn't there. Outside, she could see a man suspended in the air between the statues, trapped in the light, his arms and legs stiff, body shaking with the force. The light was blinding, making it impossible to identify the figure.

"Nathan?" Kendall screamed, running toward him.

CHAPTER FIFTEEN

JAKE GRABBED HER AND PUT HIS ARMS AROUND HER, TRAPPING her against his chest. "Stay back."

Kendall turned her head from the blinding light, clutching Jake's shirt. "Is it him?"

"If it is, there's nothing we can do now."

She looked back again, her heart pounding, the smell of ozone flooding her nostrils. The light disappeared and the body dropped to the ground. Jake let go of her and ran toward the man, who was facedown on the ground.

"Don't get too close," she warned, running to catch up. *Please don't let it be Nathan*, she prayed.

"It's not him," Jake said, examining the man from several feet away. "I've never seen this guy before." His eyes were blacked out like the thieves' who'd stolen the box.

"Do you think he was with Nathan?" Kendall asked as she approached Jake.

A click sounded behind them. Jake tensed and reached for his gun. "Don't move," a voice said.

Jake took his hand off his gun and cursed. "No, I think he was with them."

"Raise your hands and turn around...slowly."

She and Jake turned, hands raised. Four men, all dressed in the same dark clothing as the dead man, stood behind them, guns drawn, their terrified gazes darting from Jake and Kendall to the statues.

"Can you take them?" Kendall whispered.

"Not with you here," Jake whispered back.

"What are those things?" A red-haired man asked, staring nervously at the statues, keeping his gun leveled at Kendall.

"Hell if I know," a second man said. He was tall and gaunt. "Throw down your gun. Nice and slow. I'm feeling a little jumpy right now. Then get rid of your backpacks."

Jake grunted, slipped his gun from its holster at his side and dropped the gun on the ground, following it with his pack.

"How about you?" the third man asked Kendall as she dropped her backpack. He had spiky brown hair and mean eyes. "Got any weapons on you?"

"Her weapon is her mind." The fourth man had a round nervous face. "Don't look her in the eyes. I've heard she can do all kinds of crazy things."

"Seems your reputation precedes you," Jake said.

"If you have a fancy move," she whispered, "I'd do it now."

"Move away from the statues," the gaunt man said.

"Gladly," Jake said. "Wouldn't want to roast like your buddy. Did you see what those statues did to his eyes?"

Unwittingly, four pairs of eyes glanced at the dead man. Jake leapt at the red-haired man, knocking the gun out of his hand and shoving him into two of his henchmen. Three of them toppled like dominoes. "Run," he yelled to Kendall.

She hesitated, remembering her vision of him dead.

"Go!" he yelled. "What are you waiting for?"

You.

She took off, racing in the opposite direction. She heard one of the men yelling at another to go after her. There was a protest, and then the round-faced man who hadn't fallen started chasing her. She glanced back and saw him closing in. In the background, Jake was fighting the other three, holding his own.

"Stop!" The man threw himself at her and she hit the ground like a sack of flour. Rolling over, she found a gun pressed between her eyes. Any harder and he wouldn't need a bullet—the barrel would penetrate her brain. "Get up." He moved back but kept the gun aimed at her head. "Start walking."

"Where are we going?"

"That way."

He guided her away from the castle. The line of statues stretching toward the sky seemed to watch their progress as Kendall and her captor moved toward the seven pillars.

"Who are you?"

"Don't talk. Just walk toward the stones. And don't look at me."

Not the catacombs. Again.

When they arrived at the pillars, he circled around the one with the motif and pushed. The stone started moving, but this time she knew to stand back. "Down there," he ordered.

"Who are you working for? Can I at least know that?"

"I thought you knew everything."

"Not nearly enough." Maybe she could read him if she could touch something that belonged to him other than the tip of his gun. She was getting nothing from that, and he was taking pains to stay clear of her. When they reached the bottom of the steps, he stepped farther back, still keeping his gun aimed at her. "Now find the key."

"What?"

"The key, find it."

"What key?"

"The key to the box," he said, sounding exasperated.

"There's a key?"

"You think something that valuable is just kept in an unlocked box?"

"What's in the box?" She was hoping to distract him so she could find a way out.

231

"I don't know, but it must be valuable. A lot of people want it."

"I barely saw the box before your friend stole it."

He frowned. "I don't think you know as much as they say. I was just hired yesterday."

"By who? The Reaper?"

"I don't know anything about a reaper." He gave her an impatient look and nudged her with his gun. "Shut up and find the key so I can get the hell out of this place."

"Did they tell you where to look?"

The man gave a long-suffering sigh. "It's gotta be in the same place where the box was hidden."

"With the old monk?"

"If that's where it was. Take me there."

"He's not going to be happy."

"Who?"

"The monk."

"Stop that," the man said, his voice shrill. "I know you're playing with my mind."

"Who told you about me?"

"Just walk. Find the key."

So the box was locked and the bad guys didn't have the key. That was good. Nothing else was. When they reached the door, she tried again to delay.

"We can't get inside the catacombs without the cross."

The man reached under her shirt and yanked out the cross. "I'm not stupid. Open it. Now."

She inserted the cross inside the lock and turned it. The light flashed and the door began to move.

That seemed to make him even jumpier. "Hurry," he said, pushing her inside. "I don't like this place."

"I don't blame you. It's booby-trapped."

"Booby-trapped? He didn't say nothing about no booby traps."

"There are giant rocks in the ceiling. One wrong step and splat!"

"Hellfire," her captor muttered, looking overhead.

"Did he mention the ghosts?"

"Ghosts?" His flashlight jerked around the catacombs, the light landing on a skull. He yelped. "Hurry up, dammit."

If there was a key hidden on the monk, Kendall didn't want this guy to find it. She had to keep stalling. Maybe Jake would come after her. If he was alive.

"I don't remember where the coffin is. I should get help."

"From who?"

"The spirits. They might not tell me, though. They're angry because we're here. Watch out for that stone there. I think it might be a trap."

He jumped sideways. If she had been a little quicker, she might have knocked the gun out of his hand, but she waited too long. If she could get away from him, she could sneak through the narrow tunnel where she and Jake had escaped. It was unlikely that this guy knew about it.

They moved on and at each coffin she stopped and ran her hands above it, giving an imitation of a dramatic psychic that would have made Jake proud. She moaned and called on the spirits, asking for guidance to the right coffin, hoping she was speaking loudly enough for Jake to hear and praying that if there were any more booby traps, they missed her and hit her captor, who was sweating and glancing over his shoulder every few seconds.

"Be quiet," he said, interrupting her latest act. "I heard something." After a minute, he pointed to another coffin. "Try that one."

Kendall approached the wooden box and held her hands above it. "Oh spirits of the catacomb, tell me where the angry monk lies. And grant us protection from the booby traps which lie in wait to kill us." She began slowly rocking back and forth. A low moan rose in her throat, rising in volume to a piercing wail.

"Stop that."

She gasped and her eyes flew open in an expression of horror. "I hear you, angry one. Please don't kill us as you killed the man at the statues, blacking out our eyes and cursing our souls with the horror worse than death."

From the corner or her eye she saw him swipe his forehead.

"Open it," he said.

She looked at the rotting piece of wood she'd been talking to. "Why?" Did he believe this was where she had found the box?

"Open it!" he yelled.

She touched the wood, and a wave of emotion hit her like a blow. She jumped back. He grabbed her by the hair, and she felt the gun dig into her side. He cursed again and kicked the coffin. She heard a crack and he shoved the lid aside. Like most other corpses in the catacombs, the body was nothing but bones with a bit of flesh for glue. Her captor's gun lowered slightly as he peered inside. She grabbed the thigh bone and swung it at him, but he dodged the blow.

"You bitch." He hit her in the head with the gun. White lights flashed behind her eyes. Her knees buckled. She grabbed the edge of the coffin to keep from falling, and he shoved her from behind. She threw her arms out, trying to stop her fall. She landed facedown on top of the skeleton. Before she could move, the lid closed, leaving her nose to nose with the corpse in the dark.

There wasn't enough room to roll over. She was trapped. She panicked, struggling and screaming. With every breath she took she pulled death into her lungs. Every move caused the cold bones to dig into her skin. The skull, the ribs, arms, and legs.

She heard her captor's muffled voice. "Let me know when you're ready to tell me where the key is."

She closed her eyes and forced herself to stop struggling, trying to stave off the panic. But when her own thoughts calmed, she felt the corpse's memories seeping into her brain. His family.

His life. His death. Her senses were on fire, skin and body burning, mind clawing for sanity again.

Shut down. Shut down. You did it before when you needed to survive. Do it now.

She let her mind slide away from the hard, cold bones, and the damp muskiness of the bits of remaining cloth. From the smell of rotten wood. From the laughter of the corpse as a boy, from his agony in death. It was working...until she heard a muffled roar, followed by a scream. There was another roar and something crashed, followed by the sound of splintering wood. The coffin lid flew off and before she could scramble out, she was lifted off her feet. It was too dark to see. She leaned back and made out two dark shapes. The closest one had glowing eyes.

CHAPTER SIXTEEN

THE DOOR TO THE CATACOMBS WAS STILL OPEN WHEN JAKE got there. They must have come this way. He'd just entered when he heard a roar that made the hairs on his neck stand, followed by a scream. He ran past the coffins and bones lining the walls, his gun drawn. Another roar sounded. He rounded a corner and in the beam of his flashlight, he saw a man rip the lid off a coffin and fling it behind him. Jake ducked as it flew past his head and smashed into the wall.

The man lifted someone out of the coffin as easily as if she were a rag doll. It was Kendall. Jake could see her blonde hair. The man crushed her to his chest. He was going to kill her. Jake yelled out as he ran, hoping to distract the man long enough to get a clear shot. He raised his gun and the man turned. Jake saw two eyes glowing in the dark. He raised his light to the man's face. What the hell! "Nathan?"

Kendall opened her eyes and leaned back, her shocked gaze moving from Nathan to Jake. "Jake, what are you doing with that gun?"

Jake kept the gun leveled at Nathan. "Kendall, step away."

Nathan pushed Kendall clear and turned to Jake. His eyes looked normal now.

"What the hell just happened?" Jake asked. "Your eyes were glowing."

Nathan picked up a flashlight that he must have dropped in the fight. "You're imagining things."

"I didn't imagine those iron doors ripped off their hinges and that heavy coffin lid you tossed like a Frisbee."

Kendall looked at the bent doors. "You did that?" she said to Nathan.

"It was just adrenaline. I heard you scream."

Adrenaline could do strange things to a man. Jake had seen it, even felt it, but something about this felt unnatural. He remembered Nathan punching the concrete wall in the underground cell at the hotel, and his eyes shining that night at the inn, and how quickly he'd evaded Jake when he tried to follow him.

Kendall had moved around beside Jake. She touched his arm. "Put the gun down, Jake. It's just Nathan."

Jake lowered the gun, staring at Nathan. He wasn't just Nathan. Jake didn't know what he was, but this was more than adrenaline. Maybe it was this place, with its strange statues and hidden spears. They were near one of the lanterns, so Jake lit it, giving them better light.

"What happened to him?" Kendall asked, looking at her assailant.

Nathan stared at the body, his expression as stony as one of the statues.

"Looks like he broke his neck," Jake said. He guessed Nathan had done that too. He turned to Kendall. "What were you doing inside the coffin?" He saw the gleam of bones inside. Thinking of lying in there with a skeleton made Jake's stomach knot.

"He was trying to make me tell him where the key was."

Jake wished Nathan hadn't killed the guy so he could do it. But rage wouldn't do any good now. "What key?"

"He said the box won't open without it. He seemed to think it was buried with the old monk." She looked back at the coffin behind her and rubbed her arms, even though she was wearing a jacket.

"How did you find me?" Kendall asked Nathan.

"I was in the woods when I saw him move the stone," Nathan said.

"Thank you, but when we get back, I quit."

"Quit?"

"I'm not working for someone who kidnaps me because I don't go where he wants me to go. Even if you thought it was for my own good."

"I thought you were going to die. What are you doing here now?" He frowned at Jake, as if it was his fault.

"Don't look at me. I tried to keep her away. And she's not the only one quitting. You can do whatever the hell you want. I'm done with you."

"I apologize, but it was for your own good," Nathan said, his face tight. "I'm not going to be responsible for your deaths."

"My own good?" Kendall said. "I'm sick and tired of both of you telling me what's for my own good. I'm a woman, dammit, not a kid."

She looked like a witch, her hair all over the place, her face smudged with Jake didn't know what, and there was a finger bone stuck in her belt.

"How did you get away from the hotel?" Nathan said.

"Fergus is trying to save your ass," Jake said. "If it was up to me, I wouldn't bother."

"He let you out?"

"Jake escaped first," Kendall said. "Then Fergus told us where to find you."

Nathan shook his head. "I might have known."

"When I told him you were going to die, he asked us to find you."

"I'm going to die?" Nathan said.

"Another one of her visions," Jake said. "We're both going to die if she doesn't save us."

Kendall gave him one of her should-be-patented glares. "That's not exactly what I said."

"What did you see?" Nathan asked.

"Three bodies. One was yours, another was Jake's."

"Whose was the third?" Nathan asked.

"I couldn't tell. I don't know why, but I need to be here. I trust my visions…most of the time."

"Well, it looks like we're all here to save each other," Jake said. "Except him." He looked at the dead guy. "Any idea who this guy and his crew belong to?"

Nathan shook his head.

"They were well trained, whoever they were. I just got rid of his buddies."

"Did you kill them?" Nathan asked.

"No. Just incapacitated them."

"Maybe they're working with Brandi or the guy with the ring," Kendall said.

"What guy?" Nathan asked.

They explained about the mysterious guest who they believed had murdered the historian.

"I have a feeling he's your Reaper," Jake said.

"What did he look like?" Nathan asked.

"He was in disguise when I saw him. Kendall got a better look at him at the inn."

"The inn? He was there? Bloody hell."

"He was average height and weight," Kendall said. "Hard to describe, except for his ring. It was gold and it looked really old, with a big red jewel. It may have been a ruby."

"I think it's him," Nathan said. "There was a ruby ring that disappeared a few years ago. It was part of a rare collection that belonged to a well-known dealer in antiquities. I was about to buy the ring when it vanished. The dealer turned up dead, and the collection had disappeared. Everyone assumed the Reaper stole it."

"These guys must be working for him," Jake said.

Kendall shook her head, staring at the dead guy. "I don't think so. I asked him if he worked for the Reaper. He had no idea what I was talking about."

"How many people are after this thing?" Nathan rubbed his chin.

Jake noticed that Nathan's split lip had completely healed. So had his hand after punching that hotel wall. Jake's eye was still bruised from the fight. He must be testing some kind of drug. "There are at least three parties after this box, including us," Jake said. "If the Reaper had the box, I think he would have killed us. So assuming the first three thieves, including Thomas, worked for him, either party number two stole it from him or one of his thieves took it for himself."

"Thomas was undercover," Nathan said.

"Why do you say that?" Kendall asked.

"I talked to him after he was stabbed."

Kendall's mouth dropped open. "*After* he was stabbed!" she said, her eyes sparking. "Why didn't you tell us?"

"I didn't think it was important for you to know then."

Jake shook his head. "After I told you I recognized him from Iraq, you still didn't think I needed to know?"

"I was trying to sort some things out."

"It might have helped if you'd let us sort it out with you," Jake said.

"This is getting us nowhere," Kendall said. "What happened with Thomas?"

"The morning I stopped by the inn—"

"Thanks to the tracking device," Jake reminded him.

Nathan scowled and continued. "I saw someone watching the inn. Thomas came around the side. I didn't know who he was then, but when the other guy started following him I was suspicious, so I followed him as well. I found Thomas in the graveyard. He'd just been attacked. He was dying, half-conscious, and mumbling about stopping someone, saying that *he* couldn't get it and that *they* were in danger. I figured it was you two."

"And you didn't think we needed to know?" Jake clenched his fists. He wanted to punch Nathan. If Kendall hadn't been there, he probably would have.

Kendall shook her head in disgust.

"What was the point?" Nathan said. "You were supposed to be on your way home and out of this mess."

Jake glared at Nathan. "If the Reaper is who you say, I doubt we would've been any safer in Virginia."

"I can protect you in Virginia. I can't when you're running around God knows where. That's why I had my guards grab you when you didn't leave. You two are in danger."

"Everybody calm down," Kendall said. "We have to stick together until this is over. There are at least two people, maybe entire groups, who want us dead. If Thomas warned you that we were in trouble, and if 'it' referred to the box, then it sounds as if he was on our side. He was probably warning us off with that note at the hotel."

"He knew he was dying," Nathan said. "Maybe he had a change of heart. He gave me the cross. I guess the chain broke. We're still trying to find out who Thomas really is, but we keep hitting dead ends."

"Did he say anything else?" Jake asked.

"He said one more thing: 'Tell her I love her and that I'm sorry.'"

Jake looked at Kendall. "Who? Kendall?"

"He died before he could say anything else. That's why I wanted you to go home. There's too much we don't know. Finding the box isn't worth it." Nathan looked kind of sick when he said it, Jake thought.

"And you think you can handle it alone?" Kendall asked.

Had she already forgotten the coffin lid splintered into kindling and heavy iron doors being ripped from their hinges? Still, adrenaline—assuming that's what it was—would go only so far.

"I'll bring more men if I need them," Nathan said.

Kendall frowned. "I thought you said Jake was the best."

"I don't want him here."

"Why don't you want him in danger? Because he's like a brother to you?" Kendall asked, echoing what Fergus had said. "You sure as heck fight like brothers."

Brothers, right. But he couldn't help glancing at Nathan to see what his reaction was.

Nathan scowled. "I just have other things I need him to do."

"Sure," Kendall said dryly.

"I'm not leaving," Jake said. "You can do what you like with her, but good luck. She's as hard to get rid of as a tick."

"I'm staying. According to him," Kendall said glancing at the dead man, "whoever has the box still needs the key. We have to keep him from getting it."

"Marco mentioned a key as well," Nathan said. "He said it was for the box. Maybe it is with the monk."

"Marco's a strange bird," Jake said.

"He seems confused at times," Nathan agreed. "But if everyone's talking about a key, we'd better find it before they do. Someone already has the bloody box."

"Another thing to find," Jake muttered.

"If the box does contain the spear, it might be best if the key is lost," Kendall said.

Nathan shook his head. "It needs to be in a safe place."

"I think Kendall's right," Jake said.

"We find it," Nathan ordered, back to his old self.

"We can check the monk's coffin," Kendall said.

"First you might want to return this corpse's finger." Jake pointed to the bone stuck in her belt.

Any other girl would have screamed. He would have if he'd been a girl. Kendall just looked startled, and then restored the bone to its owner. They walked to the spot where the old monk lay. When they stepped over the fallen stone that had just missed crushing them Jake saw Nathan's lips thin. The old monk looked the same as when they'd found him, except his hands had been dislodged by the thieves.

Jake shifted his weight, wishing they could get out of here. "Why don't you ask him where the key is?" He turned to Nathan. "Did you know she talks to ghosts?"

"I'm not surprised."

"It doesn't work that way," Kendall said.

He still hadn't figured out how the hell it did work. She didn't seem to know either.

Kendall stepped closer and studied the skeleton. She was quiet, and Jake wondered what she was sensing. He'd seen enough to know she wasn't a fraud. She gently put the monk's hands back in place. "We have to stop whoever has the box from opening it."

Jake looked at the skeleton and swallowed. "Let me check for traps before we start digging around."

"I don't think there are any more," Kendall said. "I don't sense any danger. Not with the coffin. But if we don't stop this man—or woman—there's going to be trouble."

"I'll help you look," Jake said, grimacing at the bones.

Kendall met his gaze. "I'll do it."

"Thanks," he said gruffly.

Nathan didn't appear to have any qualms about bones. He moved beside Kendall and the two of them searched the coffin. There was no key.

"Maybe we already have the key. If the cross opens the door to the catacombs and gives safe passage through the statues, maybe it opens the box."

"Makes sense," Jake said.

"The only way we'll know is by finding the box," Nathan said. "You found it once. Think you can find it again?"

"I can try. It would be better if I had something connected to the box."

Jake looked at the grinning skull. "You could borrow a bone. What's more connected than the dead guy who was guarding it? His ghost seems to like you."

"I'm not sure this monk is the ghost I saw. But it can't hurt." She reached into the coffin and picked up a piece of rotted robe. "Let's go to the tower where we stayed. That's where I saw the ghost. I think he's attached to the room. He might lead us to the key. He led me to the box."

They decided to take the small tunnel that led to the castle in case there were more men waiting outside. Jake went first, leading the way through the narrow passage. He stepped from the column into the entryway. It was quiet, but something didn't feel right. He glanced through one of the tall windows and saw the statues outside and the bodies lying nearby. He could tell from their unnatural positions that the men were dead. He motioned toward the window. "Careful, we're not alone. Someone killed the men I knocked out."

They found two more dead men near the steps with their throats slit.

Kendall made a small sound of dismay, but she followed Jake past the bodies, upstairs to the tower bedroom. She entered first, followed by Nathan. Jake stayed at the door keeping watch.

Nathan stared at the bed, which was still rumpled. "You both slept here?"

"Yeah." Jake's satisfaction was ruined by the expression on Nathan's face as he studied the rest of the room. He looked like he was the one who'd seen a ghost.

"This is where Raphael put us," Kendall said. She looked at the bed and awkwardly sat down, immediately jumping up as if she'd been scalded. She cleared her throat and walked to the desk where she'd found the hidden letter. She sat stiffly in the chair, folded her hands on her lap while Jake and Nathan watched her. A second later she jumped up again. "This isn't working."

"Can you try someplace else?" Jake asked. He wanted Kendall out of here.

"The bathroom,"

Nathan frowned. "You think the ghost is in the bathroom?"

"No, I have to use the bathroom."

"Now?" Jake asked. "Hurry. We could have company any minute. If you hear us yell out, hide."

It was damned awkward waiting for Kendall to emerge. Jake kept watch on the hallway, occasionally glancing at the garderobe door, willing her to come out, while Nathan examined the room with that same intense look on his face that Kendall got when she was trying to decipher secrets.

Nathan looked at the bed again, his eyes narrowed.

"No," Jake said.

Nathan gave him a hard stare. "I didn't ask."

"Yes, you did."

"I hired you to protect her, not sleep with her."

"One doesn't exclude the other." Not exactly true. Sleeping with someone you were trying to protect was one of the worst things a guard could do, but the look on Nathan's face was worth the lie.

"Leave her alone," Nathan warned.

"It's not your call." Jake looked at the door. "What the hell can she be doing in a garderobe?"

"There's a garderobe?" Nathan asked, his expression haunted again.

The door opened and Kendall appeared. "The secret passage," she announced. "That's where the ghost led me. Maybe I can find him there." She looked at the bed as she passed, and Jake wondered if she was thinking about the bloody childbirth she'd sensed or her time there with him.

She walked up to the wall beside the desk and pushed something on one of the stones. A door in the wall swung open.

So this was how she'd escaped. "Not very inviting," Jake said, stepping inside. He supposed it depended on your idea of fun. Nathan and Kendall both had a rapt look on their faces that Jake equated with good sex.

"I bet this entire place is riddled with secret passages," she said.

"Don't suppose you saw any of them when you were a kid?" Jake asked.

Nathan looked like he'd swallowed a fly. "What?"

"I was here when I was a girl." Kendall slanted her head. "You didn't know?"

"How could I have known?"

"You have to admit it's a strange coincidence," Jake said. "You have her searching for a relic in a place she once visited as a child."

Nathan frowned. "When were you here?"

"I was young. I didn't remember any of this until Marco told me. I thought I recognized things, but I believed it must be a vision."

"How the bloody hell do you know Marco?"

"I talked to him at the hotel."

"How did you talk to him while you were—"

"Prisoners?" Jake supplied, following Nathan down the stone steps.

Nathan's jaw tightened. "How did you see Marco?"

Kendall ran her hand across the wall, head tilted as if listening. "He slipped into my room."

"Cell," Jake said.

"Sometimes I wish I'd never met you," Nathan said to Jake.

"You're not the only one."

"You two bicker worse than brothers." Kendall shook her head. "Marco remembered seeing me at the castle with my father. My father must have been here looking for relics. Apparently, Adam and I sneaked in someplace we weren't allowed, some sacred place, and Adam took a vow. I can't remember much about it."

Nathan stared at Kendall. "Adam?"

"He was a friend who died when I was young. Our fathers worked together."

"Adam was with you?" Nathan asked.

Kendall nodded. "He died not long after we left. Marco said breaking into the sacred place and taking the vow could be deadly. I wonder if that's what killed them."

"What kind of vow?"

"Marco didn't really say. Fergus came and made him leave. This vow must have been a big deal though. Marco said the order wasn't sure what to do about it. He was afraid of what would happen, so he helped my father sneak us out of the castle that night."

"You were close to Adam?" Nathan's voice sounded hollow in the passageway.

"He was my best friend."

Jake still didn't like the feeling he got when Kendall spoke of Adam. And it didn't make him feel any better knowing that he resented a dead boy.

"There's a door," Kendall said. "I didn't notice it the first time I came this way. This must open onto the third floor."

Nathan moved to her side. "Let me go first."

She stood back willingly, and didn't argue as she would have with Jake. That left a bad taste in his mouth.

Nathan turned the knob and opened the door. Kendall stood so close, trying to peer around him, she practically had her head under his arm.

Nathan looked inside and cursed.

Kendall ducked around him. "Oh my!" They both disappeared through the door.

Jake followed them, feeling like a third wheel until he saw what they had seen. "Damn. I think we found King Arthur's Round Table." The room was large and filled with antiques and artifacts that looked like they belonged in a medieval castle. A huge round table sat in the middle of the room, with thirteen ornate chairs. There were suits of armor and weapons: spears, swords, daggers, and guns. Shelves held books and ornaments and trophies that looked valuable, even to his uneducated eye. The Spear of Destiny would fit right in here. This area looked different from the rest of the castle. It felt like there was more life here.

Nathan and Kendall were moving around the room, eyes wide. They stopped at a large mural on the wall that showed a bunch of people in water. He couldn't tell if it was a baptism or a drowning.

He saw a glass-covered table that held a piece of paper rolled like a poster. A scroll? He lifted the top and set it aside. Carefully, he picked up the paper and began to unroll it.

"Don't touch it," Kendall yelped from across the room.

Jake quickly rolled it back up, and Kendall hurried toward him as if he were holding a baby over open flames. She took it from him with two fingers. "It's a scroll," she breathed. "Nathan, look."

Nathan came over and the two of them stared in awe.

"Should we open it?" Nathan asked.

Jake had already opened it.

"I don't know," Kendall said, still holding it between two fingers. "I want to see what's on it, but maybe we should take it back." Her voice was quick with excitement. She was obviously torn between curiosity and concern.

"It has pictures on it," Jake said.

Kendall and Nathan looked at him as if he were a gorilla in a playpen. "What kind of pictures?"

"Statues, swords, jewelry. A spear."

They both stilled. "A spear." Kendall licked her lips and looked at Nathan, who was scrubbing his hand through his hair.

"What do you think?" he asked.

"I'm afraid to expose it to the air," Kendall said, as if someone had suggested that she wave it around like a flag. "We don't have gloves or the right equipment."

"What did the spear look like?" Nathan asked.

"Sharp and pointy." They both gaped at him, and he couldn't help grin. "It was metal, with bands wound around the tip. That's all I saw before it was yanked out of my hands."

"I didn't yank it out of your hands. I'm not that careless." She sighed and put it back on the table before replacing the glass.

"Someone's coming," Jake said. He hurried to the door, which was still open, and looked out. No one. He motioned for Nathan and Kendall to stay out of sight, and then he closed the door leaving just a crack. The voices were male. They were arguing. And they seemed to be coming from the wall.

They all glanced around the room, trying to identify the source. "I think it's coming from the mural," Kendall said as the voices grew louder.

Jake told Kendall and Nathan to get behind him. Neither of them did. He leveled his gun at the mural, and the wall slid open. Fergus and Marco stepped out.

"Bloody hell," Nathan said.

"I told you it was here," Marco said.

Fergus looked like he'd been dragged through a bush backward. His suit jacket was torn, hair disheveled, and his face had some dark substance on it that Jake hoped was motor oil.

"What are you doing here?" Nathan asked.

Fergus straightened his shoulders and brushed off the lapels of his ruined jacket. "We came to help."

"Bloody hell," Nathan said again.

"We came to make sure you didn't die," Marco said.

"We were worried," Fergus said. "I know how you abhor weapons. We were afraid you weren't prepared." He opened his jacket and pulled out a gun, waving it around the room in a way that indicated his unfamiliarity with weapons.

"How did you get here so fast?" Jake asked, shifting to stay clear of the barrel.

"We drove," Fergus said, putting the gun away. "There's a road to the castle."

"A road?" Kendall said.

"That would have been nice to know," Jake said.

"I brought Marco since he knows all the secret entrances."

"Most of them," Marco said.

"Did you bring guards?" Nathan asked.

"No. They were…occupied."

"Occupied?" Nathan asked, frowning.

"There was an incident at the hotel," Fergus said.

"An explosion," Marco said.

Nathan's eyebrows rose. "Explosion?"

"It appears to have been a bomb," Fergus said. "It was set in the parking garage near the entrance to your personal rooms. The hotel management and security guards are taking care of things there."

"Was anyone hurt?" Nathan asked.

"No," Fergus said. "Marco warned us before it happened. Everyone had already been evacuated."

"How did you know there would be an explosion?" Nathan asked, his eyes narrowed with suspicion.

Jake didn't blame him. A little too much coincidence if you asked him.

"I know things," Marco said with a gentle smile. "Kendall is ill."

Jake turned. Kendall was leaning against a shelf, her face colorless. He and Nathan rushed to her side.

"We have to hurry," she said. "He's here."

"Who?" Jake asked.

"The man who stole the box."

"Do you know who he is?" Nathan asked.

She shook her head. "But he's going to the chapel," Kendall said. "Holy ground."

"How can he open the box without the key?" Jake asked.

"Keys?" Marco said. "It takes three crosses to open the box."

So the cross was the key. Kendall was right. Again.

"I know a shortcut," Marco said. "Follow me."

They did. Into the mural. Jake had to duck to get inside, and he heard a thump and muttered curses from Nathan as he entered the narrow passage.

"Why must it be opened on holy ground?" Fergus asked, his voice muffled in the tight space.

Marco shuffled ahead of them, looking uncertain about his choice of route. "It wouldn't be pleasant otherwise. The spear doesn't like to be disturbed."

The passageway came to a fork and Marco stopped. "This way. I think. Or was it…" He scratched his beard. "No, this way." He took off without looking to see whether they followed, muttering to himself all the while. They descended one more set of steps. Marco walked up to a wall, pushed something, and a door opened to a garage large enough for a fleet of cars.

"The castle has a garage," Kendall said. "And we had to use a garderobe?"

Jake's eyes caught on a sleek black car.

"Bloody hell, is that my new Lamborghini?" Nathan asked

"We needed to get here fast," Fergus said.

"That's the new model," Jake said. "It hasn't even been released." He'd give a month's pay to drive it. He looked at the other cars. Did they belong to Raphael?

"I believe we have a problem," Fergus said. "There weren't as many cars here when we arrived."

"We must hurry," Marco said. He took them to another door that led outside. They had stepped out of the side of the mountain.

"Is that an airstrip?" Jake asked.

"Yes," Marco said. "I'm afraid it's overgrown. It hasn't been used in years. The chapel is just over there."

Damn. What else didn't they know about this place? Jake was about to suggest that Nathan take Kendall and the others away from here and leave him to find the thief. He could move faster and quieter if he was alone. This troop wasn't sneaking up on anyone. Before he could speak, he heard a voice he shouldn't have been surprised to hear.

"Don't move." Brandi stepped out from behind a tree holding a gun. It was pointed at Kendall and the redhead looked like she knew how to use it.

"I suppose one of those cars is yours," Jake muttered.

"Give me the key," Brandi said.

"What key?"

"The one around Kendall's neck. Toss it to me," she said to Kendall.

Kendall didn't move. "What are you doing, Brandi?"

"Something that has to be done."

"Threatening us with a gun?" Fergus said, haughtily.

"I'm sorry. There's no other way."

Jake caught Nathan's eye and mouthed, "Protect Kendall."

Nathan gave a curt nod and Jake waited for an opening to rush Brandi. It came faster than he expected.

"I'm sorry your brother died," Kendall said.

Brandi's jaw dropped and the hand holding the gun slackened.

Jake ignored his own surprise and threw himself at Brandi. From the corner of his eye, he saw Nathan shoving Kendall clear of the gun. Brandi dropped the weapon as she fell. Jake straddled her and grabbed her hands.

After a minute she stopped struggling, but her eyes were desperate. "Please. Give me the key. I have to stop him."

Jake kept her pinned. "Stop who?"

A look of fear crossed Brandi's face. "The Reaper. I can't let him have the spear."

"Doesn't he already have it?" Nathan asked, picking up the gun Brandi had dropped.

"I don't know who has it. Thomas left it with me for safekeeping until we could figure out how to destroy it, but someone took it from my room. It must have been the Reaper. He was there at the inn."

"The man with the ring," Kendall said.

"That ring belonged to my father," Brandi said fiercely.

"You're the daughter of the antiquities dealer who died all those years ago," Nathan said. "I was supposed to buy his collection before it was stolen."

"The Reaper didn't just steal the collection. He destroyed our family. Thomas has been trying to find him ever since. Now he's dead and I'm the only one left. That's why I need the key. Without it, the Reaper can't open the box."

"Why does the Reaper want the spear?" Nathan asked.

"Power. He's collecting relics he believes will make him invincible. I don't know what he has planned, but he destroys and corrupts anything he touches. We tried to keep you from getting involved, but it was too late. Now you're tangled up in his web."

"That must be why Thomas wrote the warning note," Kendall said.

"He was trying to keep you safe."

"Did you put something in our water?" Kendall asked.

"A sedative. We hoped you would sleep long enough for Thomas to find the box and destroy it."

"Thomas was your brother's real name?" Jake asked.

Brandi nodded. "He always used his first name. He was named after our dad."

"What was Thomas doing in Iraq?" Jake asked.

"Searching for information."

On the Reaper? "Why did he shoot me?"

"He didn't. He's the one who kept you alive. Please," Brandi pleaded. "Give me the keys and I promise I'll tell you everything about Iraq. I'll tell you about the girls."

"The girls." Before Jake could ask her more questions, a swarm of men rushed at them from the trees. Jake leapt to his feet, freeing Brandi, who jumped up and ducked into the forest.

These men were better trained than the four that had jumped them earlier at the statues. Jake had just killed one man when a roar sounded behind him. He looked back and saw Nathan throw a man against a tree. When he turned, Jake was certain Nathan's eyes were glowing. A shiver went down his spine, but he kept fighting.

Kendall watched Jake launch himself at one of the men, kicking him in the knee. Next he punched him square in the jaw, dropping him in his tracks. Without stopping, he turned to the next one. Kendall was impressed but not surprised. She knew Jake was nothing to mess with. Nathan, on the other hand, was a revelation. He not only knew history and relics, he also knew how to fight. He was throwing men around like he was the Hulk. He must have had the same training as his guards. But could any of them rip iron doors off their hinges?

Behind her, Fergus was trying to protect Marco. Surprisingly, Marco was holding his own against his opponents. Maybe he had the advantage because they were shocked at the strength of the old man.

She heard another man call out "Get the girl," and a big brute rushed Kendall. Taking inspiration from Nathan and Jake, she went for his knee. Her kick didn't have the same impact, but he went down. He cursed and pulled out a gun. She saw it happen in slow motion. She lunged sideways at the same moment that Marco threw himself in front of her. His body jerked as the bullet entered his chest.

"Marco!"

"I didn't mean for you to shoot her," one of the men yelled. "He wants her alive."

Fergus was several feet away. He pulled out his big gun and, holding it in both hands, fired at Marco's assailant. The man's eyes widened as he fell.

Kendall dropped down beside Marco. A dark stain spread across his robe. "Marco, can you hear me?"

He smiled at her, his look serene amid all the shouting and fighting. "It's fine."

"You've been shot. We'll get help."

"It's fine. Everything will be fine. Adam is here."

Adam? Kendall swallowed. Did Marco really see Adam? "Can you speak to Adam?" It was selfish to consider herself when Marco was dying, but she wanted to tell Adam she was sorry.

"I'd have to yell," Marco said. "I don't think I have the strength."

Yell? "But you can see him?"

Marco nodded. "He's over there." He looked over Kendall's shoulder. She turned, expecting to see Adam's dancing eyes, sun-bleached hair, and crazy grin. Instead, she saw Nathan and Jake running toward them.

She turned back to Marco, but his eyes were closed, his face slack. She started to check for a pulse, but she heard a cry behind her. Another man was running toward her. What did they want with her? Nathan put on a burst of speed, reaching the man and taking him down with a swift blow. "Get Kendall out of here," he yelled to Jake. "I'll get rid of them."

Jake hesitated, and then grabbed her arm. "Come on. We have to go."

"We can't leave them," she said, looking back at Nathan and Fergus still fighting, and Marco, lying helpless on the ground. Was he dead?

"Boss's orders."

"When has that ever stopped you?"

"Shut up and run," he said, pulling her toward the woods.

"Where are we going?"

"The chapel."

"I didn't know you were religious," she said, running beside him. She was grateful she'd grown up a tomboy.

"I might be after this."

"You think the chapel can protect us?"

"I don't care if it's a chapel or an outhouse. It has walls I can hide behind while I pick off the enemy."

There was a roar like the one she'd heard in the catacombs before Nathan pulled her from the coffin. "What was that?" Kendall asked, trying to look back, but Jake pulled her faster.

"Hurry. Nathan will take care of them."

They reached the chapel but it was locked. Jake hit it with his shoulder but the door didn't budge. Kicking it didn't work either. "It's as strong as the door to the catacombs."

The idea hit them both at once. Jake aimed his light at the door. "There's a hole. I think it's a lock." He pulled Raphael's cross from his pocket and slipped it in the hole. There was a click. "It's open," Jake said. He put the cross back in his pocket and they opened the door.

"Far enough," a voice said behind them.

Jake and Kendall both turned and he started to step in front of her.

"Don't move."

Jake froze, staring at the man. It was too dark for Kendall to see the man's face, but she could see the red dot dancing on Jake's chest.

"How about we do this another way." The red dot left Jake and appeared over Kendall's heart. "Drop the gun if you want your girlfriend to live."

Growling beneath his breath, Jake slowly placed his gun on the ground.

The man eased forward from the shadows and moonlight fell on his face.

Edward.

CHAPTER SEVENTEEN

S TEP AWAY FROM HER," EDWARD TOLD JAKE.

"Do it," Kendall whispered when Jake hesitated. He slid a few feet to the left.

"This is an opportune moment. Here I was trying to figure out how to get inside and you two show up with the key. Now turn around and walk into the chapel," Edward said. "One wrong move and she's dead."

Jake glanced at Kendall, his eyes dark. He turned and walked into the chapel.

"Your turn." Edward nodded at Kendall. When she had stepped inside, Edward ordered Jake against the wall and pressed his gun to Kendall's head. "Since both of you are alive, I assume my men are dead."

"Not all of them...yet," Jake said.

Kendall could still hear shouts in the distance.

"Those aren't mine. I sent four in earlier. No matter. You saved me the trouble. I would have killed them anyway."

"Are you the Reaper?" Kendall asked.

Edward threw back his head and laughed. His eyes were blue now, not the muddy brown they had been when they'd first met. "No. I wish I had his money and power. But I have something the Reaper can't touch."

"So this whole thing was a setup?" Jake said.

"I needed to find the spear but didn't know precisely where to look. My ancestor saw things when he worked here. He knew the men weren't just monks. They were hiding treasure, but he didn't know where. The secret was passed down to his son and eventually to my grandfather, but everyone was too afraid to try to find the treasure, until me. And now it's my secret and my treasure."

"Is this the grandfather you murdered?" Jake asked.

"Murdered—that's an ugly word. Not entirely appropriate. Sometimes the end justifies the means. Isn't that right, Jake?"

Something dark crossed Jake's face. Kendall was certain that one of the men wouldn't leave this chapel alive. She would do whatever she could to see that it was Edward. "You set his house on fire and killed him. That's murder, pure and simple."

"Nothing's ever pure or simple. It's always clouded with gray. It was unfortunate, I agree, but they had to be eliminated. I couldn't leave loose threads."

"But they were your family," Kendall said. She felt Edward's coldness and greed through the barrel pressed against her head. If he hadn't disguised his eyes with those brown contacts perhaps she would have picked up something from him before. As she spoke, Jake slid forward so smoothly it was barely noticeable.

Edward patted a canvas bag he carried over his shoulder. "This is my family." He smiled. "*My* destiny."

"You were the one who broke into Brandi's room and stole the box. What will you do with it?"

"Sell it to the highest bidder. There are many who would pay any price for such a relic and not care how it was obtained."

"Like the Reaper?" Kendall asked.

"I don't think I'll be selling this to him."

"You were supposed to find it for him," Kendall said.

Edward moved back so the gun wasn't touching her, but it was still inches from her temple. "You are good, aren't you? I was skeptical when I first heard about your powers. I took the precaution of wearing contacts when we met, but I must admit I'm impressed."

"How did you know about my *powers*?"

"The Reaper takes a great interest in Nathan Larraby and the things that interest Nathan Larraby. An unhealthy fixation if you ask me."

"Why is he interested in Nathan?" Kendall asked.

"That would be a question for him, not me. I was merely a guide."

"Does the Reaper know you've betrayed him?"

"I expect he does by now, which means we need to hurry. If I could open the box without you, believe me, I would."

"You could break it open," Jake said.

"And risk damaging the spear?" Edward shook his head. "I don't think so. And I've heard very frightening stories about what could happen if the box isn't opened properly. That's why I came to the chapel. Part of the reason. I don't believe the spear was the only thing the Protettori were protecting. My ancestor said there were many treasures. He believed some were hidden in this very chapel. And what luck that Kendall met me here, the one person on earth who can sniff them out. I couldn't have planned it better."

More treasures? Here? "What if the spear isn't real?" Kendall asked, continuing to stall. "A lot of people think they have the real Spear of Destiny."

"Why would the Protettori protect it if it wasn't real?" But Edward's voice wasn't as confident now. "It's real, isn't it? You touched it."

"I didn't get to touch it. It was stolen before I could. Would you like me to check it now?"

She felt him wavering, weighing the value of letting her tell him for certain if it was real against the danger of letting her that close. Then Edward shrugged. "It doesn't matter if it's real, as long as someone thinks it is."

Jake was closer now, but still too far away to take out Edward or the gun. "Do you know the Reaper's real name?" Kendall asked.

"No one does. Enough talking. Where is the key?"

Jake shook his head slightly, indicating that she shouldn't tell him.

"We don't have it," Kendall said.

Edward moved quickly. He gripped her hair, yanked her head back, and shoved the gun against her temple again.

Jake had gone completely still, and she was afraid he would do something risky. "Nathan has it," he said.

Edward glanced at the door. "Then we go see Nathan."

"What about the other two keys?" Kendall asked.

Edward frowned. "What other keys?"

"It takes three to unlock the box."

She felt Edward's confidence slip again and saw Jake assessing the situation. He would know as well as she did that he couldn't get to Kendall in time to keep Edward from firing. They needed a distraction.

It roared into the room, splintering the door off its hinges. Nathan glowered at Edward, his body taut, eyes glowing. Edward was shaken, but he had the gun pointed at Kendall's head. No matter how fast the two men were, a bullet was faster.

"Either of you move a toe and I swear I'll kill her."

Nathan growled and a shiver ran up Kendall's spine. Edward shivered too. Kendall felt it, even if he didn't show it. "Give me the keys, all of them, or I'll splatter her brains all over this chapel."

Both men stood as still as the statues outside, eyes locked on Edward.

"Stop," she said. "My cross is around my neck. Jake, give him yours." Once he had the keys, he would be distracted. They might be able to take him.

Keeping the gun close to her head, Edward removed her cross. Jake pulled Raphael's from his pocket and slid it across the floor.

"Where's the third one?" Edward asked.

"I have it," Nathan said. "Marco gave it to me." He took it out of his pocket and slid it across the floor next to Jake's.

"Pick them up," Edward told Kendall.

She bent and picked up the two crosses. Edward took them from her and eased away, keeping the gun pointed at her. "Now you two, into the corner, and don't try to stop me. I don't want to kill her since she's my treasure map. But I will."

Nathan and Jake moved to the corner of the chapel. Kendall could feel their tension from across the room.

Edward put the canvas bag down. Opening it with one hand, he removed the box. Kendall leaned closer, trying to see. It looked like the one she and Jake had found; the one in Nathan's sketch. But what the sketch hadn't shown were three locks on top, hidden in three of the four circles that were etched into the corners.

Edward checked their positions and then he inserted one key. There was a click. He inserted another and there was another click. "Don't do anything stupid," he warned them again.

Kendall could have told him he was the one doing something stupid. That box shouldn't be opened.

He put the third key in. There was another click and the four circles on the box began to move. Edward's focus wavered and Kendall lunged. She grabbed for the box, and at the same time Nathan and Jake rushed to help. There was a scramble, bodies rolling on the floor, and the red dot bounced around the chapel like a laser beam. Edward grabbed the box to his chest, and then his eyes widened. A look of terror crossed his face. Kendall's hair stood on end and she couldn't help but turn. Jake and Nathan had done the same.

The ghost monk stood there, his face covered by the cowl, the chapel wall visible through him. Edward gasped, and the ghost moved toward them.

Kendall jumped up. "Get out of the way," she yelled at Nathan and Jake. They were all standing between Edward and the ghost. All three of them hurried toward the door, watching as the monk moved closer to Edward, who was cowering on the floor. He threw the box toward Kendall, probably hoping the ghost would follow. He didn't. He continued toward Edward and didn't stop, passing all the way through him. Edward gave a terrified scream and fell.

The monk turned and looked at the box lying open on the floor at Kendall's feet. The tip of a spear could be seen wrapped in a white cloth. Perhaps it was a dagger or a sword, but after what she'd witnessed, she believed it was the real spear that the Roman centurion had used to pierce Christ's side.

The monk started toward them. Nathan and Jake each moved in front of Kendall. She stepped around them and bent to pick up the box.

"What are you doing?" Jake hissed.

"Don't move," she said. She slid the spearhead back inside the box, covering it with the cloth and turned each key. Three clicks and the lid closed. She started walking toward the monk.

Jake and Nathan came after her, but the monk raised his hands and both men were thrown backward and pinned against the wall. They struggled, but they couldn't break free.

"Stop," Nathan yelled as Kendall kept walking. "Don't hurt her. Take me."

"Dammit. Come back here," Jake yelled, struggling.

The monk watched as she approached. His face was still shadowed, but she could see his eyes. Green, she thought, and wise, reminding her of her father's. The man this ghost had once been had suffered betrayal and heartbreak. Kendall stretched out her arms, offering him the spear. He continued to watch her until her arms started to hurt from the weight of the box. Then he held out his hands and she felt a rush of air as they brushed over hers. For one second, flesh and apparition were joined as they held the box. He nodded once and disappeared.

She stood for a second, shocked, the box still in her arms. She turned and saw Jake and Nathan fall free from the wall. Both men rushed to her side.

"Believe me now?" she said to Jake, and then she collapsed.

CHAPTER EIGHTEEN

A RUMBLING NOISE WOKE HER AND SHE OPENED HER EYES TO two anxious faces hovering over her, wearing matching frowns. "She's coming out of it," Jake said.

Nathan nudged him. "Move back so she can breathe."

"You're the one suffocating her," Jake said.

The past minutes—hours?—came rushing back. The box? Edward? The ghost?

Jake and Nathan moved back as she sat up, and she saw that she was lying on the altar. "Oh my God." She jumped up and moved quickly away.

"What's wrong?" Jake asked.

"The altar..." She looked at the three stones and the words engraved there. She remembered a hushed voice repeating strange words as light exploded from the stones, enveloping her and Adam. "Where's Edward?"

"Dead," Jake said.

"What about the box?"

"It's safe," Nathan said, pointing to Kendall's backpack nearby.

"What are you going to do with it?"

"Keep it safe," he said, not meeting her eyes.

"Where? Not with the rest of your collection, I hope."

"No. I'll put it somewhere no one will find it."

Jake glanced at Edward's body. "So, according to your vision, Nathan and I would have died at the hands of a ghost if you hadn't been here."

"I think the ghost would have killed you inadvertently to get to Edward. Killed all of us if we hadn't moved. All he was worried about was protecting the box."

"Is that why you thought you needed to be here?" Jake asked. "To warn us to move out of the way? Hell, you could've done that from Virginia."

"If she hadn't been here, I think he would have killed anyone who happened to be in the chapel," Nathan said.

"Maybe he knew she wanted to protect the spear," Jake said.

Nathan shook his head. "It's almost as if he recognized her."

"I think he did," Kendall said. "And the strange thing is that I felt like I knew him too." That sometimes happened with her visions.

"Our ghost could have seen you here when you were a kid," Jake said. "It's not like there were many females around."

"He saw me in the tower room where the woman gave birth. I think he loved her. Maybe I reminded him of her. At least now you believe I saw the ghost," she said to Jake.

"I've seen a lot of unbelievable things tonight," Jake said, giving Nathan a pointed look. "Not just ghosts."

"That was just adrenaline," Nathan said.

"Adrenaline doesn't make a person's eyes glow."

"Must have been your imagination or a reflection from your flashlight," Nathan said.

"Flashlight, my ass. You sure you don't have a secret lab where you're creating a drug that gives super powers?"

Nathan didn't answer. Clearly he either didn't know what was happening or wasn't ready to share his secrets. Kendall didn't buy his explanation any more than Jake did, but she had an open mind, and after the things she'd seen at this castle, it was even more open.

"How long was I out?" Kendall asked. "Has anyone checked on Marco?"

"You weren't out long. Fifteen minutes. The helicopter just took them."

That was the rumbling she'd heard. "Is he alive?"

"For now," Nathan said. "He doesn't look good. Fergus is with him."

"He took that bullet to save me. Did he say anything before he left?" She wanted to ask if he'd mentioned seeing ghosts. Particularly one named Adam.

"He was unconscious," Nathan said.

"What about Brandi? Where did she go?"

"Disappeared," Nathan said, looking at the stones behind the altar again.

"I don't think we've seen the last of her," Jake said.

Kendall suspected that he hoped for another encounter so he could find out more about Thomas's connection with his assignment in Iraq.

"She has her brother's death to avenge," Jake continued. "And I'm sure she blames the Reaper. If she wants him, she'll have to get in line."

"You're not to go after him," Nathan said. "He's too dangerous. I'll handle it."

Jake's eyes narrowed. Time to change the subject, Kendall thought. "What are we going to do with Edward's body? We can't leave it here."

The body was still on the floor, but its face had been covered by a cloth that looked remarkably like a scarf Kendall had in her bag. She hoped it was still in her bag.

"I'll have the body removed," Nathan said. He walked toward the stones.

"What are you doing?" It made her cringe to see him so close to the altar. She wasn't really superstitious, but those stones elicited sensations that she couldn't explain.

"There's something strange about these stones," Nathan said.

He was right about that, Kendall thought. She couldn't remember exactly what happened to her and Adam all those years ago, but it had something to do with this altar.

"Strange to see stones this big inside a chapel. They look like the ones near the catacombs. Except there are symbols on these."

"Writing," Kendall said, earning a surprised look from the men.

"You know what they say?" Jake asked.

Kendall touched her head, which was beginning to ache. "No."

"The stone in the middle looks different than the other two," Nathan said. "Looks like there's a disk embedded inside."

Jake added the beam from his light to Nathan's. "I think you're right. Another circle. I think they're obsessed with them."

Kendall grabbed a flashlight and joined them, trying to ignore the way her stomach flipped when she neared the stones. "It does look like a disk." With all the writing covering it, she hadn't noticed until she was up close.

"The symbols are in rows," Nathan said. "Like rings."

"None of them make sense," Jake said. "Except this one." He pointed to one of the small inner rings in the middle of the disk. "It looks like a C. It's cut deeper than the other symbols."

"There's one here as well." Nathan rubbed his finger over a symbol on the opposite side of the ring. "But the C is backward."

"It almost makes a circle," Kendall said. "Wait a minute. This center of the disk has a curved line on the top and the bottom. If we could turn the rings and line the symbols up, it would make a circle."

"And that's why she's my relic expert," Nathan said. He pressed his forefinger and thumb against the ring and attempted to turn it. "It's moving."

They aligned the rings so that the two parts faced. Kendall turned the center, filling in the rest of the circle.

"But what does it do?" Nathan asked.

"The other circles opened something," Kendall said. "Maybe this is where the four relics are hidden."

"Four relics?" Nathan asked.

Kendall studied the circle. "Marco said the Protettori protected four relics that were so powerful they had to be separated, so they're probably not here. Maybe there's something else hidden."

"When did he say that?" Nathan asked.

"When you were holding us as prisoners," Jake said.

"Are you going to remind me of that every thirty minutes?" Nathan growled.

Jake shrugged. "I might."

"Let it go," Nathan said. "I could bring up every mistake you've made."

"You're admitting kidnapping us was a mistake?"

"Can we get back to the task at hand?" Kendall asked. "Edward's ancestor thought there was treasure hidden in the chapel. Maybe this is it."

"Hidden treasure. Works for me," Jake said. "Let's give it a push and see what happens."

"We'll draw straws in case there is a trap," Kendall said.

"I'll do it," Jake offered.

Nathan shook his head. "I will. You stay with Kendall."

"We'll all draw straws," Kendall said. "The shortest one pushes the circle." Both men were scowling but they agreed. She dug in her bag and found a small tube of mascara and two tubes of lipstick. Disguising their size, she held them out and let Nathan and Jake choose first. Nathan and Jake each chose a tube of lipstick. Kendall opened her hand and showed them her tube. It was shortest.

"Best of three," Jake said.

"No." Kendall grabbed all three items and dropped them back in her bag. "Wait by the door."

They stood mutely, staring at her.

"Go to the door," she said, louder this time.

Reluctantly they moved, but their faces were tight as they walked away.

She approached the stone and let her hands hover over the mark on the disk. She looked back at Nathan and Jake. Both men had moved a few steps closer and were staring at her, their gazes dark, though Nathan's eyes seemed to be lightening. Taking a deep breath, she pushed the circle. The ring closest to the circle turned slightly, but nothing else happened.

"I guess it doesn't work," Kendall said.

The men moved behind her and they all studied the stone in disappointment. "This wasn't here before." Jake touched a small hole, which had been exposed after the ring turned.

"It looks like the keyhole in the door to the catacombs and the chapel," Kendall said.

"There's one here too," Nathan said.

"The box needed three keys," Kendall said. "What do you want to bet this does too? Look for another keyhole."

Jake scratched at something with his knife. "Bingo."

"OK, we have three." Kendall took an excited breath. "Where's my cross? Sorry, your cross," she said to Nathan.

He pulled it out of his pocket. "Try it."

She took the cross and stuck it inside the tiny hole. "It fits. We need the others."

Nathan put Marco's cross in one of the keyholes, and Jake put Raphael's in the third keyhole.

"On three," Nathan said. "One. Two. Three." They turned the keys together and light shot out of the keyholes, like it had in the catacombs.

"Get back!" Kendall yelled, but Nathan and Jake had both already jumped clear. There was a scraping sound and the entire disk started to turn. The center stone began to slide backward, revealing a set of steps leading below the chapel.

ANITA CLENNEY

"Bloody hell," Nathan said.

"Another secret room." Kendall held her light up, trying to see where the steps led. The beam cut through the darkness, picking up flashes of gold. "Edward's ancestor was right," she whispered. "I think we've found the treasure."

"Let us go first this time," Nathan said.

"We go together." She took a step. Nathan and Jake stayed beside her, each movement from their flashlights picking up the glint of silver and gold. At the bottom of the steps, they stopped, frozen in awe. "The treasure."

"There must be a light switch in this place." Jake pointed his light at the wall then pushed something. Massive torches on each side of the room flared to life. "That's cool. A fire hazard, but cool."

"The torches must burn on gas," Nathan said.

"This is unbelievable," Kendall said, walking deeper into the room. "It's like something out of a movie." The hidden room in the castle had appeared to be more of a museum, but this was a treasure hunter's dream. Trunks and shelves of treasure. Gold and jewels and coins. Very old coins. There were statues, figures of solid gold, ancient papyruses and scrolls.

The room was larger than the chapel, which appeared to have been built as a disguise. They walked around, afraid to touch anything but unable to stop themselves. Kendall picked up a wooden box filled with pieces of gold. She found another box beside it with coins and jewels that she believed to be from a shipwreck in the thirteenth century.

"Where did they get all this stuff?" Jake held a dagger embedded with a huge ruby. He took a couple of practice swings that made Kendall's stomach clench.

"Careful with that. It looks ancient." Everything in here was probably ancient.

"What are you?" Jake asked. "Some kind of Protettori proxy?"

270

"I would hate to see anything damaged. I doubt there's ever been a find like this."

"I'm starting to wonder if they were protectors or pirates," Jake said. "We have to get this stuff out of here before someone finds it. We got rid of the men outside, but they were just pawns."

"We'll see what Nathan wants to do."

Jake put the dagger away. "Where is he?"

Kendall looked around the room and saw him standing by a table with books in glass cases. "There. He's been quiet since we came down here."

Jake looked at Nathan, and a shadow darkened his eyes. "He's probably fighting his demons."

"What do you mean?"

"He's killed a lot of men today. That's not an easy thing to have on your conscience."

And he'd killed at least one of them to save her. As if he'd known they were talking about him, Nathan looked up, meeting Kendall's gaze. She felt a tingle run over her arms.

"Did you find something?" she asked.

"Just some old books." Nathan put one of the books down. Kendall thought she saw him put something in his pocket as he walked away.

"What will we do about all this?" Kendall asked after he joined them.

"We'll have to see if Marco recovers enough to tell us more about the group," Nathan said. "We need to know if there are others."

Jake picked up a goblet that appeared to be made of gold. "The treasure can't stay here."

"It's not ours to move," Kendall said.

"Too many people know about the place now," Jake said. "Edward and his men, Thomas and Brandi. The Reaper."

"Those last men must have been working for him," Kendall said. "Edward said they weren't his."

"Who knows how many others any one of them might have told," Jake said.

"If Marco dies, we'll have to move this treasure ourselves," Nathan said. "Jake's right. It's too risky to leave it here for long." He pulled in a long, steady breath. "We don't breathe a word about this."

"I thought I'd write a book," Jake said, his voice droll.

Nathan didn't smile. "If anyone found out about all this, we'd have every treasure hunter, every lunatic and every criminal in the world descending on this place."

"I think we should swear an oath of silence," Kendall said. As soon as the words left her mouth, she felt the pain hit her skull. She closed her eyes until it eased. When she opened them, she saw Nathan and Jake staring at her.

Jake scowled. "An oath? Are you kidding?"

"No, I'm not." She stretched her hand out, palm down. "I swear I won't mention the treasure, the spear, or anything else I've seen here," she said.

"This wasn't exactly what I meant." Nathan rolled his eyes, but he put his on top of hers. "I swear," he said.

Jake shook his head and put his hand over Nathan's. "Like the damned Hardy Boys. Do you know how stupid we look? I swear I won't breathe a word." Jake yanked his hand back.

CHAPTER NINETEEN

KENDALL SANK DEEPER INTO THE DREAM. HANDS SLID DOWN her arm, moving across her stomach. A kiss brushed her shoulder and she felt the tip of a warm tongue. The hand slid lower and she heard a moan. It must have been hers. She was going to take these sleeping pills more often, she thought, and then wondered how she was conscious enough to think about sleeping pills if she was really dreaming. Her eyes flew open. The hand was still there. She scrambled up and turned.

Jake grinned at her. "Sweet dreams?"

Sweet didn't really cover it, she thought, still breathless. Another minute and she might have been too far gone to care that it wasn't a dream. "What are you doing?"

"I thought that was obvious." He was fully dressed, but he had kicked off his boots.

"How did you get in here?" She frowned. "Did you pick the lock?"

"No. The door wasn't locked."

"Why are you here? You have your own room." They were at a house in Tuscany that Nathan had rented. Or maybe he owned it. She wasn't sure. Nathan had decided the three of them should stay a couple of days before heading back to Virginia. It was designed to feel like a vacation. In reality, Nathan was debriefing them and waiting to see if Marco would recover so they could move the treasure now.

Jake rolled onto his back and rested his head on his hands. "I couldn't sleep. I've gotten used to having you in my bed."

She'd gotten used to having him in her bed too. And that wasn't good. She had feelings for him that she wasn't sure what to do with, and she suspected he felt the same, but she didn't mix dating and work.

"You need to go back to your own room," Kendall said, straightening her pajamas from the effects of his roving hands. "The sun isn't even up."

"I'm going fishing. There's a river a few miles away. I thought you might want to join me. It'll be warm by afternoon. We could go skinny-dipping. It might be chilly, but I bet we could keep warm." The look in his eyes made her want to forget the river and get naked right there.

She wrangled her hormones back under control. "Jake, we can't keep doing this, whatever it is. We work together."

He sat up, his gaze steady on her, unreadable. "Guess it'll be a lonely fishing trip, then."

"You could come to the museum with Nathan and me."

"Three's a crowd, unless it's a ménage, but I don't think this particular gender arrangement would work for me."

Kendall rolled her eyes. "This museum is giving Nathan a private showing."

"How private?"

"Stop it. You know Nathan avoids public appearances."

He frowned. "Don't you find that strange? I get sick of people sometimes. A lot of the time, but what's he hiding from?"

"He's worth a lot of money. He's good looking. I can understand why he doesn't want to deal with the attention."

Jake shook his head. "I think there's more to it. Be careful. There's something strange about him. In the last couple of days

I've seen him punch a concrete wall and toss iron doors and men around like toys. And it's not adrenaline."

Kendall felt a shiver brush her neck. "What do you think it is?"

"I don't know," Jake said. "I don't believe in vampires or werewolves. I'm hoping he's a mad scientist working on a secret potion for superhuman strength."

"I'd rather he was a vampire."

"Creatures with fangs...No thanks." He looked at her and raised an eyebrow. "Don't tell me you seriously believe in that stuff?"

"My mind is open. I've seen things I can't explain, not counting my own abilities and the odd ghost here or there."

"One ghost was enough, as far as I'm concerned. Guess I'd better go. I don't want to keep the fish waiting. If you change your mind—about anything—call me." He walked to the door and turned back to her. "How do you feel about friends with benefits?"

She picked up her pillow and threw it at him. He caught it and threw it back. With a wicked grin, he disappeared out the door.

Kendall flopped back on the bed with a sigh.

CHAPTER TWENTY

I T'S YOUR OWN FAULT FOR PISSING HIM OFF," KENDALL SAID AS they waited to go through security. It seemed every tourist in Italy had decided to leave at the same time. Behind them, a child cried nonstop, not improving Jake's lousy mood.

"And you think he's happy with you? I don't see you on that private jet."

"We both know I'm just here as babysitter," she said. Which was a pain. She hadn't flown commercial since she'd started working for Nathan. She hadn't realized until now how spoiled she had become. "I guess it can't get any worse."

It could. Both of them were pulled aside and searched. Jake's pack was given intense attention.

"I'd bet my last dollar he told airline security to do it," Jake grumbled, stuffing his arms into his jacket so hard he ripped a sleeve.

"Nathan wouldn't do that," Kendall said. But he had been pissed. She'd seen a whole new side of Nathan in the past week. "You shouldn't have driven the Lamborghini without asking."

"You two were off on a damned date. What did he care?"

"It wasn't a date and you know it. We were at the museum. I work for him, remember?"

"Looked like a date to me, the way you were dressed."

"What's wrong with the way I was dressed?"

"Nothing, if you're a call girl."

"Jackass. You're in a bad mood because you know it was wrong to go for a joyride in his favorite car."

"So I borrowed a car. It's not my fault a goat ate part of the upholstery."

They finally boarded the plane and shoved their duffel bags into the overhead compartment as the child continued to wail.

Jake settled his large frame into the cramped space. He glared at Kendall then closed his eyes.

"I told you we'd find another flight," a loud voice said.

"It's your fault we missed ours," replied a quieter, irritated voice.

"I can't help it that I got diarrhea when it was time to board."

Jake's eyes flew open. "Hell no."

"Kara! Jason! Look, Gilbert. It's our honeymooners. And our seats are right across the aisle. Can you believe our luck? What did I tell you? Things always work out for the best."

Nathan leaned against the sink in the bathroom of his private jet. He stared at himself in the mirror, watching as the amber faded from his eyes. The pain in his stomach was easing. This time it had hit him for no reason. He splashed water on his face and dried it with a monogrammed towel.

There was a tap on the door. "Are you all right?"

Nathan opened the bathroom door and walked out. Fergus watched him, frowning.

"You've had another episode, haven't you? They're coming closer together now. You must see a doctor."

"What kind of doctor, Fergus? A witch doctor? A voodoo priestess? Someone from Area Fifty-One? I don't know what the bloody hell is wrong with me."

Fergus tilted his head, making the line of his nose almost parallel with the floor. A testament to his strict upbringing. "I would start with your regular physician, sir." He poured Nathan a glass of wine.

Sir? Fergus wasn't happy. What now? "What's the latest on Marco?" Nathan asked.

"He's still in a coma." Fergus paused before handing Nathan the glass. "He saved Kendall's life, you know."

"I know." It didn't help the pain in his stomach to think what might have happened if Marco hadn't been that close. Nathan should have been there beside her. "Let me know if anything changes."

"Certainly, sir."

He gave Fergus a sharp glance as he took the glass. "What have I done to displease you now, Fergus?"

Fergus cleared his throat. "Well, if you must ask. You know I never intrude in your business—"

"Fergus, you've intruded in my business at least twice a week for the past decade. If there's an afterlife, I'm sure you'll find your way there so you can torment me as well."

Fergus straightened his shoulders and gave a sound of disapproval. "I didn't agree with your kidnapping Kendall and Jake."

"I know that, Fergus. You made your opinion very clear, but I had my reasons."

"Yes, you care for them, even if you won't admit it, sir. I understand that, but what you've done now is surely going too far. This man isn't your family. Have you stopped to think of the ramifications this could have? This could cause an international incident."

"Stop calling me sir. Do you mean Marco?"

"No, I don't mean Marco...sir. You know very well whom I mean."

How the devil did Fergus know about that? "How did you find out?"

"I see things," Fergus said, his shoulders stiffening.

Nathan's hand tightened on the glass. "I had no choice, Fergus. He could be the answer to my problem. I have to know who he really is."

And why his eyes look like mine.

"One day your money is going to be your doom, *sir*. Now if you'll excuse me."

Fergus closed the door, leaving Nathan alone. He took a seat and looked out the window of the jet, watching as Italy grew smaller on the horizon. He set the wine down and rubbed a knuckle over his chin. Had he gone too far? He didn't know what else to do. He had to figure out what was wrong with him. What these bloody dreams were about.

He pulled the piece of paper he'd found in the secret room from his pocket and laid it on the table in front of him. Then he took out the journal, staring at the familiar leather cover stained with years of hopes and dreams. He didn't know who it belonged to or why Thomas had had it, or where Jake had gotten the page of sketches, but Nathan would bet his soul that the sketches were somehow connected to the curse.

He opened the journal for the hundredth time, staring at the words written in code. Pulling out the loose page he'd found in Jake's pack, he laid it beside the first paper and studied them side by side. The first sketch on both pages appeared to be a knife. But now he knew it was a spearhead. He moved on to the other sketches, comparing each one. He felt excitement stirring his blood. These must be the four relics. He was one step closer to his goal. His phone rang and he picked it up.

"We've arrived," his security chief said.

"I'll be there in a few hours," Nathan said. "Keep him under guard, but don't hurt him." He turned to the panel of monitors and touched the one labeled "Virginia." An image popped on the screen. Five guards were on each side of a tall, muscular man, escorting him inside the lower level of the estate. The man turned and looked at the camera, amber eyes locking with Nathan's for several seconds, as if he could see him watching from thousands of miles away. The man's tattoos looked dark, his face even more hostile than it had seemed in person.

"OK, Raphael," Nathan whispered to himself. "Let's see how you managed to come back from the dead, and then you can tell me where the other three relics are."

ACKNOWLEDGMENTS

T HERE ARE SO MANY PEOPLE I NEED TO THANK FOR HELPING me as I wrote this book. My family, of course. Without their support, I wouldn't be writing at all. Dana Rodgers, my critique partner and friend, for her wonderful help with brainstorming, revising, and editing. Keep those pancakes coming! Lori McDermeit, a beta reader who has an excellent understanding of my stories. Tamie Holman, another beta reader who has eyes like a hawk. Nancy Barone Wythe for her "Italian" help. Clarence Haynes for his creative insights. Marcus Trower for the expert copyedits, my agent, Christine Witthohn who has helped me get this far, and finally Kelli Martin, my wonderful Montlake editor and the entire Montlake team. Thank you!

ABOUT THE AUTHOR

NEW YORK TIMES AND USA TODAY bestselling author Anita Clenney writes mysteries and paranormal romantic suspense novels, including the bestselling Connor Clan series. Clenney grew up an avid reader, devouring Nancy Drew and Hardy Boys books before moving on to mysteries and romance. It was only after several successful but wildly different careers—including work as an executive assistant, a real estate agent, a teacher's assistant, and a brief stint in a pickle factory—that she discovered her untapped passion for writing. Clenney's first novel, *Awaken the Highland Warrior*, won the Single Titles Reviewers' Choice Award. She lives with her husband and two children in suburban Virginia.